This book belongs to

Little Amelia

Classic Animal Stories

Compiled by Tig Thomas

Miles
KeLLy

First published in 2013 by Miles Kelly Publishing Ltd
Harding's Barn, Bardfield End Green, Thaxted, Essex, CM6 3PX, UK

This edition printed 2017

2 4 6 8 10 9 7 5 3 1

Publishing Director *Belinda Gallagher*
Creative Director *Jo Cowan*
Editorial Director *Rosie Neave*
Assistant Editor *Amy Johnson*
Designers *Jo Cowan, Joe Jones, Venita Kidwai, Simon Lee*
Production *Elizabeth Collins, Caroline Kelly*
Reprographics *Stephan Davis, Jennifer Cozens, Thom Allaway*
Assets *Lorraine King*

ISBN 978-1-78617-312-6

Printed in China

British Library Cataloguing-in-Publication Data
A catalogue record for this book is available from the British Library

ACKNOWLEDGEMENTS

The publishers would like to thank the following artists
who have contributed to this book:
Cover
Marcela Calderón at Advocate Art

Inside pages
Frank Endersby
Beehive Illustration: Irisz Agocs, Neil Chapman, John Dillow,
Mike Phillips, Elena Selivanova, Rupert Van Wyk
The Bright Agency: Marsela Hajdinjak

Made with paper from a sustainable forest

www.mileskelly.net

CONTENTS

FRIENDS AND COMPANIONS

MYTHS AND WONDERS

TRICKS, TRAPS AND MISCHIEF

THE HUNTERS

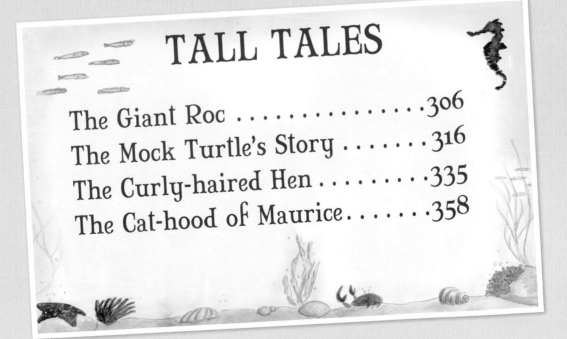

TALL TALES

ABOUT THE AUTHORS

Learn more about some of the famous authors behind these much-loved stories.

Kenneth Grahame
1859–1932

Grahame was born in Edinburgh, Scotland. His mother died when he was five, and he and his siblings were raised by their grandmother. Unable to afford to go to university, Grahame took a job in the Bank of England. He began to write about the characters that would later appear in *The Wind in the Willows* in letters to his son.

Dulce Domum • The Piper at the Gates of Dawn

James Baldwin
1841–1925

Baldwin was born in Indiana, USA, and was largely self-educated. Aged 41, he published his first book, *The Story of Siegfried*, and went on to write or edit more than fifty others – mostly stories for children on themes of mythology, biography, fable, legend and literature.

*Bucephalus • The Horse and the Olive • The Story of Arachne
Bellerophon and Pegasus*

Rudyard Kipling
1865–1936

Kipling was born in India, and his earliest years were very happily spent there. At the age of seven he was sent to live in England, a miserable experience that he never forgot. He was encouraged to write by his headmaster, and on returning to India he became a journalist, writing poems and stories in his spare time that were published alongside his other work.

How the Leopard Got His Spots • The Elephant's Child
Rikki-tikki-tavi • Tiger! Tiger! • The White Seal

Richard Jefferies
1848–1887

Jefferies grew up on a small farm in Wiltshire, UK, where he spent much of his time roaming the countryside. He became a journalist, and his writing is characterized by a love of nature and close observations of its smallest details.

The Spider and the Toad

Anna Sewell
1820–1878

Born into a devout Quaker family, Anna Sewell lived a quiet, religious life. Lamed in an accident at the age of fourteen, she often travelled by carriage, and hated the cruel treatment of the carriage horses. She wrote *Black Beauty* in response to this, saying its special aim was "to induce sympathy, kindness and an understanding treatment of horses".

Black Beauty's Final Home

E Nesbit
1858–1924

Edith Nesbit used the initial 'E' rather than 'Edith' to disguise the fact that she was a woman. She wrote more than forty books for children, and created the idea of mixing real-life characters and settings with magical elements. Her best-known books include *The Railway Children*, *Five Children and It* and *The Treasure Seekers*.

The Circus • *The Cat-hood of Maurice*

About the Artists

Mike Phillips For the past 15 years Mike has been illustrating children's books from his home in North Devon, UK. His work ranges from full-colour picture books to gruesome cartoons.
How the Leopard Got His Spots

Rupert Van Wyk Working between the UK and Italy, Rupert illustrates by using an ink dip pen and then adding watercolours to bring his images to life. The work of Quentin Blake is always a wonderful source of inspiration to him.
Bucephalus • The Horse and the Olive • Bellerophon and Pegasus
The Spider and the Toad • The Giant Roc • The Mock Turtle's Story
The Cat-hood of Maurice • The Circus

Marsela Hajdinjak Marsela contributes to children's magazines and has created characters and scenography for several animated films. In 2005, she received the Grigor Vitez Award in recognition of her illustrations for the books *Water Sprite* and *Old Pear Tree*.
The Wonderful Weaver

FRIENDS AND COMPANIONS

Dulce Domum

From *The Wind in the Willows*
by Kenneth Grahame

*One day, bored by his spring cleaning, the Mole clambered
out of his hole and took a walk instead. He met the Water Rat,
who introduced him to the pleasures of the outdoor, riverside life. The
Mole moved in with Ratty and has never gone back to his old house.*

They were returning across country after a long
day's outing with Otter, hunting and exploring
on the wide uplands where certain streams tributary
to their own River had their first small beginnings,
and the shades of the short winter day were closing in
on them, and they had still some distance to go.
Plodding at random across the plough, they had
heard the sheep and had made for them, and now,

leading from the sheep-pen, they found a beaten track that made walking a lighter business, and responded, moreover, to that small inquiring something which all animals carry inside them, saying unmistakably, 'Yes, quite right – this leads home!'

"It looks as if we were coming to a village," said the Mole somewhat dubiously, slackening his pace, as the track, that had in time become a path and then had developed into a lane, now handed them over to the charge of a road.

"Oh, never mind!" said the Rat. "At this season of the year they're all safe indoors by this time, sitting round the fire – men, women, and children, dogs and cats and all. We shall slip through alright, without any bother or unpleasantness, and we can have a look at them through their windows if you like, and see what they're doing."

The rapid nightfall of mid-December had quite beset the little village as they approached it on soft feet over a first thin fall of powdery snow. Little was visible but squares of a dusky orange-red on either side of the street, where the firelight or lamplight of each cottage overflowed through the casements into the dark world without.

FRIENDS AND COMPANIONS

Most of the low windows were innocent of blinds, and to the lookers-in from outside, the inmates, gathered round the tea-table, absorbed in handiwork, or talking with laughter and gesture, had each that happy grace which goes with perfect unconsciousness of observation.

But it was from one little window, with its blind drawn down, a mere blank transparency on the night, that the sense of home and the little curtained world within walls most pulsated. Close against the white blind hung a bird-cage, clearly silhouetted, every wire, perch, and appurtenance distinct and recognizable, even to yesterday's dull-edged lump of sugar. On the middle perch the fluffy occupant, head tucked well into feathers, seemed so near to them as to be easily stroked, had they tried – even the delicate tips of his plumped-out plumage pencilled plainly on the illuminated screen.

As they looked, the sleepy little fellow stirred uneasily, woke, shook himself, and raised his head. They could see the gape of his tiny beak as he yawned in a bored sort of way, looked round, and then settled his head into his back again, while the ruffled feathers gradually subsided into perfect stillness.

Then a gust of bitter wind took them in the back of the neck, a small sting of frozen sleet on the skin woke them as from a dream, and they knew their toes to be cold and their legs tired, and their own home distant a weary way. Once beyond the village, where the cottages ceased abruptly, on either side of the road they could smell through the darkness the friendly fields again, and they braced themselves for the last long stretch, the home stretch, the stretch that we know is bound to end, some time, in the rattle of the door latch, the sudden firelight, and the sight of familiar things greeting us as long-absent travellers from far over sea.

They plodded along steadily, each of them thinking his own thoughts. The Mole's ran a good deal on supper.

As for the Rat, he was walking a little way ahead, as his habit was, his shoulders hunched against the cold, his eyes fixed on the straight grey road in front of him, so he did not notice poor Mole when suddenly the summons reached him, and took him just like an electric shock. We others, who have long lost the more subtle of the physical senses, have not even the proper terms to express an animal's inter-communications with his surroundings, living or otherwise, and have only the word 'smell', for instance, to include the whole range of delicate thrills which murmur in the nose of the animal night and day, summoning, warning, inciting, repelling.

It was one of these mysterious fairycalls from out the void that suddenly reached Mole in the darkness, making him tingle through and through with its very familiar appeal, even while yet he could not clearly remember what it was. He stopped dead in his tracks, his nose searching hither and thither in its efforts to recapture the fine filament, the telegraphic current, that had so strongly moved him.

A moment, and he had caught it again, and with it this time came recollection in fullest flood – home! That was what they meant, those caressing appeals, those soft touches wafted through the air, those invisible little hands pulling and tugging, all one way! Why, it must be quite close by him at that moment, his old home that he had hurriedly forsaken and never sought again, that day when he first found the river! And now it was sending out its scouts and its messengers to capture him and bring him in.

Since his escape on that bright morning he had hardly given it a thought, so absorbed had he been in his new life, in all its pleasures, its surprises, its fresh and captivating experiences. Now, with a rush of old memories, how clearly it stood up before him, in the darkness! Shabby indeed, and small and poorly furnished, and yet his, the home he had made for himself, the home he had been so happy to get back to after his day's work. And the home had been happy with him, too, evidently, and was missing him, and wanted him back, and was telling him so, through his nose, sorrowfully, reproachfully, but with no bitterness or anger, only with plaintive reminder that it was there, and wanted him. The call was clear, the summons was plain. He must obey it instantly, and go.

"Ratty!" he called, full of joyful excitement, "Hold on! Come back! I want you, quick!"

"Oh, come along, Mole, do!" replied the Rat cheerfully over his shoulder, still plodding along.

"Please stop, Ratty!" pleaded the poor Mole, in

anguish of heart. "You don't understand! It's my home, my old home! I've just come across the smell of it, and it's close by here, really quite close. And I must go to it, I must, I must! Oh, come back, Ratty! Please, please come back!"

The Rat was by this time very far ahead, too far to hear clearly what the Mole was calling, too far to catch the sharp note of painful appeal in his voice. And he was much taken up with the weather, for he too could smell something – something suspiciously like approaching snow.

"Mole, we mustn't stop now, really!" he called back. "We'll come for it tomorrow, whatever it is you've found. But I daren't stop now – it's late, and the snow's coming on again, and I'm not sure of the way! And I want your nose, Mole, so come on quick, there's a good fellow!" And the Rat pressed forward on his way without waiting for an answer.

Poor Mole stood alone in the road, his heart torn asunder, and a big sob gathering somewhere low down inside him, to leap up to the surface presently, he knew, in passionate escape. But even under such a test as this his loyalty to his friend stood firm. With a wrench that tore his very heartstrings he set his face down the road and followed submissively in the track of the Rat, while faint, thin little smells, still dogging his retreating nose, reproached him for his new friendship and his callous forgetfulness.

With an effort he caught up to the unsuspecting Rat, who began chattering cheerfully about what they would do when they got back, and how jolly a fire of logs in the parlour would be, and what a supper he meant to eat – never noticing his companion's silence. At last, however, when they had gone some considerable way further, and were passing some tree-stumps at the edge of a copse that bordered the road, he stopped and said kindly, "Look here, Mole old chap, you seem dead tired. No talk left in you, and your feet dragging like lead. We'll sit down here for a minute and rest. The snow has held off so far, and the best part of our journey is over."

The Mole subsided forlornly on a tree-stump and tried to control himself, for he felt it surely coming. The sob he had fought with so long refused to be beaten. Up and up, it forced its way to the air, and then another, and another, and others thick and fast, till poor Mole at last gave up the struggle, and cried freely and helplessly and openly, now that he knew it

was all over and he had lost what he could hardly be said to have found.

The Rat was astonished and dismayed at the violence of Mole's paroxysm of grief. At last he said, very quietly and sympathetically, "What is it, old fellow? Whatever can be the matter? Tell us your trouble, and let me see what I can do."

Poor Mole found it difficult to get any words out between the upheavals of his chest that followed one upon another so quickly and held back speech and choked it as it came.

"I know it's a – shabby, dingy little place," he sobbed forth at last, brokenly. "Not like – your cosy quarters – or Toad's beautiful hall – or Badger's great house – but it was my own little home – and I was fond of it – and I went away and forgot all about it – and then I smelt it suddenly – on the road, when I called and you wouldn't listen, Rat – and everything came back to me with a rush – and I wanted it! Oh dear, Oh dear! And when you wouldn't turn back, Ratty – and I had to leave it, though I was smelling it all the time – I thought my heart would break. We might have just gone and had one look at it, Ratty – only one look – it was close by – but you wouldn't turn back, Ratty, you wouldn't turn back! Oh dear, Oh dear!"

Recollection brought fresh waves of sorrow, and sobs again took full charge of him, preventing further speech. The Rat stared straight in front of him, saying nothing, only patting Mole gently on the shoulder.

After a time he muttered gloomily, "I see it all now! What a pig I have been! A pig – that's me! Just a pig – a plain pig!"

He waited till Mole's sobs became gradually less stormy and more rhythmical, he waited till at last sniffs were frequent and sobs only intermittent. Then he rose from his seat, and, remarking carelessly, "Well, now we'd better be getting on, old chap!" set off up the road again, over the toilsome way they had come.

"Wherever are you – *hic* – going to – *hic* – Ratty?" cried the tearful Mole, looking up in alarm.

"We're going to find that home of yours, old fellow," replied the Rat pleasantly, "so you had better come along, for it will take some finding, and we shall want your nose."

"Oh, come back, Ratty, do!" cried the Mole, getting up and hurrying after him. "It's no good, I tell you! It's too late, and too dark, and the place is too far off, and the snow's coming! And – and I never meant to let you know I was feeling that way about it – it was all an accident and a mistake! And think of River Bank, and your supper!"

"Hang River Bank, and supper too!" said the Rat heartily. "I tell you, I'm going to find this place now, if I stay out all night. So cheer up, old chap, and take my arm, and we'll very soon be back there again."

Still snuffling, pleading, and reluctant, Mole suffered himself to be dragged back along the road by his imperious companion, who by a flow of cheerful talk and anecdote endeavoured to beguile his spirits back and make the weary way seem shorter. When at last it seemed to the Rat that they must be nearing that part of the road where the Mole had been, "Hold up," he said. "Now, no more talking. Business! Use your nose, and give your mind to it."

They moved on in silence for some little way, when suddenly the Rat was conscious, through his arm that was linked in Mole's, of a faint sort of electric thrill that was passing down that animal's body. Instantly he disengaged himself, fell back a pace, and waited, all attention. The signals were coming through! Mole stood a moment rigid, while his uplifted nose, quivering slightly, felt the air. Then a short, quick run forward – a fault – a check – a try back, and then a slow, steady, confident advance.

The Rat, much excited, kept close to his heels as the Mole, with something of the air of a sleep-walker, crossed a dry ditch, scrambled through a hedge, and nosed his way over a field open and trackless and bare in the faint starlight. Suddenly, without giving warning, he dived, but the Rat was on the alert, and promptly followed him down the tunnel to which his unerring nose had faithfully led him. It was close and airless, and the earthy smell was strong, and it seemed a long time to Rat before the passage ended and he could stand erect and stretch and shake himself.

The Mole struck a match, and by its light the Rat saw that they were standing in an open space, neatly swept and sanded underfoot, and directly facing them was Mole's little front door, with 'Mole End' painted over the bell-pull at the side.

Mole reached down a lantern from a nail on the wall and lit it, and the Rat, looking round him, saw that they were in a sort of forecourt. A garden seat stood on one side of the door, and on the other a roller – for the Mole, who was a tidy animal when at home, could not stand having his ground kicked up by other animals into little runs that ended in earth-heaps. On the walls hung wire baskets with ferns in them, alternating with brackets carrying plaster statuary – Garibaldi, and the infant Samuel, and Queen Victoria, and other heroes of modern Italy.

Down on one side of the forecourt ran a skittle alley, with benches along it and little wooden tables marked with rings that hinted at beer mugs. In the middle was a small round pond containing goldfish and surrounded by a cockleshell border. Out of the centre of the pond rose a fanciful erection clothed in more cockleshells and topped by a large silvered glass

ball that reflected everything all wrong and had a very pleasing effect.

Mole's face beamed at the sight of all these objects so dear to him, and he hurried Rat through the door, lit a lamp in the hall, and took one glance round his old home. He saw the dust lying thick on everything, saw the cheerless, deserted look of the long-neglected house, and its narrow, meagre dimensions, its worn and shabby contents – and collapsed again on a hall chair, his nose to his paws.

"Oh Ratty!" he cried dismally, "Why ever did I do it? Why did I bring you to this poor, cold little place, on a night like this, when you might have been at River Bank by this time, toasting your toes before a blazing fire, with all your own nice things about you!"

The Rat paid no heed to his doleful self-reproaches. He was running here and there, opening doors, inspecting rooms and cupboards, and lighting lamps and candles and sticking them up everywhere.

"What a capital little house this is!" he called out cheerily. "So compact! So well planned! Everything here and everything in its place! We'll make a jolly night of it. The first thing we want is a good fire – I'll see to that, I always know where to find things. So this is the parlour? Splendid! Your own idea, those little sleeping-bunks in the wall? Capital! Now, I'll fetch the wood and the coals, and you get a duster, Mole – you'll find one in the drawer of the kitchen table – and try and smarten things up a bit. Bustle about, old chap!"

Encouraged by his companion, the Mole roused himself and dusted and polished with energy and heartiness, while the Rat, running to and fro with armfuls of fuel, soon had a cheerful blaze roaring up the chimney. He hailed the Mole to come and warm himself, but Mole promptly had another fit of the blues, dropping down on a couch in dark despair and burying his face in his duster.

"Rat," he moaned, "How about your supper, you poor, cold, hungry, weary animal? I've nothing to give you – nothing – not a crumb!"

"What a fellow you are for giving in!" said the Rat reproachfully. "Why, only just now I saw a sardine-opener on the kitchen dresser, quite distinctly, and everybody knows that means there are sardines about somewhere in the neighbourhood. Rouse yourself! Pull yourself together, and come with me and forage."

They went and foraged accordingly, hunting

through every cupboard and turning out every drawer. The result was not so depressing after all, though it might have been better – a tin of sardines, a box of captain's biscuits (nearly full) and a German sausage encased in silver paper.

"There's a banquet for you!" observed the Rat, as he arranged the table. "I know some animals who would give their ears to be sitting down to supper with us tonight!"

"No bread!" groaned the Mole, "No butter, no—"

"No pate de foie gras, no champagne!" continued the Rat, grinning. "And that reminds me – what's that little door at the end of the passage? Your cellar, of course! Every luxury in this house! Just you wait a minute."

He made for the cellar door, and presently reappeared, somewhat dusty, with a bottle of beer in each paw and another under each arm. "Self-indulgent beggar you seem to be, Mole," he observed. "Deny yourself nothing. This is really the jolliest little place I ever was in. Now, wherever did you pick up those prints? Make the place look so home-like, they do. No wonder you're so fond of it, Mole. Tell us all about it, and how you came to make it what it is."

Then, while the Rat busied himself fetching plates, and knives and forks, and mustard – which he mixed in an egg-cup – the Mole, his bosom still heaving with the stress of his recent emotion, related – somewhat shyly at first, but with more freedom as he warmed to his subject – how this was planned, and how that was thought out, and how this was got through a windfall from an aunt, and that was a wonderful find and a bargain, and this other thing was bought out of laborious savings and a certain amount of 'going without'.

At last the Rat succeeded in decoying him to the table, and had just got seriously to work with the sardine-opener when sounds were heard from the forecourt without – sounds like the scuffling of small feet in the gravel and a confused murmur of tiny voices, while broken sentences reached them: "Now, all in a line – hold the lantern up a bit, Tommy – clear your throats first – no coughing after I say 'one, two, three'. Where's young Bill? Here, come on, do, we're all a-waiting—"

"What's up?" inquired the Rat, pausing briefly in his labours.

"I think it must be the field mice," replied the Mole, with a touch of pride in his manner. "They go round carol-singing regularly at this time of the year. They're quite an institution in these parts. And they never pass me over – they come to Mole End last of all, and I used to give them hot drinks, and supper too sometimes, when I could afford it. It will be like old times to hear them again."

"Let's have a look at them!" cried the Rat, jumping up and running to the door.

It was a pretty sight, and a seasonable one, that met their eyes when they flung the door open. In the forecourt, lit by the dim rays of a horn lantern, some eight or ten little field mice stood in a semicircle, red worsted comforters round their throats, their fore paws thrust deep into their pockets, their feet jigging

Dulce Domum

for warmth. With
bright beady eyes they
glanced shyly at each other,
sniggering a little, sniffing and
applying coat sleeves a good deal. As the
door opened, one of the elder ones that
carried the lantern was just saying, "Now
then, one, two, three!" and forthwith their
shrill little voices rose on the air, singing one of the
old-time carols that their forefathers composed in
fields that were fallow and held by frost, or when
snow-bound in chimney corners, and handed down
to be sung in the miry street to lamp-lit windows at
Yule-time.

FRIENDS AND COMPANIONS

Then, from up above and far away, down the tunnel they had so lately travelled was borne to their ears in a faint musical hum the sound of distant bells ringing a joyful and clangorous peal.

"Very well sung, boys!" cried the Rat heartily as the cheerful song ended. "And now come along in, all of you, and warm yourselves by the fire, and have something hot!"

"Yes, come along, field mice," cried the Mole eagerly. "This is quite like old times! Shut the door after you. Pull up that settle to the fire. Now, you just wait a minute, while we—Oh, Ratty!" he cried in despair, plumping down on a seat, with tears impending. "Whatever are we doing? We've nothing to give them!"

"You leave all that to me," said the masterful Rat. "Here, you with the lantern! Come over this way. I want to talk to you. Now, tell me, are there any shops open at this hour of the night?"

"Why, certainly, sir," replied the field mouse respectfully. "At this time of the year our shops keep open to all sorts of hours."

"Then look here!" said the Rat. "You go off at once, you and your lantern, and you get me—"

36

Here much muttered conversation ensued, and the Mole only heard bits of it, such as – "Fresh, mind! – no, a pound of that will do – see you get Buggins', for I won't have any other – no, only the best – if you can't get it there, try somewhere else – yes, of course, home-made, no tinned stuff – well then, do the best you can!"

Finally, there was a chink of coin passing from paw to paw, the field mouse was provided with an ample basket for his purchases, and off he hurried, he and his lantern. The rest of the field mice, perched in a row on the settle, their small legs swinging, gave themselves up to enjoyment of the fire, and toasted their chilblains till they tingled, while the Mole, failing to draw them into easy conversation, plunged into family history and made each of them recite the names of his numerous brothers, who were too young, it appeared, to be allowed to go out a-carolling this year, but looked forward very shortly to winning the parental consent.

The Rat, meanwhile, was busy examining the label on one of the beer-bottles. "I perceive this to be Old Burton," he remarked approvingly. "Sensible Mole! The very thing! Now we shall be able to mull some ale!

Get the things ready, Mole, while I draw the corks."

It did not take long to prepare the brew and thrust the tin heater well into the red heart of the fire, and soon every field mouse was sipping and coughing and choking (for a little mulled ale goes a long way) and wiping his eyes and laughing and forgetting he had ever been cold in all his life.

Under the generalship of Rat, everybody was set to do something or to fetch something. In a very few minutes supper was ready, and Mole, as he took the head of the table in a sort of a dream, saw a lately barren board set thick with savoury comforts, saw his little friends' faces brighten and beam as they fell to without delay, and then let himself loose – for he was famished indeed – on the provender so magically provided, thinking what a happy home-coming this had turned out, after all.

Dulce Domum

As they ate, they talked of old times, and the field mice gave him the local gossip up to date, and answered as well as they could the hundred questions he had to ask them. The Rat said little or nothing, only taking care that each guest had what he wanted, and plenty of it, and that Mole had no trouble or anxiety about anything. They clattered off at last, very grateful and showering wishes of the season, with their jacket pockets stuffed with remembrances for the small brothers and sisters at home. When the door had closed on the last of them and the chink of the lanterns had died away, Mole and Rat kicked the fire up, drew their chairs in, brewed themselves a last nightcap of mulled ale, and discussed the events of the long day.

At last the Rat, with a tremendous yawn, said, "Mole, old chap, I'm ready to drop. Sleepy is simply not the word. That your own bunk over on that side? Very well, then, I'll take this. What a ripping little house this is! Everything so handy!"

He clambered into his bunk and rolled himself well up in the blankets, and slumber gathered him forthwith, as a swathe of barley is folded into the arms of the reaping machine. The weary Mole also was glad to turn in without delay, and soon had his head on his pillow, in great joy and contentment. But before he closed his eyes he let them wander round his old room, mellow in the glow of the firelight that played or rested on familiar and friendly things which had long been unconsciously a part of him, and now smilingly received him back, without rancour.

He was now in just the frame of mind that the tactful Rat had quietly worked to bring about in him. He saw clearly how plain and simple – how narrow, even – it all was, but clearly, too, how much it all meant to him. He did not at all want to abandon the new life and its splendid spaces, to turn his back on sun and air and all they offered him and creep home and stay there – the upper world was all too strong, it called to him still, even down there, and he knew he must return to the larger stage. But it was good to think he had this to come back to, this place which was all his own, these things which were so glad to see him again and could always be counted upon for the same simple welcome.

Bucephalus

By James Baldwin

Philonicus of Thessaly was the most famous horse-raiser of his time. His stables were talked about from the Adriatic Sea to the Persian Gulf, and many of the best war steeds in Greece and Asia Minor had been bred and partially trained by him. He prided himself particularly on his 'ox-headed' horses – strong, knowing, high-spirited creatures, just the kind for war steeds, and that was about all that horses were valued for in those days.

Among these 'ox-heads' there was one which excelled all others in courage, beauty, and size, but seemed to be altogether untameable. Although he was now fourteen years old, there was not a horseman in Greece who had ever been able to mount him. He was a handsome creature – coal-black, with a white star in his forehead. One eye was grey and the other brown. Everybody admired him, and people came great distances to see him. Had Philonicus been less shrewd, he would have sold him for half the price of a common steed, and been glad that he was rid of him. But instead he kept the horse's untameableness a secret, and was careful that only his good points should be exhibited. Everybody who had any use for such an animal wanted to buy him.

"What is the price?"

"Thirteen thousand dollars."

That answer usually put an end to the talk, for an ordinary horse might be bought at that time for about seventy dollars, and a thoroughbred war steed for two hundred. There were rich men who made Philonicus some very handsome offers – a thousand dollars, five thousand, eight thousand – but he held steadily to his first price, and the longer he held to it the more anxious everybody became to buy.

At last, however, after the horse had reached middle age, Philonicus got his price. King Philip of

Bucephalus

Macedon was the purchaser. Philonicus, after hearing the gold pieces jingle in his strong-box, led Bucephalus up to the Macedonian capital and left him safely housed in the king's stalls. He was careful to get back into his own country before Philip had had time to give the steed any kind of examination.

Of course, when the horse was brought out upon the parade ground the skilfullest riders in Macedon could not mount him. He reared and plunged, and beat around with his sharp hoofs, until until no one dared approach him. The greatest horse-tamers of the country were called, but they could do nothing.

"Take him away!" cried the king, at last, in great rage. "Philonicus has sold me an utterly wild and unbroken beast – but he shall rue it."

But Bucephalus would not be led away. The horse-tamers tried to throw ropes over him, they beat him with long poles, they pelted him with stones. "What a shame to spoil so fine a horse! The awkward cowards know nothing about handling him!" cried the king's son, Alexander, who was standing by.

"Are you finding fault with men wiser than yourself?" asked the king, growing more angry. "Do you, a boy of twelve, pretend to know more about handling horses than these experts?"

"I can certainly handle this horse better," the prince replied.

"How much will you forfeit if you try, and fail?"

"I will forfeit the price which you paid for the horse," answered Alexander.

Everybody laughed, but the king said, "Stand away, and let the lad try his skill."

Alexander ran to the horse and turned his head toward the sun, for he had noticed that the animal was afraid of his own shadow. Then he spoke gently to him, and stroked his neck. The horse seemed to know that he had found a friend, and little by little his uneasiness left him. Soon the lad leaped nimbly upon his back, and allowed him to start off at his own gait. Then, when he saw that the horse was no longer afraid, but only proud of his speed, he urged him with voice and spur to do his utmost. The king and his attendants expected every moment to see the boy unseated and dashed to the ground. But when he turned and rode back, proud of his daring feat, everybody cheered and shouted – everybody but his father, who wept for joy, and said, "You must look for a kingdom which is worthy of you, my son, for

Bucephalus

Macedonia is too small for you."

After that, nobody but Alexander dared touch Bucephalus. He would even kneel to his young master, so that he might mount more easily. For sixteen years he served him faithfully. He was with Alexander when he conquered Persia, and carried him into more than one hard-fought battle. Once, in Hyrcania, he was stolen. But his master made proclamation that unless he were returned within a certain time, every person in the province should be put to death, and he was soon brought back.

In the great battle that was fought with King Porus, of India, Alexander recklessly rode too far into the enemy's ranks. The horse and his rider were a target for every spear, and for a time it seemed as if neither could escape. But the gallant Bucephalus, pierced by many weapons, and with streams of blood flowing from his neck and sides, turned about and, overriding the foes which beset them, rushed back to a place of safety. When he saw that his master was out of danger and among friends, the horse sank down upon the grass and died. Historians say that this happened in the year 327 BC, and that Bucephalus had reached the good old age – for a horse – of thirty years. Alexander mourned for him as for his dearest friend, and the next city which he founded he named Bucephalia, in honor of the steed that had served him so well.

How the Leopard Got His Spots

By Rudyard Kipling

*L*ong, long ago, the Leopard lived in the 'sclusively bare, hot, shiny High Veldt, where there was sand and sandy-coloured rock and 'sclusively tufts of sandy-yellowish grass. The Giraffe and the Zebra and the Eland and the Koodoo and the Hartebeest lived there, and they were 'sclusively sandy-yellow-brownish all over. But the Leopard, he was the 'sclusivest sandiest-yellowish-brownest of them all – a greyish-yellowish catty-shaped kind of beast, and he matched the 'sclusively yellowish-greyish-brownish colour of the High Veldt to one hair.

This was very bad for the Giraffe and the Zebra

and the rest of them, for he would lie down by a 'sclusively yellowish-greyish-brownish stone or clump of grass, and when the Giraffe or the Zebra or the Eland or the Koodoo or the Bush-Buck or the Bonte-Buck came by he would surprise them out of their jumpsome lives!

There was an Ethiopian with bows and arrows (a 'sclusively greyish-brownish-yellowish man he was then), who lived on the High Veldt with the Leopard. The two used to hunt together till the Giraffe and the Eland and the Koodoo and the Quagga and all the rest of them didn't know which way to jump!

After a long time, the animals learned to avoid anything that looked like a Leopard or an Ethiopian, and bit by bit – the Giraffe first, because his legs were the longest – they went away from the High Veldt.

They scuttled for days till they came to a great forest, 'sclusively full of trees and bushes and stripy, speckly, patchy-blatchy shadows, and there they hid. After another long time, what with standing half in the shade and half out of it, the Giraffe grew blotchy, the Zebra grew stripy, and the Eland and the Koodoo grew darker, with little wavy grey lines on their backs like bark on a tree. And so, though you could hear

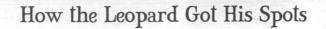

them and smell them, you could very seldom see them, and then only when you knew where to look.

They had a beautiful time in the 'sclusively speckly-spickly shadows of the forest. Meanwhile the Leopard and the Ethiopian ran about over the 'sclusively greyish-yellowish-reddish High Veldt outside, wondering where their breakfasts and their dinners and their teas had gone.

At last they were so hungry that they ate rats and beetles and rock-rabbits, and then they both had tummy-ache. Then they met Baviaan – the dog-headed, barking Baboon, who is quite the wisest animal in All South Africa.

Said Leopard to Baviaan, "Where has the game gone?"

Then said Baviaan, "The game has gone into other spots. My advice to you, Leopard, is to go into other spots as soon as you can. And my advice to you, Ethiopian, is to change as soon as you can."

That puzzled the Leopard and the Ethiopian, but they set off to look. Presently, after ever so many days, they saw a great, high, tall forest full of tree trunks all 'sclusively speckled and sprottled and spotted, dotted and splashed with shadows.

"What is this," said the Leopard, "that is so 'sclusively dark, and yet so full of pieces of light?"

"I don't know," said the Ethiopian, "but I can smell Giraffe, and I can hear Giraffe, but I can't see Giraffe."

"That's curious," said the Leopard. "I can smell Zebra, and I can hear Zebra, but I can't see Zebra."

"Wait," said the Ethiopian. "It's a long time since we've hunted 'em. Perhaps we've forgotten what they were like."

"Fiddle!" said the Leopard. "I remember them perfectly, especially their marrowbones. Giraffe is seventeen feet high, of a 'sclusively golden-yellow from head to heel. Zebra is four and a half feet high, of a 'sclusively grey-fawn colour from head to heel."

"Umm," said the Ethiopian, looking into the speckly-spickly shadows of the forest. "Then they ought to show up in this dark place like ripe bananas in a smokehouse."

How the Leopard Got His Spots

But they didn't. The Leopard and the Ethiopian hunted all day, and though they could smell them and hear them, they never saw one of them.

So they waited till dark, and then the Leopard heard something breathing sniffily in the starlight that fell all stripy through the branches.

He jumped at the noise, and it smelled like Zebra, and it felt like Zebra, and when he knocked it down it kicked like Zebra, but he couldn't see it. So he said, "Be quiet, O you person without any form. I am going to sit on your head till morning, because there is something about you that I don't understand."

Presently the Ethiopian called out, "I've caught a thing that I can't see. It smells like Giraffe, and it kicks like Giraffe, but it hasn't any form."

"Don't trust it," said the Leopard. "Sit on its head till the morning, same as me. They haven't any form – any of 'em."

So they sat down on them hard till morning time. Then Leopard said, "What have you, Brother?"

The Ethiopian said, "It ought to be Giraffe, but it is covered all over with blotches. What have you, Brother?"

The Leopard said, "It ought to be Zebra, but it is covered with stripes. What have you been doing, Zebra? If you were on the High Veldt I could see you ten miles off."

"Yes," said the Zebra, "but this isn't the High Veldt. Can't you see, Leopard?"

"I can now," said the Leopard. "But I couldn't all yesterday. How is it done?"

"Let us up," said the Zebra, "and we will show you."

They let the Zebra and the Giraffe get up. The Zebra moved away to some little thorn bushes where the sunlight fell all stripy, and Giraffe moved off to some tallish trees where the shadows fell all blotchy.

"Now watch us," said the Zebra and the Giraffe. "This is the way it's done. One – two – three! Where's your breakfast?"

Leopard stared, and Ethiopian stared, but all they could see were stripy and blotched shadows in the forest – but not a sign of Zebra and Giraffe. They had just walked off and hidden themselves in the shadowy, speckled forest.

"Hi! Hi!" said the Ethiopian. "That's a trick worth learning. Take a lesson by it, Leopard. You show up in this dark place like a bar of soap in a coal bucket."

"Ho! Ho!" said the Leopard. "Would it surprise you very much to know that you show up in this dark place like a mustard plaster on a sack of coals?"

"Well, calling names won't catch dinner," said the Ethiopian. "The long and the little of it is that we don't match our backgrounds. Baviaan's told me I ought to change, and as I've nothing to change except my skin, I'm going to change that."

"What will you change it to?" said the Leopard, tremendously excited.

"I will change it to a nice working blackish-brownish colour, with a little purple in it, and touches of slaty-blue. It will be the very thing for hiding in hollows and behind trees."

He changed his skin then and there, and the Leopard was more excited than ever.

"But what about me?" he said, when the Ethiopian had worked his last little finger into his fine new black skin.

"You take Baviaan's advice too. He told you to go into spots. I'll make 'em with the tips of my fingers," said the Ethiopian. "There's plenty of black left on my skin."

Then the Ethiopian put his five fingers close together and pressed them all over the Leopard. Wherever the five fingers touched they left five little black marks, all close together. If you look closely at any Leopard now you will see that there are always five spots – off five black fingertips.

"Now you are a beauty!" said the Ethiopian. "You can lie out on the ground and look like pebbles. You can lie out on the rocks and look like a stone. You can lie out on a leafy branch and look like sunshine sifting through leaves, and you can lie across a path and look like nothing in particular. Now come along – we'll

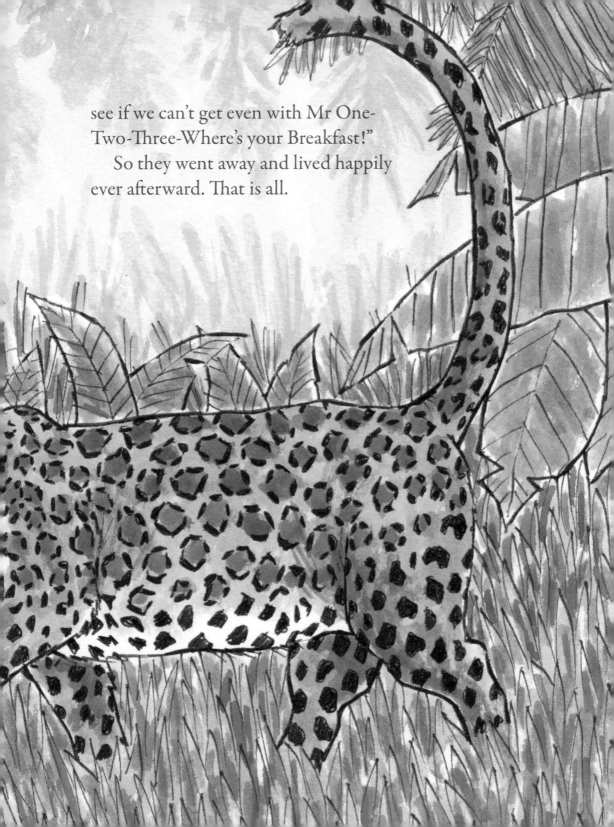

see if we can't get even with Mr One-Two-Three-Where's your Breakfast!"

So they went away and lived happily ever afterward. That is all.

Black Beauty's Final Home

From *Black Beauty*
by Anna Sewell

Black Beauty is a horse. He has had many masters, but has never forgotten his first home, and the kind stable boy who once accidentally made him ill by giving him cold water to drink when he was overheated. His owners have sometimes treated him badly and sometimes kindly, but he has always worked hard.

*I*was sold to a corn dealer and baker, and with him he thought I should have good food and fair work. In the first he was quite right, and if my master had always been on the premises I do not think I should have been overloaded, but there was a foreman who was always hurrying and driving everyone, and frequently when I had quite a full load he would order something else to be taken on. My carter, whose name was Jakes, often said it was more than I ought to take, but the other always overruled him. Jakes, like the other carters, always had the check-rein up, which prevented me from drawing easily, and by the time I had been there three or four months I found the work telling very much on my strength.

One day I was loaded more than usual, and part of the road was a steep uphill. I used all my strength, but I could not get on, and was obliged continually to stop. This did not please my driver, and he laid his whip on badly. "Get on, you lazy fellow," he said, "or I'll make you."

Again I started the heavy load, and struggled on a few yards, again the whip came down, and again I struggled forward. The pain of that great cart whip was sharp, but my mind was hurt quite as much as my poor sides. To be punished and abused when I was doing my very best was so hard it took the heart out of me. A third time he was flogging me cruelly, when a lady stepped quickly up to him, and said in a sweet, earnest voice, "Oh! Pray do not whip your good horse any more, I am sure he is doing all he can, and the road is very steep. I am sure he is doing his best."

"If doing his best won't get this load up he must do

something more than his best, ma'am," said Jakes.

"But is it not a heavy load?" she said.

"Yes, yes, too heavy," he said, "The foreman came just as we were starting, and would have three hundredweight more put on to save him trouble, and I must get on with it as well as I can."

He was raising the whip again, when the lady said, "Pray, stop – I think I can help if you will let me. You see," she said, "you do not give him a fair chance – he cannot use all his power with his head held back with that check-rein. If you take it off I am sure he would do better – do try it," she said persuasively, "I should be very glad if you would."

"Well," said Jakes, with a laugh, "anything to please a lady. How far would you wish it down, ma'am?"

"Quite down, give him his head altogether."

The rein was taken off, and in a moment I put my head down to my very knees. What a comfort it was! Then I tossed it up and down several times to get the aching stiffness out of my neck.

"Poor fellow! That is what you wanted," said she, patting me with her gentle hand. "Now if you will speak kindly to him and lead him on I believe he will be able to do better."

Jakes took the rein. "Come on, Blackie."

I put down my head, and threw my whole weight against the collar. The load moved on, and I pulled it steadily up the hill, and then stopped to take breath.

The lady had walked along the footpath, and now came across into the road. She stroked and patted my neck, as I had not been patted for many a long day.

"You see he was quite willing when you gave him the chance – I am sure he is a fine-tempered creature, and I dare say he has known better days. You won't put that rein on again, will you?"

"Well, ma'am, I can't deny that having his head has helped him up the hill, and I'll remember it another time, and thank you, ma'am, but if he went without a check-rein I should be the laughing-stock of all the carters – it is the fashion, you see."

"Is it not better," she said, "to lead a good fashion than to follow a bad one? A great many gentlemen do not use check-reins now. Our carriage horses have not worn them for fifteen years, and work with much less fatigue than those who have them. Besides," she added in a very serious voice, "we have no right to distress any of God's creatures without a very good reason – we call them dumb animals, and so they are, for they cannot tell us how they feel, but they do not suffer less because they have no words. But I must not detain you now. I thank you for trying my plan with your good horse, and I am sure you will find it far better than the whip. Good-day." And with another soft pat on my neck she stepped lightly across the path, and I saw her no more.

"That was a real lady," said Jakes to himself. "She spoke just as polite as if I was a gentleman, and I'll try her plan, uphill, at any rate." And I must do him the justice to say that he let my rein out several holes, and going uphill after that, he always gave me my head, but the heavy loads went on. Good feed and fair rest will keep up one's strength under full work, but no horse can stand against overloading, and I was getting so thoroughly pulled down from this cause that a younger horse was bought in my place, and I was sold to a large cab owner.

My new master I shall never forget. He had black eyes and a hooked nose, his mouth was as full of teeth as a bulldog's, and his voice was as harsh as the grinding of cart wheels over gravelled stones. His name was Nicholas Skinner.

Skinner had a low set of cabs and a low set of drivers. He was hard on the men, and the men were hard on the horses. In this place we had no Sunday rest, and it was in the heat of summer.

Sometimes on a Sunday morning a party of men would hire the cab for the day, four of them inside and another with the driver, and I had to take them ten or fifteen miles out into the country, and back again. Never would any of them get down to walk up a hill, let it be ever so steep, or the day ever so hot – unless, indeed, when the driver was afraid I should not manage it – and sometimes I was so fevered and worn that I could hardly touch my food.

My driver was just as hard as his master. He had a cruel whip with something so sharp at the end that it sometimes drew blood, and he would even whip me under the belly, and flip the lash out at my head. Indignities like these took the heart out of me terribly, but still I did my best and never hung back.

My life was now so utterly wretched that I wished I might drop down dead at my work and be out of my misery, and one day my wish very nearly came to pass.

I went on the stand at eight in the morning, and had done a good share of work, when we had to take a fare to the railway. A train was expected in, so my driver pulled up at the back of some of the outside cabs to take the chance of a return fare. It was a heavy train, and all the cabs were soon engaged. There was a party of four: a noisy, blustering man with a lady, a little boy and a young girl, and a great deal of luggage. While the man ordered about the luggage the young girl came and looked at me.

"Papa," she said, "I am sure this poor horse cannot take us and all our luggage so far, he is so very weak and worn up. Do look at him."

"Oh! He's all right, miss," said my driver, "he's strong enough."

The porter, who was pulling about some heavy boxes, suggested to the gentleman, as there was so much luggage, that he might take a second cab.

"Can your horse do it, or can't he?" said the man.

"Oh! He can do it all right, sir. Send up the boxes, porter." And he helped to haul up a box so heavy that I could feel the springs go down.

"Papa, papa, do take a second cab," said the young

girl in a beseeching tone. "I am sure it is very cruel."

"Nonsense, Grace, get in at once, and don't make all this fuss – a pretty thing it would be if a man of business had to examine every cab-horse before he hired it – the man knows his own business of course. There, get in and hold your tongue!"

My gentle friend had to obey, and box after box was dragged up and lodged on the top of the cab or settled by the side of the driver. At

last all was ready, and with his usual jerk at the rein and slash of the whip he drove out of the station.

The load was very heavy and I had had neither food nor rest since morning, but I did my best, as I always had done, in spite of cruelty and injustice.

I got along till we came to Ludgate Hill, but there

the load and my own exhaustion were too much. I was struggling to keep on, goaded by constant chucks of the rein and use of the whip, when in a single moment – I cannot tell how – my feet slipped from under me, and I fell heavily to the ground on my side. The suddenness and the force with which I fell seemed to beat all the breath out of my body. I lay perfectly still, indeed, I had no power to move, and I thought now I was going to die. I heard a sort of confusion round me, loud, angry voices, and the getting down of the luggage, but it was all like a dream. I thought I heard that sweet voice saying, "Oh, that poor horse! It is all our fault."

Someone came and loosened the throat strap of my bridle, and undid the traces which kept the collar so tight upon me. Someone said, "He's dead, he'll never get up again."

Then I could hear a policeman giving orders, but I did not even open my eyes. I could only draw a gasping breath now and then. Some cold water was thrown over my head, and some cordial was poured into my mouth, and something was covered over me. I cannot tell how long I lay there, but I found my life coming back, and a kind-voiced man was patting me

and encouraging me to rise. After one or two
attempts, I staggered to my feet, and was gently led to
some stables which were close by. Here I was put into
a well-littered stall, and some warm gruel was brought
to me, which I drank thankfully.

In the evening I was sufficiently recovered to be led
back to Skinner's stables, where I think they did the
best for me they could. In the morning Skinner came
with a farrier to look at me. The farrier examined me
and said: "This is a case of overwork. If you could give
him a run off for six months he would be able to work
again, but now there is no strength left in him."

"Then he must just go to the dogs," said Skinner.
"I have no meadows to nurse sick horses in. My plan
is to work 'em as long as they'll go, and then sell 'em
for what they'll fetch, at the knacker's or elsewhere."

"If he was broken-winded," said the farrier, "you
had better have him killed out of hand, but he is not.
There is a sale of horses coming off in about ten days.
If you rest him and feed him up he may pick up, and
you may get more than his skin is worth, at any rate."

Upon this advice Skinner, rather unwillingly, I
think, gave orders that I should be well fed and cared
for, and the stable man, happily for me, carried out

the orders with a much better will than his master had in giving them. Ten days of perfect rest, plenty of good oats, hay, bran mashes with boiled linseed mixed in them, did more to get up my condition than anything else could have done. Those linseed mashes were delicious, and I began to think, after all, it might be better to live than go to the dogs. When the twelfth day after the accident came, I was taken to the sale, a few miles out of London. I felt that any change from my present place must be an improvement, so I held up my head, and hoped for the best.

At this sale, I found myself with the broken-down horses – some lame, some old, and some that I am sure it would have been merciful to shoot.

Many of the buyers and sellers looked not much better off than the poor beasts they were bargaining about. There were poor old men, trying to get a horse or a pony for a few pounds, that might drag about some little wood or coal cart. There were poor men trying to sell a worn-out beast for two or three pounds, rather than have the greater loss of killing him. Some of them looked as if poverty and hard times had hardened them, but there were others that I would have willingly used the last of my strength in serving – poor and shabby, but kind and human, with voices that I could trust. There was one little old man who took a great fancy to me, and I to him, but I was not strong enough – it was an anxious time! Coming from the better part of the fair, I noticed a man who looked like a gentleman farmer, with a young boy by his side. He had a broad back and round shoulders, and a kind face. When he came up to me and my companions he stood still and gave a pitiful look round upon us. I saw his eye rest on me – I had still a good mane and tail, which did something for my appearance. I pricked my ears and looked at him.

"There's a horse, Willie, that has known better days than these."

"Poor old fellow!" said the boy, "Do you think, grandpapa, he was ever a carriage horse?"

"Oh, yes! My boy," said the farmer, coming closer, "He might have been anything – look at his nostrils and his ears, the shape of his neck and shoulder – there's a deal of breeding about that horse." He gave me a kind pat on the neck. I put out my nose in answer to his kindness. The boy stroked my face.

"Poor old fellow! See, grandpapa, how well he understands kindness. Could not you buy him and

make him young again as you did with Ladybird?"

"My dear boy, I can't make all old horses young. Besides, Ladybird was not so very old, as she was run down and badly used."

"Well, grandpapa, I don't believe he is old – look at his mane and tail. I wish you would open his mouth and look – then you could tell. Though he is so thin, his eyes are not sunk like some old horses."

The old gentleman laughed. "Bless the boy! He is as horsey as his old grandfather."

"But do look at his mouth, grandpapa, and ask the price of him. I am sure he would be able to grow young in our meadows."

The man who had brought

me for sale now put in his word. "The young gentleman's a real knowing one, sir. Now the fact is, this 'ere hoss is just pulled down with overwork in the cabs. He's not an old one, and I heerd as how the vetenary should say that a six months' run off would set him right up. I've had the tending of him these ten days past, and a gratefuller, pleasanter animal I never met with, and 'twould be worth a gentleman's while to give a five-pound note for him, and let him have a chance. I'll be bound he'd be worth twenty pounds next spring."

The farmer slowly felt my legs, which were much swelled and strained. Then he looked at my mouth. "Thirteen or fourteen, I should say. Just trot him out, will you?"

I arched my thin neck, raised my tail, and threw out my legs as well as I could, for they were very stiff.

"What is the lowest you will take for him?" said the farmer as I came back.

"Five pounds, sir – that was the lowest price my master set."

"'Tis a speculation," said the old gentleman, shaking his head and drawing out his purse, "quite a speculation! Have you any more business here?" he said, counting the sovereigns into his hand.

"No, sir, I can take him for you to the inn, if you would like me to."

"Do so, I am now going there."

They walked forward, and I was led behind. The boy could hardly control his delight. I had a good feed at the inn, and was then gently ridden home by a servant of my new master's, and turned out into a large meadow.

Mr Thoroughgood, for that was the name of my benefactor, gave orders that I should have hay and oats every night and morning, and the run of the meadow in the day. "You, Willie," said he, "must take the oversight of him. I give him in charge to you."

The boy was proud of his charge, and undertook it in all seriousness. He visited me every day, sometimes picking me out from among the other horses and giving me a bit of carrot, or sometimes standing by me while I ate my oats. He always came with kind words and caresses, and I grew very fond of him. He called me 'Old Crony', as I used to come to him in the field and follow him about. Sometimes he brought his grandfather, who always looked closely at my legs.

"This is our point, Willie," he would say, "but he is

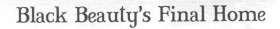

improving so steadily that I think we shall see a
change for the better in the spring."

The perfect rest, the good food, the soft turf, and
gentle exercise soon began to tell on my condition
and my spirits. During the winter my legs improved
so much that I began to feel quite young again. One
day in March Mr Thoroughgood determined that he
would try me in the carriage. I was well pleased, and
he and Willie drove me a few miles. My legs were not
stiff now, and I did the work with perfect ease.

"He's growing young, Willie. We must give him a
little gentle work now, and by mid-summer he will be
as good as Ladybird. He has a beautiful mouth and
good paces, they can't be better."

"Oh, grandpapa, how glad I am you bought him!"

"So am I, my boy, but he has to thank you more
than me. We must now be looking out for a quiet,
genteel place for him, where he will be valued."

One day during this summer the groom cleaned
and dressed me with extraordinary care, so I thought
some new change must be at hand. He trimmed my
fetlocks and legs, passed the tarbrush over my hoofs,
and even parted my forelock. I think the harness had
an extra polish. Willie seemed half-anxious, half-

merry, as he got into the chaise with his grandfather.

"If the ladies take to him," said the old gentleman, "they'll be suited and he'll be suited. We can but try."

At the distance of a mile or two from the village we came to a pretty, low house, with a lawn and shrubbery at the front and a drive up to the door. While Willie stayed with me, Mr Thoroughgood went into the house. In about ten minutes he returned, followed by three ladies – one tall, pale lady, wrapped in a white shawl, leaned on a younger lady, with dark eyes and a merry face. The other – a very stately-looking person – was Miss Blomefield.

They all came and looked at me and asked questions. The younger lady – that was Miss Ellen – took to me very much, saying she was sure she should like me, I had such a good face. The tall lady said that she should be nervous in riding behind a horse that had once been down, as I might come down again, and if I did she should never get over the fright.

"You see, ladies," said Mr Thoroughgood, "many first-rate horses have had their knees broken through the carelessness of their drivers without any fault of their own. From what I see of this horse I should say that is his case, but I do not wish to influence you. If

you incline you can have him on trial, and then your coachman will see what he thinks of him."

"You have always been such a good adviser to us about our horses," said the stately lady, "that your recommendation would go a long way with me, and if my sister Lavinia sees no objection we will accept your offer of a trial, with thanks."

It was then arranged that I should be sent for the next day.

In the morning a smart-looking young man came for me. At first he looked pleased, but when he saw my knees he said in a disappointed voice, "I didn't think, sir, you would have recommended my ladies a blemished horse like that."

"Handsome is that handsome does," replied my master. "You are only going to take him on trial, and I am sure you will do fairly by him, young man. If he is not as safe as any horse you ever drove then by all means send him back."

I was led to my new home, placed in a comfortable stable, fed, and left to myself. The next day, when the groom was cleaning my face, he said, "That is just like the star that Black Beauty had. He is much the same height, too. I wonder where he is now."

Black Beauty's Final Home

A little further on he came to the place in my neck where I was bled and where a little knot was left in the skin. He almost started, and began to look me over carefully, talking to himself.

"White star in the forehead, one white foot on the off side, this little knot just in that place," then looking at the middle of my back—"and, as I am alive, there is that little patch of white hair that John used to call 'Beauty's three-penny bit'. It must be Black Beauty! Why, Beauty! Beauty! Do you know me? Little Joe Green, that almost killed you?" And he began patting and patting and stroking me as if he was quite overjoyed.

I could not say that I remembered him, for now he was a fine grown young fellow, with black whiskers and a man's voice, but I was sure he knew me, and that he was Joe Green, and I was very glad. I put my nose up to him, and tried to say that we were friends. I never saw a man so pleased.

"Give you a fair trial! I should think so! I wonder who the rascal was that broke your knees, my Beauty! You must have been badly served somewhere. Well, well, it won't be my fault if you haven't good times of it now. I wish John Manly was here to see you."

FRIENDS AND COMPANIONS

That afternoon I was put into a low park chair and brought to the door. Miss Ellen was going to try me, and Joe Green went with her. She was a good driver, and she seemed pleased with me. I heard Joe telling her about me, and that he was sure I was old 'Black Beauty' that had once belonged to Squire Gordon.

When we returned the other sisters came out to hear how I had behaved. Miss Ellen told them what she had heard from Joe Green, and said, "I shall write to Mrs Gordon, and tell her that her favourite horse has come to us. How pleased she will be!"

After this I was driven every day for a week or so, and as I appeared to be quite safe, Miss Lavinia at last ventured out in the small close carriage. After this it was quite decided to keep me and call me by my old name of 'Black Beauty'.

I have now lived in this happy place a whole year. Joe is the best and kindest of grooms. My work is very pleasant, and I feel my spirits coming back again. Mr Thoroughgood said to Joe the other day, "In your place he will last till he is twenty – perhaps more."

Willie always speaks to me when he can, and treats me as his special friend. My ladies have promised that I shall never be sold, so I have nothing to fear. And here my story ends. My troubles are over, and I am at home, and often before I am quite awake, I fancy I am still in the orchard at Birtwick, standing with my old friends under the apple-trees.

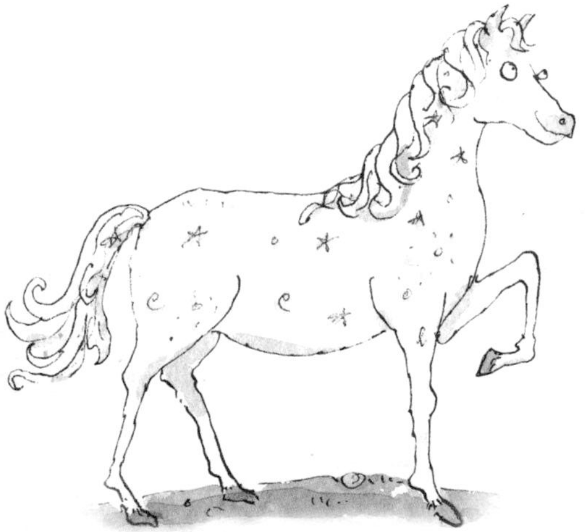

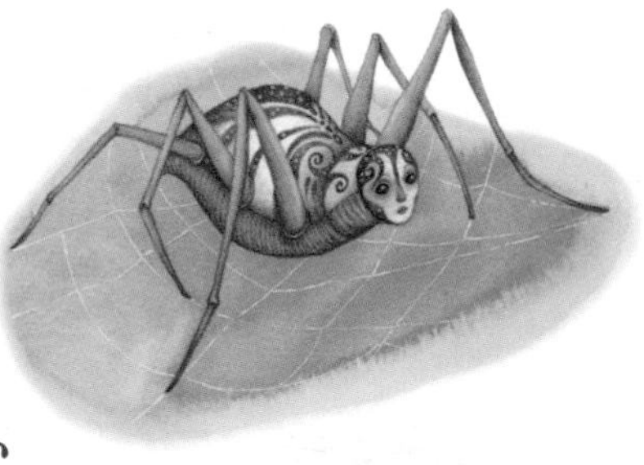

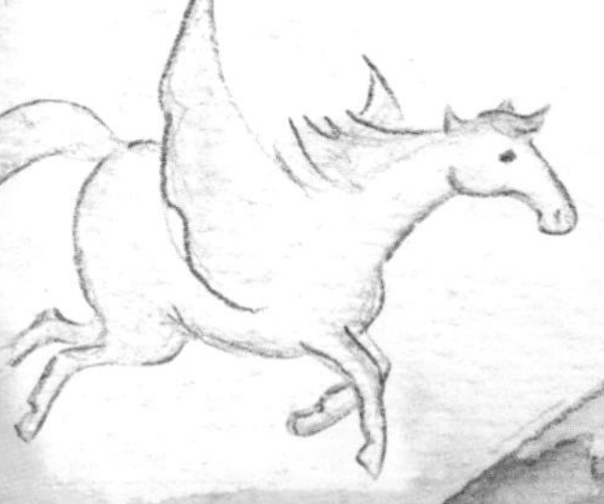

MYTHS AND WONDERS

The Horse and the Olive

By James Baldwin

On a steep stony hill in Greece there lived in early times a few very poor people who had not yet learned to build houses. They made their homes in little caves, which they dug in the earth or hollowed out among the rocks, and their food was the flesh of wild animals, which they hunted in the woods, with now and then a few berries or nuts. They did not even know how to make bows and arrows, but used slings and clubs and sharp sticks for weapons, and the little clothing they had was made of skins.

They lived on the top of the hill, because they were safe there from the savage beasts of the great forest around them, and safe also from the wild men who sometimes roamed through the land. The hill was so steep on every side that there was no way of climbing it save by a single narrow footpath which was always guarded by someone at the top.

One day when the men were hunting in the woods, they found a strange youth. His face was so fair and he was dressed so beautifully that they could hardly believe him to be a man like themselves. He moved so nimbly among the trees that they fancied him to be a serpent in the guise of a human being, and they stood still in wonder and alarm. The young man spoke to them, but they could not understand a word that he said. Then he made signs to them that he was hungry, and they gave him food and were no longer afraid. Had they been like the wild men of the woods, they might have killed him at once.

But they wanted their women and children to see the serpent man, as they called him, and hear him talk, and so they took him home with them to the top of the hill. They thought that after they had made a show of him for a few days, they would kill him and offer his body as a sacrifice to the unknown being whom they dimly fancied to have some sort of control over their lives.

But the young man was so fair and gentle that, after they had all taken a look at him, they began to think it would be a great pity to harm him. So they gave him food and treated him kindly, and he sang songs to them and played with their children, and made them happier than they had been for many a day. In a short time he learned to talk in their language, and he told them that his name was Cecrops, and that he had been shipwrecked on the coast not far away. Then he told them many strange things about the land from which he had come and to which he would never be able to return. The poor people listened and wondered, and it was not long until they began to love him and to look up to him as one wiser than themselves. Then they came to ask him about everything that was to be done, and there was not one of them who refused to do his bidding.

So Cecrops – the serpent man, as they still called him – became the king of the people on the hill. He taught them to make bows and arrows, and to set nets for birds, and to take fish with hooks. He led them against the savage wild men of the woods, and helped them kill the fierce beasts that had been so great a terror to them. He showed them how to build houses of wood and to thatch them with the reeds which grew in the marshes. He taught them to live in families instead of herding together like senseless beasts as they had always done before. And he told them about great Jupiter and the Mighty Folk who lived amid the clouds on the mountain top.

By and by, instead of the wretched caves among the rocks, there was a little town on the top of the hill, with neat houses and a market-place. Around it was a strong wall with a single narrow gate just where the footpath began to descend to the plain. But as yet the place had no name.

One morning while the king and his wise men were sitting together in the market-place and planning how to make the town become a rich, strong city, two strangers were seen in the street. Nobody could tell how they came there. The guard at the gate had not seen them, and no man had ever dared to climb the narrow footway without his leave. But there the two strangers stood. One was a man, the other a woman, and they were so tall, and their faces were so grand and noble, that those who saw them stood still and wondered and said not a word.

MYTHS AND WONDERS

The man had a robe of purple and green wrapped round his body, and he bore in one hand a strong staff with three sharp spear points at one end. The woman was not beautiful, but she had wonderful grey eyes, and in one hand she carried a spear and in the other a shield of curious workmanship.

"What is the name of this town?" asked the man.

An old man answered, "It has no name. We who live on this hill used to be called Cranæ, but since King Cecrops came, we have been so busy that we have had no time to think of names."

"Where is this King Cecrops?" asked the woman.

"He is in the market-place with the wise men," was the old man's answer.

"Lead us to him at once," said the man.

When Cecrops saw the two strangers coming into the market-place, he stood up and waited for them to speak. The man spoke first. "I am Neptune," said he, "and I rule the sea."

"And I am Athena," said the woman, "and I give wisdom to men."

"I hear that you are planning to make your town become a great city," said Neptune, "and I have come to help you. Give my name to the place, and let me be your protector and patron, and the wealth of the whole world shall be yours. Ships from every land shall bring you merchandise and gold and silver, and you shall be the masters of the sea."

"My uncle makes you fair promises," said Athena, "but listen to me. Give my name to your city, and let me be your patron, and I will give you that which gold cannot buy – I will teach you how to do a thousand things of which you now know nothing. I will make your city my favourite home, and I will give you wisdom that shall sway the minds and hearts of all men until the end of time."

The king bowed, and turned to the people, who had all crowded into the market-place.

"Which of these mighty ones shall we elect to be the protector and patron of our city?" he asked. "Neptune offers us wealth, Athena promises us wisdom. Which shall we choose?"

"Neptune and wealth!" cried many.

"Athena and wisdom!" cried as many others.

At last when it was plain that the people could not agree, an old man whose advice was always heeded stood up and said, "These mighty ones have only given us promises, and they have promised things of which we are ignorant. For who among us knows what wealth is or what wisdom is? Now, if they would give us some real gift which we can see and handle, we should know better how to choose."

"That is true! That is true!" cried the people.

"Very well, then," said the strangers, "we will each give you a gift, right now and right here, and then you may choose between us."

Neptune gave the first gift. He stood on the highest point of the hill where the rock was bare, and bade the people see his power. He raised his three-pointed spear high in the air, and then brought it down with great force. Lightning flashed, the earth shook, and the rock was split halfway down to the bottom of the hill. Then out of the yawning crevice there sprang a wonderful creature, white as milk, with long slender legs, an arching neck, and a mane and tail of silk.

The people had never seen anything like it before, and they thought perhaps it a new kind of bear or wolf or wild boar that had come out of the rock to devour them.

Some of them ran and hid in their houses, while others climbed upon the wall, and still others grasped their weapons in alarm. But when they saw the creature stand quietly by the side of Neptune, they lost their fear and came closer to see and admire its beauty.

"This is my gift," said Neptune. "This animal will carry your burdens for you, he will draw

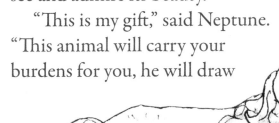

your chariots, he will pull your wagons and your plows, he will let you sit on his back and will run with you faster than the wind."

"What is his name?" asked the king.

"His name is Horse," answered Neptune.

Then Athena came forward. She stood a moment on a green grassy plot where the children of the town liked to play in the evening. Then she drove the point of her spear deep down in the soil. At once the air was filled with music, and out of the earth there sprang a tree with slender branches and dark green leaves and white flowers and beautiful violet green fruit.

"This is my gift," said Athena. "This tree will give you food when you are hungry, it will shelter you from the sun when you are faint, it will beautify your city, and the oil from its fruit will be sought by all the world."

"What is it called?" asked the king.

"It is called Olive," answered Athena.

Then the king and his wise men began to talk about the two gifts.

"I do not see that Horse will be of much use to us," said the old man who had spoken before. "For, as to the chariots and wagons and plows, we have none of them, and indeed do not know what they are. And who among us will ever want to sit on this creature's back and be borne faster than the wind? But Olive will be a thing of beauty and a joy for us and our children forever."

"Which shall we choose?" asked the king, turning to the people.

"Athena has given us the best gift," they all cried, "and we choose Athena and wisdom!"

"Be it so," said the king, "and the name of our city shall be Athens."

From that day the town grew and spread, and soon there was not room on the hilltop for all the people. Then houses were built in the plain around the foot of the hill, and a great road was built to the sea, three miles away, and in all the world there was no city more fair than Athens.

In the old market-place on the top of the hill the people built a temple to Athena, the ruins of which may still be seen. The olive tree grew and flourished, and, when you visit Athens, people will show you the very spot where it stood. Many other trees sprang from it, and in time became a blessing both to Greece and to all the other countries round the great sea. As for the horse, he wandered away across the plains towards the north and found a home at last in distant Thessaly beyond the River Peneus. And I have heard it said that all the horses in the world have descended from that one which Neptune brought out of the rock – but of the truth of this story there may be some doubts.

The Wonderful Weaver

From *Old Greek Stories* by James Baldwin

There was once a young girl in Greece whose name was Arachne. Her face was pale but beautiful, and her eyes were big and blue, and her hair was long and like gold. All that she cared to do from morn till noon was to sit in the sun and spin, and all that she cared to do from noon till night was to sit in the shade and weave.

And oh, how fine and fair were the things which she wove in her loom! Flax, wool, silk – she worked with them all – and when they came from her hands, the cloth which she had made of them was so thin and soft and bright that men came from all parts of the world to see it. And they said that cloth so rare could not be made of flax, or wool, or silk, but that the warp was of rays of sunlight and the woof was of threads of gold.

Then, as day by day, the girl sat in the sun and span, or sat in the shade and wove, she said to herself, "In all the world there is no yarn so fine as mine, and in all the world there is no cloth so soft and smooth, nor silk so bright and rare."

"Who taught you to spin and weave so well?" someone asked.

"No one taught me," she said. "I learned how to do it by myself as I sat in the sun and the shade, but no one showed me."

"But it may be that Athena, the queen of the air, taught you, and you did not know it."

"Athena, the queen of the air? No!" said Arachne. "How could she teach me? Can she spin such skeins of yarn as these? Can she weave goods like mine? I should like to see her try to match me. I can teach her a thing or two."

Then she looked up and saw in the doorway a tall woman wrapped in a long cloak. Her face was fair to see, but stern, oh, so stern! Her grey eyes rested on

Arachne, and they were so sharp and bright that
Arachne could not bring herself to meet her gaze.

"Arachne," said the woman, "I am Athena, the
queen of the air, and I have heard your boast. Do you
still mean to say that I have not taught you how to
spin and weave?"

"No one has taught me," said Arachne, "and I
thank no one for what I know." And she stood up,
straight and proud, by the side of her loom.

"And do you still think that you can spin and
weave as well as I?" said Athena.

Arachne's cheeks grew white, but she said, "Yes.
I can weave as well as you."

"Then let me tell you what we will do," said
Athena. "Three days from now we will both weave –
you on your loom, and I on mine. We will ask all the
world to come and see us, and great Jupiter, who sits
in the clouds, shall be the judge. And if your work is
the best, then I will weave no more so long as the
world shall last. But if my work is best, then you shall
never use loom or spindle or distaff again. Do you
agree to this?"

"I agree," said Arachne.

"It is well," said Athena. And she was gone.

When the time came for the contest in weaving, all the world was gathered there to see it, and great Jupiter himself sat among the clouds and looked on from above.

Arachne had set up her loom in the shade of a mulberry tree, where butterflies were flitting and grasshoppers chirping all through the livelong day. But Athena had set up her loom in the sky, where the breezes were blowing and the summer sun was shining, for she was the queen of the air.

Then Arachne took her skeins of finest silk and began to weave. And she wove a web of marvellous beauty, so thin and light that it would float in the air, and yet so strong that it could hold a lion in its meshes, and the threads were of many colours, so beautifully arranged and mingled one with another that all who saw it were filled with delight.

"No wonder that the maiden boasted of her skill," said the people.

And Jupiter himself nodded.

Then Athena began to weave. And she took of the bright sunbeams that gilded the highest mountain top, and of the snowy fleece of the light summer clouds, and of the deep blue of the summer sky, and

94

of the fresh green of the summer fields, and of the royal purple of the autumn woods – and what do you suppose she wove?

The web which she wove in the sky was full of enchanting pictures of flowers and gardens, and of castles and towers, and of mountain heights, and of men and beasts, and of giants and dwarfs, and of the mighty beings who dwell in the clouds with Jupiter.

And all those who looked upon it were so filled with wonder and delight, that they forgot all about the beautiful web which Arachne had woven. And Arachne herself was ashamed and afraid when she saw it, and she hid her face in her hands and wept.

"Oh, how can I live," she cried, "now that I must never again use loom or spindle or distaff?" And she kept on, weeping and weeping and weeping, and saying, "How can I live?"

Then, when Athena saw that the poor maiden would never have any joy unless she were allowed to spin and weave, she took pity on her and said, "I would free you from your bargain if I could, but that is a thing which no one can do. You must hold to your agreement never to touch loom or spindle again. And yet, since you will never be happy again unless you can spin and weave, I will give you a new form so that you can carry on your work with neither spindle nor loom."

Then she touched Arachne with the tip of the spear which she sometimes carried, and the maiden was changed at once into a nimble spider, which ran into a shady place in the grass and began merrily to spin and weave a beautiful web.

I have heard it said that all the spiders which have been in the world since then are the children of Arachne, but I doubt whether this be true. Yet, for all I know, Arachne still lives and spins and weaves – and the very next spider you see may be she herself.

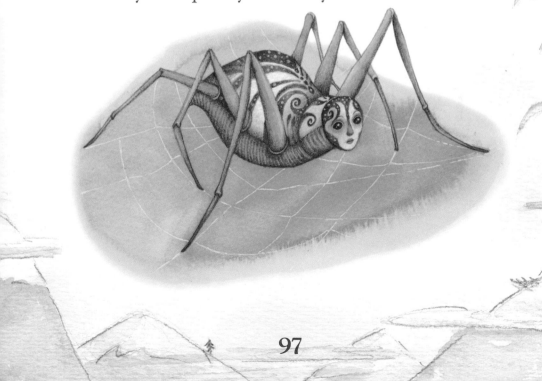

Bellerophon and Pegasus

By James Baldwin

*P*eople said that the gods sent him to the earth, but to this day nobody knows anything about his origin. When first seen he was simply a beautiful horse with wings like a great bird's, and he could travel with equal ease in the air and on the ground.

A good many years ago – so many that we shall not bother about the date – this wonderful animal alighted at a pleasant spot near the foot of Mount Helicon, in Boeotia. He was thirsty, and having seen some reeds growing at that spot, he hoped that he would find there a stream of water, from which he could drink. But there wasn't a drop of water to be seen – nothing but a little patch of boggy ground. In his anger he spread his wings and gave the earth a tremendous kick with both of his hind feet together. The ground was soft, and the force of the blow was such that a deep trench was opened in the boggy soil. Instantly a stream of water, cool and sweet and clear, poured out and filled the trench and ran as a swift brook across the plain toward the distant river. The horse drank his fill from the pleasant fountain which he himself had thus hollowed out, and then, greatly refreshed, unfolded his wings again and rose high in the air, ready for a flight across the sea to the distant land of Lycia.

Men were not long in finding out that the waters of the new spring at the foot of Mount Helicon had some strange properties, filling their hearts with a wonderful sense of whatever is beautiful and true and good, and putting music into their souls and new songs into their mouths. And so they called the spring Hippocrene, meaning Fountain of the Horse, and poets from all parts of the world went there to drink. But in later times the place fell into neglect, and nobody cared to drink from Hippocrene. And so the fountain was allowed to become choked with the stones and dirt that rolled down from the mountain, and soon wild grass and tall reeds hid the spot from view, and nobody from that day to this has been able to point out just where it is. But the horse?

We left him poised high in the air, with his head turned toward the sea and the distant land of Lycia. I do not know how long it took him to fly across, nor does it matter, but one day he alighted on the great road that runs eastward a little way from the capital city of Lycia. So softly had he descended, and so quietly had he folded his great wings and set his feet upon the ground, that a young man who was walking thoughtfully along the way did not know of his presence until he had cantered up quite close to him.

The young man stopped and turned to admire the beautiful animal, and when he came quite near reached out his hand to stroke his nose. But the horse wheeled about and was away again as quick as an arrow sent speeding from a bow. The young man walked on again, and the horse soon returned and gambolled playfully around him, sometimes trotting swiftly back and forth along the road, sometimes rising in the air and sailing in circles round and round him. At last, after much whistling and the offer of a handful of sweetmeats, the young man coaxed the horse so near to him that by a sudden leap he was able to throw himself astride of his back just in front of his great grey wings.

"Now, my handsome fellow," he cried, "carry me straight forward to the country that lies beyond the great northern mountains. I would not be afraid of all the wild beasts in Asia if I could be sure of your help."

But the horse did not seem to understand him. He flew first to the north, then to the south, then to the north again, and sailed hither and thither gaily among the white clouds. At the end of an hour he alighted at the very spot from

101

which he had risen, and his rider, despairing of
making any progress with him, leapt to the ground
and renewed his journey on foot. But the horse, who
seemed to have taken a great liking to the young man,
followed him, frisking hither and thither like a
frolicsome dog, not afraid of him in the least, but
very timid of all other travellers on the road. Late in
the afternoon, when they had left the pleasant
farmlands of Lycia behind them and had come to the
border of a wild, deserted region, an old man, with a
long white beard and bright glittering eyes, met them
and stopped, as many others had already done, to
admire the beautiful animal.

"Who are you, young man," he inquired, "and
what are you doing with so handsome a steed here in
this place?"

"My name is Bellerophon," answered the young
man, "and I am going by order of King Iobates to the
country beyond the northern mountains, where I
expect to slay the Chimaera, which lives there. But as
for this horse, all I know is that he has followed me
since early morning. Whose he is and from whence
he came I cannot tell."

The old man was silent for a few moments as if in

deep thought, while Bellerophon, very weary with his long walk, sat down on a stone to rest, and the horse strolled along by the roadside nipping the short grass.

"Do you see the white roof over there among the trees?" asked the old man finally. "Well, under it there is a shrine to the goddess Athena, of which I am the keeper. A few steps beyond it is my own humble cottage, where I spend my days in study and meditation. If you will go in and lodge with me for the night, I may be able to tell you something about the task that you have undertaken."

Bellerophon was very glad to accept the old man's invitation, for the sun had already begun to dip below the western hills. The hut contained only two rooms, but everything about it was very clean and cosy, and the kind host spared no pains to make his guest comfortable and happy. After they had eaten supper and were still reclining on couches at the side of the table, the old man looked Bellerophon sharply in the face and said, "Now tell me all about yourself and your kindred, and why you are going thus alone and on foot into the country of the Chimaera."

"My father," answered Bellerophon, "is Glaucus, the king of Corinth. He has great wealth in horses and in ships. My grandfather was Sisyphus – I see you have heard of him – for he was famed all over the world for his craftiness and his fine business qualities, that made him the richest of men.

"I was brought up in my father's house, and it was intended that I should succeed him as king of Corinth, but three years ago a sad misfortune happened to me. My younger brother and I were hunting among the wooded hills of Argos, and we were having fine sport, for we had taken much game. We had started home with our booty, and I, who was the faster walker, was some distance ahead of my brother, when suddenly, a deer sprang up between me and the sun. I was half-blinded by the light, but I turned and let fly an arrow quickly. The creature bounded swiftly away, unhurt, but a cry of anguish from the low underbrush told me that I had slain my brother by mistake.

"Vainly did I try to staunch the flow of blood, vainly did I call upon the gods to save him and me. He raised his eyes to mine, smiled feebly, pressed my hand as in forgiveness, and was no more.

"I knew that I dared not return home – the laws of our country are very severe against anyone who, even by accident, causes the death of another. Indeed, until I could be purified from my brother's blood, I dared not look any man in the face. For a long time I wandered in the loneliest of places, like a hunted beast, avoiding the sight of every human being, and living upon nuts and fruits and such small game as I could bring down with my arrows. At length I thought that perhaps old King Proteus of Tiryns, in whose land I then was, might purify me, or if not, he might at least slay me at the altar, which would be better than living longer as a fugitive. So, under the cover of night, I went down into Tiryns, and entering the temple with my cloak thrown over my head, knelt down at the shrine where penitent men are wont to seek purification.

"There King Proteus found me. He purified me and took me into his own house and treated me for a long time as his own son. But a few weeks ago I noticed that a great change had come over him, for he no longer showed me the kind attention which I had learned to expect of him. The queen, too, seemed to have become my enemy, and treated me with the haughtiest disdain. Indeed, I began to suspect that she was urging her husband to put me out of the way, and I should not have been surprised if he had banished me from his court. I was, of course, uncomfortable, and was trying to think of some excuse for leaving Tiryns, when the king, very early one morning, called me into his private chamber. He held in his hand a wooden tablet, sealed with his own signet, and he seemed to be greatly excited about something. 'Bellerophon,' he said, 'I have written on this tablet a letter of very great importance, which I wish to send to my father-in-law, King Iobates, of Lycia, beyond the sea. You are the only man whom I can trust to carry this letter, and so I beg that you will get ready to go at once. A ship is in the harbour already manned for the voyage, and the wind is fair. Before the sun rises you may be well out at sea.'

"I took the tablet and embarked, as he wished, without so much as saying goodbye to the friends I had made there. A good ship and fresh breezes carried me over the sea to Lycia, where I was welcomed most kindly by your good king Iobates. For he had known both my father and my grandfather, and he said that he owed me honour for their sakes. For nine days he held a great feast in his palace, and all the most famous philosophers, merchants and warriors were invited to his table, in order that I might meet them and hear them talk.

"I had not forgotten the tablet that King Proteus had given me, and several times I had made a start to give it to Iobates, but I knew that it would be bad taste to speak of business at such a time. On the tenth day, however, after all the guests had gone home, he said to me, 'Now tell me what message you have brought from my son-in-law Proteus and my dear daughter Anteia. For I know that they have sent me some word.'

"Then I gave him the tablet. He untied the ribbon which bound the two blocks of wood together, and when he had broken the seal he lifted them apart and read that which was engraved on the wax between them. I do not know what this message was, but it must have been something of great importance, for the king's face grew very pale, and he staggered as if he would fall. Then he left the room very quickly, and

I did not see him again until this morning, when he called me into his council-chamber. I was surprised to notice how haggard and worn he was, and how very old he seemed to have become, just within the past three days.

"'Young man,' he said, speaking rather sharply, I thought. 'Young man, they tell me that you are brave and fond of hunting wild beasts, and that you are anxious to win fame by doing some daring deed. I have word, only this morning, that the people who live on the other side of the northern mountains are in great dread of a strange animal that comes out of the caves and destroys their flocks, and sometimes carries their children off to its lair. Some say it is a lion, some a dragon, and some laugh at the whole affair and call it a goat. I think myself that it must be the very same beast that infested the mountain valleys some years ago, and was called by our wise men a Chimaera, and for the sake of the good people whom it persecutes, I should like to have it killed. Everyone to whom I have spoken about it, however, is afraid to venture into its haunts.'

"'I am not afraid,' said I. 'I will start to the mountains this very hour, and if I don't bring you the head of the Chimaera to hang up in your halls, you may brand me as a coward.'

"'You are a brave young man,' said the king, 'and I will take you at your word, but I would advise you to lose no time in starting.'

"Although I was surprised at the way in which the king dismissed me, and the longer I thought about the matter the stranger it all seemed, there was only one thing I could do. I walked out of the king's palace, found the shortest road to Mount Climax, and here I am!"

"Do you have any idea what it was that King Proteus wrote to King Iobates?" asked the old man.

"Why should I?"

"Then I will tell you. He wrote to say that you had been accused of treasonable crimes in Tiryns, and that, not wishing to harm you himself, he had sent you to Lycia to be put to death. King Iobates was loath to have this done, and so he has sent you out against the Chimaera, knowing that no man ever fought with that monster and lived. For she is a more terrible beast than you would believe. All the region beyond the mountains has been laid waste by her, hundreds of people have been slain by her fiery breath alone, and a whole army that was lately sent out against her was routed and put to flight. The king knows very well that she will kill you."

"But what kind of a beast is this Chimaera?" asked Bellerophon.

"She is a strange kind of monster," was the answer. "Her head and shoulders are those of a lion, her body is that of a goat, and her hinder parts are those of a dragon. She fights with her hot breath and her long tail, and she stays on the mountains by night, and goes down into the valleys by day."

"If I had only a shield, and my bow and arrows, and could ride the good winged horse whithersoever I wished him to go, I would not be afraid of all the Chimaeras in the world," said Bellerophon.

"Let me tell you something," said the old man. "Go out to the little temple in the grove before us and lie down to sleep at the foot of the shrine. Everybody knows that to people who are in need of help Athena often comes in dreams to give good advice. Perhaps she will favour you with her counsel and aid, if you only show that you have faith in her."

Bellerophon went at once to the little temple and stretched himself out on the floor close to the shrine of the goddess. The winged horse, who had been feeding on the grass, followed him to the door, and then lay down on the ground outside.

It was nearly morning when Bellerophon dreamed that a tall and stately lady, with large round eyes, and long hair that fell in ringlets upon her shoulders, came into the temple and stood beside him.

"Do you know who the winged steed is that waits outside the door for you?" she asked.

"Truly, I do not," answered Bellerophon. "But if I had some means of making him understand me, he might be my best friend and helper."

"His name is Pegasus," said the lady, "and he was born near the shore of the great western ocean. He has come to help you in your fight with the Chimaera, and you can guide him anywhere you wish if you will only put this ribbon into his mouth, holding on to the ends yourself."

With these words, she placed a beautiful bridle in Bellerophon's hands, and, turning about, walked silently away.

When the sun had risen and Bellerophon awoke, the bridle was lying on the floor beside him, and near it were a longbow with arrows and a shield. It was the first bridle that he had ever seen – some people say that it was the first that was ever made – and Bellerophon examined it with great curiosity. Then he went out and quickly slipped the ribbon bit into the mouth of Pegasus, and leapt upon his back. To his great joy, he saw that now the horse understood all his wishes.

"Here are your bow and arrows and your shield," cried the old man, handing them to him. "Take them, and may Athena be with you in your fight with the Chimaera!"

At a word from Bellerophon, Pegasus rose high in the air, and then, turning, made straight northward toward the great mountains. It was evening when they reached Mount Climax, and quite dark when they at last hovered over the spot which the Chimaera was said to visit at

night. Bellerophon would have passed on without seeing her, had not a burning mountain sent out a great sheet of flame that lighted up the valleys and gave him a plain view of the monster crouching in the shadow of a cliff. He fitted an arrow quickly in his bow and, as Pegasus paused above the edge of the cliff, he let fly directly at her fearful head. The arrow missed the mark, however, and struck the beast in the throat, giving her an ugly wound. Then you should have seen the fury of the Chimaera! She reared herself on her hind feet, made great leaps into the air, and beat the rocks with her long, scaly dragon's tail. She puffed and fumed and roared and blew her fiery breath toward Pegasus, hoping to scorch his wings or smother both horse and rider with its poisonous fumes. Bellerophon, when he saw her in her mad rage, could no longer wonder that the whole country had been in terror of her.

"Now, my good Pegasus," he said, stroking the horse's mane, "steady yourself just out of her reach, and let me send her another keepsake!"

This time the arrow struck the beast in the back, and instead of killing her, only made her more furious than ever. She attacked everything that was in her reach, clawed the rocks, knocked trees down with her tail, and filled all the mountain-valleys with the noise of her mad roarings. The third arrow, however, was sent with a better aim, and the horrid creature, pierced to the heart, fell backward lifeless, and rolled over and over down the steep mountainside, and far out into the valley below.

Bellerophon slept on the mountain that night, while his steed kept watch by his side. In the morning he went down and found the Chimaera lying stiff and dead in the spot where she had rolled, and a score of gaping countrymen standing around – at a safe distance – rejoicing that the monster which had destroyed their fields and desolated their homes had at last been slain. Bellerophon cut off the creature's head, and remounting Pegasus, flew off to return to King Iobates.

Of course old Iobates was astonished to see Bellerophon come back with the monster's head in his arms. All that he did was to thank the young hero for the great service which he had done for his country, and then he began to study up some other means of putting him out of the way.

At last, Bellerophon decided that, since this world was beset with so many distressing things – worse even than Chimaeras – he would leave it and ride on the back of Pegasus all the way to heaven. There is no knowing what might have happened next, had not Zeus, just in the nick of time, sent a gadfly to sting the horse. Pegasus made a wild plunge to escape the fly, and Bellerophon, taken by surprise, was tumbled back to earth. Strange to say, the hero was not killed, but only blinded by his fall, and he never heard of Pegasus again.

The Piper at the Gates of Dawn

From *The Wind in the Willows*
By Kenneth Grahame

Mole lives with his good friend Ratty by the edge of the River. They have other friends, especially Toad, Badger and the Otter, who has a large family.

The Willow-Wren was twittering his thin little song, hidden in the dark selvedge of the river bank. Though it was past ten o'clock at night, the sky still clung to and retained some lingering skirts of light from the departed day, and the sullen heats of the torrid afternoon broke up and rolled away at the dispersing touch of the cool fingers of the short midsummer night. Mole lay stretched on the bank, still panting from the stress of the fierce day that had been cloudless from dawn to late sunset, and waited for his friend to return. He had been on the river with some companions, leaving the Water Rat free to keep an engagement of long standing with Otter, and he had come back to find the house dark and deserted, and no sign of Rat, who was doubtless keeping it up late with his old comrade. It was still too hot to think of staying indoors, so he lay on some cool dock-leaves, and thought over the past day and its doings, and how very good they all had been.

The Rat's light footfall was presently heard approaching over the parched grass. "Oh, the blessed coolness!" he said, and sat down, gazing thoughtfully into the river, silent and preoccupied.

"You stayed to supper, of course?" asked the Mole.

"Simply had to," said the Rat. "They wouldn't hear of my going before. You know how kind they always are. And they made things as jolly for me as ever they could, right up to the moment I left. But I felt a brute all the time, as it was clear to me they were very unhappy, though they tried to hide it. Mole, I'm afraid they're in trouble. Little Portly is missing again, and you know what a lot his father thinks of him, though he never says much about it."

"What, that child?" said the Mole lightly. "Well, suppose he is – why worry about it? He's always straying off, and turning up again – he's so adventurous. But no harm ever happens to him. Everybody knows him and likes him, just as they do old Otter, and you may be sure some animal or other will come across him and bring him back again all right. Why, we've found him ourselves, miles from home, and quite self-possessed and cheerful!"

"Yes, but this time it's more serious," said the Rat gravely. "He's been missing for some days now, and the Otters have hunted everywhere, high and low, without finding a trace. And they've asked every animal, too, for miles around, and no one knows anything about him. Otter's evidently more anxious than he'll admit. I got out of him that young Portly hasn't learnt to swim very well yet, and I can see he's thinking of the weir. There's a lot of water coming down still, and the place always had a fascination for the child. And then there are – well, traps and things – you know. Otter's not the fellow to be nervous about any son of his before it's time. And now he is nervous. When I left, he came out with me – said he wanted some air, and talked about stretching his legs. But I could see it wasn't that, so I drew him out and pumped him, and got it all from him at last. He was going to spend the night watching by the ford. You know the place where the old ford used to be, before they built the bridge?"

"I know it well," said the Mole. "But why should Otter choose to watch there?"

"Well, it seems that it was there he gave Portly his first swimming lesson," continued the Rat. "From that shallow, gravelly spit near the bank. And it was there he used to teach him fishing, and there young Portly caught his first fish, of which he was so very proud. The child loved the spot, and Otter thinks that if he came wandering back from wherever he is, he might make for the ford, or if he came across it he'd remember it well, and stop there and play, perhaps. So Otter goes there every night and watches – on the chance, you know, just on the chance!"

They were silent for a time, both thinking of the same thing – the lonely, heart-sore animal, crouched by the ford, watching and waiting, the long night through – on the chance.

"Well, well," said the Rat presently, "I suppose we ought to be thinking about turning in." But he never offered to move.

"Rat," said the Mole, "I simply can't go and turn in, and go to sleep, and do nothing, even though there doesn't seem to be anything to be done. We'll get the boat out, and paddle upstream. The moon will be up in an hour or so, and then we will search as well as we can – anyhow, it will be better than going to bed and doing nothing."

"Just what I was thinking myself," said the Rat. "It's not the sort of night for bed anyhow, and daybreak is not so very far off, and then we may pick up some news of him from early risers as we go along."

They got the boat out, and the Rat took the sculls, paddling with caution. Out in midstream, there was a clear, narrow track that faintly reflected the sky, but wherever shadows fell on the water from bank, bush, or tree, they were as solid to all appearance as the banks themselves, and the Mole had to steer with judgement accordingly.

Dark and deserted as it was, the night was full of small noises, song and chatter and rustling, telling of the busy little population who were up and about, plying their trades and vocations through the night till sunshine should fall on them at last and send them off to their well-earned repose. The water's own noises, too, were more apparent than by day, its gurglings and 'cloops' more unexpected and near at hand, and constantly they started at what seemed a sudden clear call from an actual articulate voice.

The line of the horizon was clear and hard against the sky, and in one particular quarter it showed black against a silvery climbing phosphorescence that grew and grew. At last, over the rim of the waiting earth the moon lifted with slow majesty till it swung clear of the horizon and rode off, free of moorings, and once more they began to see surfaces – meadows wide-spread, and quiet gardens, and the river itself

from bank to bank, all softly disclosed, all washed clean of mystery and terror, all radiant again as by day, but with a difference that was tremendous. Their old haunts greeted them again in other raiment, as if they had slipped away and put on this pure new apparel and come quietly back, smiling as they shyly waited to see if they would be recognized again under it.

Fastening their boat to a willow, the friends landed in this silent, silver kingdom, and patiently explored the hedges, the hollow trees, the ditches and dry water-ways. Embarking again and crossing over, they worked their way up the stream in this manner, while the moon, serene and detached in a cloudless sky, did what she could to help them in their quest, till her hour came and she sank earthwards reluctantly, and left them, and mystery once more held field and river.

Then a change began slowly to declare itself. The horizon became clearer, field and tree came more into sight, and somehow with a different look. A bird piped suddenly, and a light breeze sprang up and set the reeds and bulrushes rustling. Rat, who was in the stern of the boat, while Mole sculled, sat up suddenly and listened with an intentness. Mole, who was just keeping the boat moving while he scanned the banks, looked at him with curiosity.

"It's gone!" sighed the Rat, sinking back in his seat again. "So beautiful and strange and new. Since it was to end so soon, I almost wish I had never heard it. For it has roused a longing in me that is pain, and nothing seems worthwhile but just to hear that sound once more and go on listening to it for ever. No! There it is again!" he cried, alert once more. Entranced, he was silent for a long space, spellbound.

"Now it passes on and I begin to lose it," he said presently. "Oh Mole! The beauty of it! The merry bubble and joy, the thin, clear, happy call of the distant piping! Such music I never dreamed of, and the call in it is stronger even than the music is sweet! Row on, Mole, row! For the music and the call must be for us."

The Mole obeyed. "I hear nothing myself," he said, "but the wind playing in the reeds and rushes."

The Rat never answered, if indeed he heard. Rapt, transported, trembling, he was possessed in all his senses by this new divine thing that caught up his helpless soul and swung and dandled it, a powerless but happy infant in a strong sustaining grasp.

In silence Mole rowed steadily, and soon they

came to a point where the river divided, a long backwater branching off to one side. With a slight movement of his head Rat, who had long dropped the rudder-lines, directed the rower to take the backwater. The creeping tide of light gained and gained, and now they could see the colour of the flowers that gemmed the water's edge.

"Clearer and nearer still," cried the Rat joyously. "Now you must surely hear it! Ah – at last – I can see you do!"

Breathless and transfixed the Mole stopped rowing as the liquid run of that glad piping broke on him like a wave, caught him up, and possessed him utterly. He saw the tears on his comrade's cheeks, and bowed his head and understood. For a space they hung there, brushed by the purple loosestrife that fringed the bank, then the clear imperious summons that marched hand-in-hand with the intoxicating melody imposed its will on Mole, and mechanically he bent to his oars again. And the light grew steadily stronger, but no birds sang as they were wont to do at the approach of dawn, and but for the heavenly music all was marvellously still.

On either side of them, as they glided onwards, the

rich meadow-grass seemed that morning of a freshness and a greenness unsurpassable. Never had they noticed the roses so vivid, the willowherb so riotous, the meadowsweet so odorous and pervading. Then the murmur of the approaching weir began to hold the air, and they felt a consciousness that they were nearing the end, whatever it might be, that surely awaited their expedition.

A wide half-circle of foam and glinting lights and shining shoulders of green water, the great weir closed the backwater from bank to bank, troubled all the quiet surface with twirling eddies and floating foam streaks, and deadened all other sounds with its solemn and soothing rumble. In midmost of the stream, embraced in the weir's shimmering arm-spread, a small island lay, fringed close with willow and silver birch and alder. Reserved, shy, but full of significance, it hid whatever it might hold behind a veil, keeping it till the hour should come, and, with the hour, those who were called and chosen.

Slowly, but with no doubt or hesitation whatever, and in something of a solemn expectancy, the two animals passed through the broken tumultuous water and moored their boat at the flowery margin of the island. In silence they landed, and pushed through the blossom and scented herbage and undergrowth that led up to the level ground, till they stood on a little lawn of a marvellous green, set round with Nature's own orchard trees – crab apple, wild cherry, and sloe.

"This is the place of my song-dream, the place the music played to me," whispered the Rat, as if in a trance. "Here, in this holy place, here if anywhere, surely we shall find Him!"

Then suddenly the Mole felt a great awe fall upon him, an awe that turned his muscles to water, bowed his head, and rooted his feet to the ground. It was no panic terror – indeed he felt wonderfully at peace and happy – but it was an awe that smote and held him and, without seeing, he knew it could only mean that some august presence was very, very near. With difficulty he turned to look for his friend and saw him at his side, cowed, stricken, and trembling violently. And still there was utter silence in the populous bird-haunted branches around them, and still the light grew and grew.

Perhaps he would never have dared to raise his eyes, but that, though the piping was now hushed, the call and the summons seemed still dominant and imperious. He might not refuse, were Death himself waiting to strike him instantly, once he had looked with mortal eye on things rightly kept hidden. Trembling he obeyed, and raised his humble head.

Then, in that utter clearness of the imminent dawn, while Nature, flushed with fullness of incredible colour, seemed to hold her breath for the event, he looked in the very eyes of the Friend and Helper, saw the backward sweep of the curved horns, gleaming in the growing daylight, saw the stern, hooked nose between the kindly eyes that were looking down on them humorously, while the bearded mouth broke into a half-smile at the corners, saw the rippling muscles on the arm that lay across the broad chest, the long supple hand still holding the pan-pipes only just fallen away from the parted lips, saw the splendid curves of the shaggy limbs disposed in majestic ease on the sward, saw, last of all, nestling between his very hooves, sleeping soundly in entire peace and contentment, the little, round, podgy, childish form of the baby otter. All this he saw, for one moment breathless and intense, vivid on the morning sky, and still, as he looked, he lived. And still, as he lived, he wondered.

"Rat!" he found breath to whisper, shaking. "Are you afraid?"

"Afraid?" murmured the Rat, his eyes shining with unutterable love. "Afraid! Of him? Oh, never, never! And yet – and yet – Oh, Mole, I am afraid!"

Then the two animals, crouching to the earth, bowed their heads and did worship.

Sudden and magnificent, the sun's broad golden disc showed itself over the horizon facing them, and the first rays, shooting across the level water-meadows, took the animals full in the eyes and dazzled them. When they were able to look once more, the vision had vanished, and the air was full of the carol of birds that hailed the dawn.

As they stared blankly in dumb misery, deepening as they slowly realized all they had seen and all they had lost, a capricious little breeze, dancing up from the surface of the water, tossed the aspens, shook the dewy heads of the roses and blew lightly and caressingly in their faces, and with its soft touch came instant oblivion. For this is the last, best gift that the kindly demi-god is careful to bestow on those to whom he has revealed himself in their helping: the

gift of forgetfulness. Lest the awful remembrance should remain and grow, and overshadow mirth and pleasure, and the great haunting memory should spoil all the after-lives of little animals helped out of difficulties, in order that they should be happy and lighthearted as before.

Mole rubbed his eyes and stared at Rat, who was looking about him in a puzzled sort of way. "I beg your pardon, what did you say, Rat?" he asked.

"I think I was only remarking," said Rat slowly, "that this was the right sort of place, and that here, if anywhere, we should find him. And look! Why, there he is, the little fellow!" And with a cry of delight he ran towards the slumbering Portly.

But Mole stood still a moment, held in thought. As one wakened suddenly from a beautiful dream, who struggles to recall it, and can recapture nothing but a dim sense of the beauty of it – the beauty! But eventually that, too, fades away in its turn, and the dreamer bitterly accepts the hard, cold waking and all its penalties. So Mole, after struggling with his memory for a brief moment, shook his head sadly and followed the Rat.

Portly woke up with a joyous squeak, and wriggled

with pleasure at the sight of his father's friends, who had played with him so often in past days. In a moment, however, he fell to hunting round in a circle with pleading whine. As a child that has fallen happily asleep in its nurse's arms, and wakes to find itself alone in a strange place, and runs from room to room, despair growing silently in its heart, even so Portly searched the island and searched, dogged and unwearying, till at last the black moment came for giving it up, and sitting down and crying bitterly.

The Mole ran to comfort the little animal, but Rat looked long and doubtfully at hoof-marks deep in the grass. "Some great animal has been here," he murmured thoughtfully, and then stood musing, his mind strangely stirred.

"Come along, Rat!" called the Mole. "Think of poor Otter, waiting up there by the ford!"

Portly had soon been comforted by the promise of a treat – a jaunt on the river in Mr Rat's real boat – and the two animals conducted him to the water's

side, placed him securely between them in the bottom of the boat, and paddled off down the backwater. The sun was up by now, birds sang, and flowers smiled and nodded, but somehow – so thought the animals – with less of richness and blaze of colour than they seemed to remember seeing quite recently somewhere – they wondered where.

The main river reached again, they turned the boat upstream, towards the point where they knew their friend was keeping his vigil. As they drew near the ford, the Mole took the boat in to the bank. They lifted Portly out onto the towpath, gave him a friendly farewell pat on the back, and shoved out into midstream. They watched the little animal as he waddled along the path contentedly.

They saw his muzzle suddenly lift and his waddle break into a clumsy amble as he quickened his pace with shrill whines of recognition. Looking up the river, they could see Otter start up, tense and rigid, from out of the shallows where he crouched, and could hear his amazed and joyous bark as he bounded up through the willow shoots onto the path. Then the Mole swung the boat round and let the full stream bear them down again whither it would, their quest now happily ended.

"I feel strangely tired, Rat," said the Mole, leaning wearily over his oars as the boat drifted. "It's being up all night, you'll say, but that's nothing. We do as much half the nights of the week, at this time of the year. No – I feel as if I had been through something exciting and terrible, and it was over, and yet nothing much has happened."

"Or something very surprising and splendid and beautiful," murmured the Rat, leaning back and closing his eyes. "I feel just as you do, Mole, simply dead tired, though not body tired. It's lucky we've got the stream with us, to take us home. Isn't it jolly to feel the sun again, soaking into one's bones! And hark to the wind playing in the reeds!"

"It's like music – far away music," said the Mole drowsily.

"So I was thinking," murmured the Rat, dreamful and languid. "Dance music – the lilting sort – it passes into words and out of them again – I catch them at intervals – then it is dance music once more, and then nothing but the reeds' soft thin whispering."

"You hear better than I," said the Mole sadly. "I cannot catch the words."

"Let me try and give you them," said the Rat softly, his eyes still closed. "Now it is turning into words again – faint but clear:

"*Lest the awe should dwell*
And turn your frolic to fret
You shall look on my power at the helping hour
But then you shall forget!'

"Now the reeds take it up – '*forget, forget,*' and it dies away in a whisper. Then the voice returns:

"*Lest limbs be reddened and rent*
I spring the trap that is set
As I loose the snare you may glimpse me there
For surely you shall forget!'

"Row nearer, Mole, nearer to the reeds! It is hard to catch, and grows each minute fainter:

"*Helper and healer, I cheer*
Small waifs in the woodland wet
Strays I find in it, wounds I bind in it
Bidding them all forget!'

"Nearer, Mole, nearer! No, it is no good, the song has died away into reed-talk."

"But what do the words mean?" asked the wondering Mole.

"That I do not know," said the Rat simply. "I passed them on to you as they reached me. Ah! Now they return again, and this time full and clear! This time, at last, it is the real, the unmistakable thing, simple – passionate – perfect—"

"Well, let's have it, then," said the Mole, after he had waited patiently for a few minutes, half-dozing in the hot sun.

But no answer came. He looked, and understood the silence. With a smile of much happiness on his face, and something of a listening look still lingering there, the weary Rat was fast asleep.

TRICKS, TRAPS AND MISCHIEF

The Elephant's Child

From *Just So Stories*
by Rudyard Kipling

In the high and far-off times, the Elephant, oh best beloved, had no trunk. He had only a blackish, bulgy nose, as big as a boot, that he could wriggle about from side to side, but he couldn't pick up things with it. But there was one Elephant – a new Elephant – an Elephant's Child – who was full of 'satiable curtiosity, and that means he asked ever so many questions. And he lived in Africa, and he filled all Africa with his 'satiable curtiosities. He asked his tall aunt, the Ostrich, why her tail feathers grew just so, and his tall aunt the Ostrich spanked him with her hard, hard claw.

The Elephant's Child

He asked his broad aunt, the Hippopotamus, why her eyes were red, and his broad aunt, the Hippopotamus, spanked him with her broad, broad hoof. And he asked his hairy uncle, the Baboon, why melons tasted the way that they did, and his hairy uncle, the Baboon, spanked him with his hairy, hairy paw. And still he was full of 'satiable curtiosity! He asked questions about everything that he saw, or heard, or felt, or smelt, or touched, and all his uncles and his aunts spanked him. And still he was full of 'satiable curtiosity!

One fine morning in the middle of the Precession of the Equinoxes this 'satiable Elephant's Child asked a new question that he had never asked before. He asked, "What does the Crocodile have for dinner?"

Then everybody said, "Hush!" in a loud and dreadful tone, and they spanked him immediately and directly, without stopping, for a long time.

By and by, when that was finished, he came upon Kolokolo Bird sitting in the middle of a wait-a-bit thorn-bush, and he said, "My father has spanked me, and my mother has spanked me, and all my aunts and uncles have spanked me because of my 'satiable curtiosity, and still I want to know what the

Crocodile has for dinner!"

Then Kolokolo Bird said, with a mournful cry, "Go to the banks of the great grey-green, greasy Limpopo River, all set about with fever-trees, and find out."

That very next morning, when there was nothing left of the Equinoxes, because the Precession had preceded according to precedent, this 'satiable Elephant's Child took a hundred pounds of bananas (the little short red kind), and a hundred pounds of sugar-cane (the long purple kind), and seventeen melons (the greeny-crackly kind), and said to all his dear families, "Goodbye. I am going to the great grey-green, greasy Limpopo River, all set about with fever-trees, to find out what the Crocodile has for dinner." And they all spanked him once more for luck, though he asked them most politely to stop.

Then he went away, a little warm, but not at all astonished, eating melons, and throwing the rind about, because he could not pick it up.

The Elephant's Child went from Graham's Town to Kimberley, and from Kimberley to Khama's Country, and from Khama's Country he went east by north, eating melons all the time, till at last he came

to the banks of the great grey-green, greasy Limpopo
River, all set about with fever-trees, precisely as
Kolokolo Bird had said it would be.

Now you must know and understand, Oh Best
Beloved, that till that very week, and day, and
hour, and minute, this 'satiable Elephant's
Child had never seen a Crocodile,
and did not know what one
was like. It was all his
'satiable curtiosity.

The first thing
that he found was
a Bi-Coloured-
Python-Rock-Snake
curled round a rock.

"'Scuse me," said the
Elephant's Child most
politely, "but have you seen such a thing as a
Crocodile in these parts?"

"Have I seen a Crocodile?" said the Bi-Coloured-
Python-Rock-Snake, in a voice of dreadful scorn.
"What will you ask me next?"

"'Scuse me," said the Elephant's Child, "but could
you kindly tell me what he has for dinner?"

Then the Bi-Coloured-Python-Rock-Snake uncoiled himself very quickly from the rock, and spanked the Elephant's Child with his scalesome, flailsome tail.

"That is odd," said the Elephant's Child, "because my father and my mother, and my uncle and my aunt, not to mention my other aunt, the Hippopotamus, and my other uncle, the Baboon, have all spanked me for my 'satiable curtiosity – and I suppose this is the same thing."

So he said goodbye very politely to the Bi-Coloured-Python-Rock-Snake, and helped to coil him up on the rock again, and went on, a little warm, but not at all astonished, eating melons, and throwing the rind about, because he could not pick it up, till he trod on what he thought was a log of wood at the very edge of the great grey-green, greasy Limpopo River, all set about with fever-trees.

But it was really the Crocodile, Oh Best Beloved, and the Crocodile winked one eye – like this!

"'Scuse me," said the Elephant's Child most politely, "but do you happen to have seen a Crocodile in these promiscuous parts?"

Then the Crocodile winked the other eye, and

lifted half his tail out of the mud, and the Elephant's Child stepped back most politely, because he did not wish to be spanked again.

"Come hither, Little One," said the Crocodile. "Why do you ask such things?"

"'Scuse me," said the Elephant's Child most politely, "but my father has spanked me, my mother has spanked me, not to mention my tall aunt, the Ostrich, and my tall uncle, the Giraffe, who can kick ever so hard, as well as my broad aunt, the Hippopotamus, and my hairy uncle, the Baboon, and even including the Bi-Coloured-Python-Rock-Snake, with the scalesome, flailsome tail, just up the bank, who spanks harder than any of them, and so, if it's quite all the same to you, I don't want to be spanked any more."

"Come hither, Little One," said the Crocodile, "for I am the Crocodile," and he wept crocodile-tears to show it was quite true.

Then the Elephant's Child grew all breathless, and panted, and kneeled down on the bank and said, "You are the very person I have been looking for all these long days. Will you please tell me what you have for dinner?"

"Come hither, Little One," said the Crocodile, "and I'll whisper."

Then the Elephant's Child put his head down close to the Crocodile's musky, tusky mouth, and the Crocodile caught him by his little nose, which up to that very week, day, hour, and minute, had been no bigger than a boot, though much more useful.

"I think," said the Crocodile – and he said it between his teeth, like this – "I think today I will begin with Elephant's Child!"

At this, Oh Best Beloved, the Elephant's Child was much annoyed, and he said, speaking through his nose, like this, "Led go! You are hurtig be!"

Then the Bi-Coloured-Python-Rock-Snake scuffled down from the bank and said, "My young friend, if you do not now, immediately and instantly, pull as hard as ever you can, it is my opinion that your acquaintance in the large-pattern leather ulster" (and by this he meant the Crocodile) "will jerk you into yonder limpid stream before you can say Jack Robinson." (This is the way Bi-Coloured-Python-Rock-Snakes always talk.)

The Elephant's Child

Then the Elephant's Child sat back on his little haunches, and pulled, and pulled, and pulled, and his nose began to stretch. And the Crocodile floundered into the water, making it all creamy with great sweeps of his tail, and he pulled, and pulled, and pulled.

And the Elephant's Child's nose kept on stretching, and the Elephant's Child spread all his little four legs and pulled, and pulled, and his nose kept on stretching, and the Crocodile threshed his tail like an oar, and he pulled, and pulled, and pulled, and at each pull the Elephant's Child's nose grew longer and longer – and it hurt him terribly!

Then the Elephant's Child felt his legs slipping, and he said through his nose, which was now nearly five feet long, "This is too butch for be!"

Then the Bi-Coloured-Python-Rock-Snake came down from the bank, and knotted himself in a double-clove-hitch round the Elephant's Child's hind legs, and said, "Rash and inexperienced traveller, we will now seriously devote ourselves to a little high tension, because if we do not, it is my impression that yonder self-propelling man-of-war with the armour-plated upper deck" (and by this, Oh Best Beloved, he meant the Crocodile), "will permanently vitiate your future career." (That is the way all Bi-Coloured-Python-Rock-Snakes always talk.)

So he pulled, and the Elephant's Child pulled, and the Crocodile pulled, but the Elephant's Child and the Bi-Coloured-Python-Rock-Snake pulled hardest, and at last the Crocodile let go of the Elephant's Child's nose with a plop that you could hear all up and down the Limpopo.

Then the Elephant's Child sat down with a bump most hard and sudden, but first he was careful to say "Thank you" to the Bi-Coloured-Python-Rock-Snake, and next he was kind to his poor pulled nose, and wrapped it all up in cool banana leaves, and hung it in the great grey-green, greasy Limpopo to cool.

"What are you doing that for?" asked the Bi-Coloured-Python-Rock-Snake.

"'Scuse me," replied the Elephant's Child, "but my poor nose is badly out of shape, and I am waiting for it to shrink."

"Then you will have to wait a long time," said the Bi-Coloured-Python-Rock-Snake. "Some people do not know what is good for them."

The Elephant's Child sat there for three days waiting for his nose to shrink. But it never grew any shorter, and, besides, it made him squint. For, Oh Best Beloved, you will see and understand that the Crocodile had pulled it out into a really truly trunk, same as all Elephants have today.

At the end of the third day a fly came and stung him on the shoulder, and before he knew what he was doing he lifted up his trunk and hit that fly dead with the end of it.

"'Vantage number one!" said the Bi-Coloured-Python-Rock-Snake. "You couldn't have done that with a mere-smear nose. Try and eat a little now."

Before he thought what he was doing the Elephant's Child put out his trunk and plucked a large bundle of grass, dusted it clean against his fore-legs, and stuffed it into his own mouth.

"'Vantage number two!" said the Bi-Coloured-Python-Rock-Snake. "You couldn't have done that with a mear-smear nose. Don't you think the sun is very hot here?"

"It is," said the Elephant's Child, and before he thought what he was doing he schlooped up a schloop of mud from the banks of the great grey-green, greasy Limpopo, and slapped it on his head, where it made a cool schloopy-sloshy mud-cap all trickly behind his ears.

"'Vantage number three!" said the Bi-Coloured-Python-Rock-Snake. "You couldn't have done that with a mere-smear nose. Now how do you feel about being spanked again?"

"'Scuse me," said the Elephant's Child, "but I should not like it at all."

"How would you like to spank somebody?" said the Bi-Coloured-Python-Rock-Snake.

"I should like that very much," replied the Elephant's Child.

"Well," said the Bi-Coloured-Python-Rock-Snake, "your new nose will be useful to spank people with."

"Thank you," said the Elephant's Child, "I'll remember that. And now I'll go home to my dear families and try."

So the Elephant's Child went home across Africa, frisking and whisking his trunk. When he wanted fruit to eat he pulled fruit down from a tree, instead of waiting for it to fall as he used to do. When he wanted grass he plucked grass up from the ground, instead of going on his knees as he used to do. When the flies bit him he broke off the branch of a tree and used it as fly-whisk, and he made himself a new, cool, slushy-squishy mud-cap whenever the sun was hot. When he felt lonely walking through Africa he sang to himself down his trunk, and the noise was louder than several brass bands.

He went especially out of his way to find a broad Hippopotamus (she was no relation of his), and he spanked her very hard, to make sure that the Bi-Coloured-Python-Rock-Snake had spoken the truth about his new trunk. The rest of the time he picked up the melon rinds that he had dropped on his way to the Limpopo – for he was a Tidy Pachyderm.

One dark evening he came back to all his dear families, and he coiled up his trunk and said, "How do you do?" They were very glad to see him, and immediately said, "Come here and be spanked for your 'satiable curtiosity."

"Pooh," said the Elephant's Child. "I don't think you peoples know anything about spanking, but I do, and I'll show you." Then he uncurled his trunk and knocked two of his dear brothers head over heels.

"Oh Bananas!" said they. "Where did you learn that trick, and what have you done to your nose?"

"I got a new one from the Crocodile on the banks of the great grey-green, greasy Limpopo River," said the Elephant's Child. "I asked him what he had for dinner, and he gave me this to keep."

"It looks very ugly," said his hairy uncle, the Baboon.

"It does," said the Elephant's Child. "But it's very useful," and he picked up his hairy uncle, the Baboon, by one hairy leg, and hove him into a hornet's nest.

Then that bad Elephant's Child spanked all his dear families for a long time, till they were very warm and greatly astonished. He pulled out his tall Ostrich aunt's tail feathers, and he caught his tall uncle, the Giraffe, by the hind-leg, and dragged him through a thorn-bush, and he shouted at his broad aunt, the Hippopotamus, and blew bubbles into her ear when she was sleeping in the water after meals, but he never let any one touch Kolokolo Bird.

At last things grew so exciting that his dear families went off one by one in a hurry to the banks of the great grey-green, greasy Limpopo River, all set about with fever-trees, to borrow new noses from the Crocodile. When they came back nobody spanked anybody any more, and ever since that day, Oh Best Beloved, all the Elephants you will ever see, besides all those that you won't, have trunks precisely like the trunk of the 'satiable Elephant's Child.

The Spider and the Toad

From *Wood Magic*
by Richard Jefferies

*Bevis is a child growing up in Victorian England. He loves
to play for hours in his garden and the fields surrounding it,
watching the animals and learning about their lives.*

One morning as little 'Sir' Bevis (such was his pet
name) was digging in the farmhouse garden, he
saw a daisy, and throwing aside his spade, he sat down
on the grass to pick the flower to pieces. He pulled
the pink-tipped petals off one by one, and as they
dropped they were lost. Next he gathered a bright
dandelion, and squeezed the white juice from the
hollow stem, which drying presently, left his fingers
stained with brown spots. Then he drew forth a

bennet from its sheath, and bit and sucked it till his teeth were green from the sap. Lying at full length, he drummed the earth with his toes, while the tall grass blades tickled his cheeks.

Presently, rolling on his back, he drummed again with his heels. He looked up at the blue sky, but only for a moment, because the glare of light was too strong in his eyes. After a minute, he turned on his side, thrust out one arm, placed his head on it, and drew up one knee, as if going to sleep. His little brown wrist, bared by the sleeve shortening as he extended his arm, bent down the grass, and his still browner fingers played with the blades, and every now and then tore one off.

A flutter of wings sounded among the blossom on an apple tree close by, and instantly Bevis sat up, knowing it must be a goldfinch thinking of building a nest in the branches. If the trunk of the tree had not been so big, he would have tried to climb it at once, but he knew he could not do it, nor could he see the bird for the leaves and bloom. A puff of wind came and showered the petals down upon him. They fell like snowflakes on his face and dotted the grass.

Buzz! A great humble-bee, with a band of gold

across his back, flew up, and hovered near, wavering to and fro in the air as he stayed to look at a flower.

Buzz! Bevis listened, and knew very well what he was saying. It was, "This is a sweet little garden – all grass and daisies, and apple trees, and narrow patches with flowers and fruit trees one side, and a wall and currant bushes another side, and a low box-hedge and a haha, where you can see the high mowing grass quite underneath you, and a round summerhouse in the corner, painted as blue inside as a hedge-sparrow's egg is outside, and then another haha with iron railings, which you are always climbing up, Bevis, on the fourth side, with stone steps leading down to a meadow, where the cows are feeding, and where they have left all the buttercups standing as tall as your waist, sir.

"The gate in the iron railings is not fastened, and besides, there is a gap in the box-hedge, and it is easy to drop down the haha wall, but that is mowing grass there. You know very well you could not come to any harm in the meadow – they said you were not to go outside the garden, but that's all nonsense, and very stupid. I am going outside the garden, Bevis. Good morning, dear. Buzz!" And the great humble-bee flew slowly between the iron railings, out among the buttercups, and away up the field.

Bevis went to the railings, and stood on the lowest bar. Then he opened the gate a little way, but it squeaked so loud upon its rusty hinges that he let it shut again. He walked round the garden along beside the box-hedge to the patch by the lilac trees – they were single lilacs, which are much more beautiful than the double, and all bowed down with a mass of bloom. Some rhubarb grew there, and to bring it up the faster, they had put a round wooden box on it, hollowed out from the sawn butt of an elm, which was rotten within and easily scooped. The top was covered with an old board, and every time that Bevis passed he lifted up the corner of the board and peeped in, to see if the large red, swelling knobs were yet bursting.

One of these round wooden boxes had been split

and spoilt, and half of it was left lying on the ground. Under this shelter a Toad had his house. Bevis peered in at him, and touched him with a twig to make him move an inch or two, for he was so lazy, and sat there all day long, except when it rained. Sometimes the Toad told him a story, but not very often, for he was a silent old philosopher, and not very fond of anybody. He had a nephew, quite a lively young fellow, in the cucumber frame on the other side of the lilac bushes, at whom Bevis also peered nearly every day after they had lifted the frame and propped it up with wedges.

The gooseberries were no bigger than beads, but he

tasted two, and then a thrush began to sing on an ash tree in the hedge of the meadow. "Bevis! Bevis!" said the thrush, and he turned round to listen. "My dearest Bevis, have you forgotten the meadow, and the buttercups, and the sorrel? You know the sorrel, don't you, that tastes so pleasant if you nibble the leaf? And I have a nest in the bushes, not very far up the hedge, and you may take just one egg, there are only two yet. But don't tell any more boys about it, or we shall not have one left. That is a very sweet garden, but it is very small. I like all these fields to fly about in, and the swallows fly ever so much farther than I can, so far away and so high, that I cannot tell you how they find their way home to the chimney. But they will tell you, if you ask them. Good morning! I am going over the brook."

Bevis went to the iron railings and got up two bars, and looked over, but he could not yet make up his mind, so he went inside the summerhouse, which had one small round window. All the lower part of the blue walls was scribbled and marked with pencil, where he had written and drawn, and put down his ideas and notes. The lines were somewhat intermingled, and crossed each other, and some stretched out long distances, and came back in sharp angles. But Bevis knew very well what he meant when he wrote it all. Taking a stump of cedar pencil from his pocket, one end of it much gnawn, he added a few scrawls to the inscriptions, and then stood on the seat to look out of the round window, which was darkened by an old cobweb.

Once upon a time there was a very cunning Spider, a very cunning Spider indeed. The old Toad by the rhubarb told Bevis there had not been such a cunning Spider for many summers. He knew almost as much about flies as the old Toad, and caught such a great number that the Toad began to think there would be none left for him. Now the Toad was extremely fond of flies, and he watched the Spider with envy, and grew more angry about it every day.

As he sat blinking and winking by the rhubarb in his house all day long, the Toad never left off thinking, thinking, thinking about this Spider. And as he kept thinking, thinking, thinking, so he told Bevis, he recollected that he knew a great deal about a good many other things besides flies. So one day, after several weeks of thinking, he crawled out of his house in the sunshine, which he did not like at all, and went across the grass to the iron railings, where the Spider had then got his web. The Spider saw him coming, and being very proud of his cleverness, began to taunt and tease him.

"Your back is all over warts, and you are an old toad," he said. "You are so old, that I heard the swallows saying their great, great, great grandmothers, when they built in the chimney, did not know when you were born. And you have got foolish, and past doing anything, and so stupid that you hardly know when it is going to rain. Why, the sun is shining bright, you stupid old toad, and there isn't a chance of a single drop falling. You look very ugly down there in the grass. Don't you wish you were me, and could catch more flies than you could eat? I can catch wasps and bees, and tie them up so tight with my threads that they cannot sting nor even move their wings, nor so much as wriggle their bodies. I am the very cleverest and most cunning spider that ever lived."

"Indeed, you are!" replied the Toad. "I have been thinking so all the summer, and so much do I admire you, that I have come all this way, across in the hot sun, to tell you something."

"Tell me something!" said the Spider, much

offended. "I know everything."

"Oh, yes, honoured sir," said the Toad, "you have such wonderful eyes, and such a sharp mind, it is true that you know everything about the sun, and the moon, and the earth, and flies. But, as you have studied all these great and important things, you could hardly see all the very little trifles like a poor old toad."

"Oh yes, I can. I know everything there is to know – everything!"

"But, sir," went on the Toad so humbly, "this is such a very little thing, and a spider like you in such a high position of life, could not mind me telling you such a mere nothing."

"Well, I don't mind," said the Spider, "you may go on, and tell me, if you like."

"The fact is," said the Toad, "while I have been sitting in my hole, I have noticed that such a lot of the flies that come into this garden presently go into the summerhouse there, and when they are in the summerhouse, they always go to that little round window, which is sometimes quite black with them, for it is the nature of flies to buzz over glass."

"I do not know so much about that," said the

The Spider and the Toad

Spider, "for I have never lived in houses, being an independent insect, but it is possible you may be right. At any rate, it is not of much consequence. You had better go up into the window, old toad." Now this was a sneer on the part of the Spider.

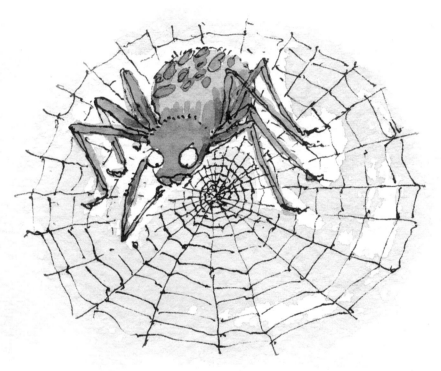

"But I can't climb up into the window," said the Toad. "All I can do is to crawl about the ground, but you can run up a wall quickly. How I do wish I was a spider!" Then the Toad turned round, after bowing to the clever Spider, and went back to his hole.

Now the Spider was secretly very much mortified and angry with himself, because he had not noticed this about the flies going to the window in the summerhouse. At first he said to himself that it was not true, but he could not help looking that way now and then, and every time he looked, there was the window crowded with flies. They had all the garden to buzz about in, and all the fields, but instead of wandering under the trees, and over the flowers, they preferred to go into the summerhouse and crawl over the glass of the little window, though it was very dirty from so many feet. For a long time, the Spider was too proud to go there too, but one day such a splendid bluebottle fly got in the window and made such a tremendous buzzing, that he could no longer resist climbing up there.

So he left his web by the railings, and walked up the blue-painted wall, over Bevis' writings and marks, and spun such a web in the window as had never before been seen. It was the largest and the finest, and the most beautiful web that had ever been made, and it caught such a number of flies that the Spider grew fatter every day. In a week's time he was so big that he

could no longer hide in the crack he had chosen, he
was quite a giant, and the Toad came across the grass
one night and looked at him, but the Spider was now
so bloated he would not recognize the Toad.

But one morning a robin came to the iron railings,
and perched on the top, and put his head a little on
one side, to show his black eye the better. Then he
flew inside the summerhouse, alighted in the window,
and gobbled up the Spider in an instant. The old
Toad shut his eye and opened it again, and went on
thinking, for that was just what he knew would
happen. Ever so many times in his very long life he
had seen spiders go up there, but no sooner had they
got fat than a robin or a wren came in and ate them.
Some of the clever Spider's web was there still when
Bevis looked out of the window, all dusty and
draggled, with the skins and wings of some gnats and
a dead leaf entangled in it.

Rikki-tikki-tavi

From *The Jungle Book*
by Rudyard Kipling

Rikki-tikki was a mongoose, rather like a little cat in his fur and his tail, but quite like a weasel in his head and his habits. His eyes and the end of his restless nose were pink. He could scratch himself anywhere he pleased with any leg, front or back, that he wished to use. He could fluff up his tail 'til it looked like a bottle brush, and his war cry as he scuttled through the long grass was, "Rikk-tikk-tikki-tikki-tchk!"

One day, a high summer flood washed him out of the burrow where he lived with his father and mother, and carried him, kicking and clucking, down a roadside ditch. He found a little wisp of grass floating there, and clung to it till he lost his senses. When he revived, he was lying in the hot sun on the middle of a garden path, very 'draggled indeed, and a small boy was saying, "Here's a dead mongoose. Let's have a funeral."

"No," said his mother, "let's take him in and dry him. Perhaps he isn't really dead."

They took him into the house, and a man picked him up between his finger and thumb and said he was not dead but half-choked. They wrapped him in cotton wool, warmed him over a fire, and he opened his eyes and sneezed.

"Now," said the big man, "don't frighten him, and we'll see what he'll do."

It is the hardest thing in the world to frighten a mongoose, because he is eaten up from nose to tail with curiosity. The motto of all the mongoose family is 'Run and find out', and Rikki-tikki was a true mongoose. He looked at the cotton wool, decided that it was not good to eat, ran all round the table, sat up and put his fur in order, scratched himself, and jumped on the small boy's shoulder.

"Don't be frightened, Teddy," said his father.

"That's his way of making friends."

"Ouch! He's tickling under my chin," said Teddy.

Rikki-tikki looked down between the boy's collar and neck, snuffed at his ear, and climbed down to the floor, where he sat rubbing his nose.

"Good gracious," said Teddy's mother, "and that's a wild creature! I suppose he's so tame because we've been kind to him."

"All mongooses are like that," said her husband. "If Teddy doesn't pick him up by the tail, or try to put him in a cage, he'll run in and out of the house all day long. Let's give him something to eat."

They gave him a little piece of raw meat. Rikki-tikki liked it immensely, and when it was finished he went out into the veranda and sat in the sunshine and fluffed up his fur to make it dry to the roots. Then he felt better.

"There are more things to find out about in this house," he said to himself, "than all my family could find out in all their lives. I shall certainly stay and find out."

He spent all that day roaming over the house. He nearly drowned himself in the bathtubs, put his nose into the ink on a writing table, and burned it on the end of the big man's cigar, for he climbed up in the man's lap to see how writing was done. At nightfall he ran into Teddy's nursery to watch how kerosene lamps were lighted, and when Teddy went to bed Rikki-tikki climbed up too. But he was a restless companion, because he had to get up and attend to every noise all through the night, and find out what made it. Teddy's mother and father came in, the last thing, to look at their boy, and Rikki-tikki was awake on the pillow.

"I don't like that," said Teddy's mother. "He may bite the child."

"He'll do no such thing," said the father. "Teddy's safer with that little beast than if he had a bloodhound to watch him. If a snake came into the nursery now—" But Teddy's mother didn't want to think about anything so awful.

Early in the morning Rikki-tikki came to early breakfast in the veranda riding on Teddy's shoulder, and they gave him banana and some boiled egg. He sat on all their laps one after the other, because every well-brought-up mongoose always hopes to be a house mongoose some day and have rooms to run about in, and Rikki-tikki's mother (she used to live in the general's house at Segowlee) had carefully told Rikki what to do if ever he came across white men.

Then Rikki-tikki went out into the garden to see what was to be seen. It was a large garden, only half-cultivated, with bushes, as big as summerhouses, of Marshal Niel roses, lime and orange trees, clumps of bamboos, and thickets of high grass. Rikki-tikki licked his lips. "This is a splendid hunting-ground," he said, and his tail grew bottle-brushy at the thought of it, and he scuttled up and down the garden, snuffing here and there till he heard very sorrowful voices in a thorn-bush.

It was Darzee, the Tailorbird, and his wife. They had made a beautiful nest by pulling two big leaves together and stitching them up the edges with fibres, and had filled the hollow with cotton and downy fluff. The nest swayed to and fro, as they sat on the rim and cried.

"What is the matter?" asked Rikki-tikki.

"We are feeling very miserable," said Darzee. "One of our babies fell out of the nest yesterday and

Nag ate him."

"H'm!" said Rikki-tikki, "that is very sad – but I am a stranger here. Who is Nag?"

Darzee and his wife only cowered down in the nest without answering, for from the thick grass at the foot of the bush there came a low hiss – a horrid cold sound that made Rikki-tikki jump back two clear feet. Then inch by inch out of the grass rose up the head and spread hood of Nag, the big black cobra, and he was five feet long from tongue to tail. When he had lifted one-third of himself clear of the ground, he stayed balancing to and fro exactly as a dandelion tuft balances in the wind, and he looked at Rikki-tikki with the wicked snake's eyes that never change their expression, whatever the snake may be thinking of.

"Who is Nag?" said he. "I am Nag. The great God Brahm put his mark upon all our people, when the first cobra spread his hood to keep the sun off Brahm as he slept. Look, and be afraid!"

He spread out his hood more than ever, and Rikki-tikki saw the spectacle-mark on the back of it that looks exactly like the eye part of a hook-and-eye fastening. He was afraid for the minute, but it is

impossible for a mongoose to stay frightened for any length of time, and though Rikki-tikki had never met a live cobra before, his mother had fed him on dead ones, and he knew that all a grown mongoose's business in life was to fight and eat snakes. Nag knew that too and, at the bottom of his cold heart, he was also afraid.

"Well," said Rikki-tikki, and his tail began to fluff up again, "marks or no marks, do you think it is right

170

for you to eat fledglings out of a nest?"

Nag was thinking to himself, and watching the least little movement in the grass behind Rikki-tikki. He knew that mongooses in the garden meant death sooner or later for him and his family, but he wanted to get Rikki-tikki off his guard. So he dropped his head a little, and put it on one side.

"Let us talk," he said. "You eat eggs. Why should not I eat birds?"

"Behind you! Look behind you!" sang Darzee.

Rikki-tikki knew better than to waste time in staring. He jumped up in the air as high as he could go, and just under him whizzed by the head of Nagaina, Nag's wicked wife. She had crept up behind him as he was talking, to make an end of him. He heard her savage hiss as the stroke missed. He came down almost across her back, and if he had been an old mongoose he would have known that then was the time to break her back with one bite, but he was afraid of the terrible lashing return stroke of the cobra. He bit, indeed, but did not bite long enough, and he jumped clear of the whisking tail, leaving Nagaina torn and angry.

"Wicked, wicked Darzee!" said Nag, lashing up as

high as he could reach toward the nest in the thorn-bush. But Darzee had built it out of reach of snakes, and it only swayed to and fro.

Rikki-tikki felt his eyes growing red and hot (when a mongoose's eyes grow red, he is angry), and he sat back on his tail and hind legs like a little kangaroo, and looked all round him, and chattered with rage. But Nag and Nagaina had disappeared into the grass. So he trotted off to the gravel path near the house, and sat down to think. It was a serious matter for him.

Rikki-tikki knew he was a young mongoose, and it made him all the more pleased to think that he had managed to escape a blow from behind. It gave him confidence in himself, and when Teddy came running down the path, Rikki-tikki was ready to be petted.

But just as Teddy was stooping, something wriggled a little in the dust, and a tiny voice said, "Be careful. I am Death!" It was Karait, the dusty brown snakeling that lies for choice on the dusty earth, and his bite is as dangerous as the cobra's. But he is so small that nobody thinks of him, and so he does the more harm to people.

Rikki-tikki's eyes grew red again, and he danced up to Karait with the peculiar rocking, swaying motion that he had inherited from his family. It looks very funny, but it is so perfectly balanced a gait that you can fly off from it at any angle you please, and in dealing with snakes this is an advantage. If Rikki-tikki had only known, he was doing a much more dangerous thing than fighting Nag, for Karait is so small, and can turn so quickly, that unless Rikki bit him close to the back of the head, he would get the return stroke in his eye or his lip. But Rikki did not know. His eyes were all red, and he rocked back and forth, looking for a good place to hold. Karait struck out. Rikki jumped sideways and tried to run in, but the wicked little dusty grey head lashed within a fraction of his shoulder, and he had to jump over the body, and the head followed his heels close.

Teddy shouted to the house, "Oh, look here! Our mongoose is killing a snake." And Rikki-tikki heard a scream from Teddy's mother. His father ran out with a stick, but by the time he came up, Karait had lunged out once too far, and Rikki-tikki had sprung, jumped on the snake's back, dropped his head far between his forelegs, bitten as high up the back as he could get hold, and rolled away. That bite paralyzed Karait, and Rikki-tikki was just going to eat him up from the tail when he remembered that a full meal makes a slow mongoose, and if he wanted all his strength and quickness ready, he must keep himself thin.

Teddy's mother picked him up from the dust and hugged him, crying that he had saved Teddy from death. Rikki-tikki was rather amused at all the fuss, which, of course, he did not understand. Teddy's mother might just as well have petted Teddy for playing in the dust. Rikki-tikki was thoroughly enjoying himself.

That night at dinner, walking to and fro among the wine-glasses on the table, he might have stuffed himself three times over with nice things. But he remembered Nag and Nagaina.

Teddy carried him off to bed, and insisted on Rikki-tikki sleeping under his chin. Rikki-tikki was too well bred to bite or scratch, but as soon as Teddy was asleep he went off for his nightly walk round the house, and in the dark he ran up against Chuchundra, the muskrat, creeping around by the wall. Chuchundra is a broken-hearted little beast, and he whimpers and cheeps all the night.

"Don't kill me," said Chuchundra, almost weeping. "Rikki-tikki, don't kill me!"

"Do you think a snake-killer kills muskrats?" said Rikki-tikki scornfully.

"Those who kill snakes get killed by snakes," said Chuchundra, more sorrowfully than ever. "And how am I to be sure that Nag won't mistake me for you some dark night?"

"There's not the least danger," said Rikki-tikki. "For Nag is in the garden, and I know you don't go out there."

"My cousin Chua, the rat, told me—" said Chuchundra, and then he stopped.

"Told you what?"

"H'sh! Nag is everywhere, Rikki-tikki. You should have talked to Chua in the garden."

"I didn't – so you must tell me!"

Chuchundra sat down and cried till the tears rolled off his whiskers. "H'sh! I mustn't tell you anything. Can't you hear, Rikki-tikki?"

Rikki-tikki listened. The house was as still as still, but he thought he could just catch the faintest scratch-scratch in the world – the dry scratch of a snake's scales on brick-work. "That's Nag or Nagaina," he said to himself, "and he is crawling into the bathroom sluice."

He stole off to Teddy's bathroom, but there was nothing there, and then to Teddy's mother's bathroom. At the bottom of the smooth plaster wall there was a brick pulled out to make a sluice for the bath water, and as Rikki-tikki stole in, he heard Nag and Nagaina whispering outside.

"When the house is emptied of people," said Nagaina to her husband, "he will have to go away, and then the garden will be our own again. Go in quietly, and remember that the big man who killed Karait is the first one you should bite. Then we will hunt for Rikki-tikki together."

"But are you sure that there is anything to be gained by killing the people?" said Nag.

"Everything. When there were no people in the bungalow, did we have any mongoose in the garden? So long as the bungalow is empty, we are king and queen of the garden. As soon as our eggs in the melon bed hatch (as they may tomorrow), our children will need room and quiet."

"I had not thought of that," said Nag. "I will go, but there is no need that we should hunt for Rikki-tikki afterward. I will kill the big man and his wife, and the child if I can, and come away quietly. Then the bungalow will be empty, and Rikki-tikki will go."

Rikki-tikki tingled all over with rage and hatred at this, and then Nag's head came through the sluice, and his five feet of cold body followed it. Nag coiled himself up, raised his head, and Rikki could see his eyes glitter.

"Now, if I kill him here, Nagaina will know, and if I fight him on the open floor, the odds are in his favour. What am I to do?" said Rikki-tikki-tavi.

Nag waved to and fro, and then Rikki-tikki heard him drinking from the water jar that was used to fill the bath.

"That is good," said the snake. "Now, when Karait was killed, the big man had a stick. He may have that stick still, but when he comes in to bathe in the morning he will not have a stick. I shall wait here till he comes."

There was no answer from outside, so Rikki-tikki

knew Nagaina had gone away. Nag coiled himself
down, coil by coil, round the bulge at the bottom of
the water jar, and Rikki-tikki stayed still as death.
After an hour he began to move, muscle by muscle,
toward the jar. Nag was asleep, and Rikki-tikki looked
at his big back, wondering which would be the best
place for a good hold.

"If I don't manage to break his back at the first
jump," said Rikki, "he can still fight." He looked at the
thickness of the neck below the hood, but that was
too much for him, and a bite near the tail would only
make Nag savage.

"It must be the head," he said to himself at last,
"the head above the hood. And, when I am once
there, I must not let go."

Then he jumped. The head was lying a little clear
of the water jar, under the curve of it, and, as his teeth
met, Rikki braced his back against the bulge of the
red earthenware to hold down the head. This gave
him just one second's purchase, and he made the most
of it. Then he was battered to and fro as a rat is
shaken by a dog, but his eyes were red and he held on
as the body cart-whipped over the floor, upsetting the
tin dipper and the soap dish and the flesh brush, and

banged against the tin side of the bath. As he held he closed his jaws tighter and tighter – for the honour of his family, he preferred to be found with his teeth locked. He was dizzy, and felt shaken to pieces when something went off like a thunderclap just behind him. A hot wind knocked him senseless and red fire singed his fur. The big man had been wakened by the noise, and had fired both barrels of a shotgun into Nag just behind the hood.

Rikki-tikki held on with his eyes shut, for now he was quite sure he was dead. But the head did not move, and the big man picked him up and said, "It's the mongoose again, Alice. The little chap has saved our lives now."

Then Teddy's mother came in with a very white face, and saw what was left of Nag, and Rikki-tikki dragged himself to Teddy's bedroom and spent half the rest of the night shaking himself tenderly to find out whether he really was broken into forty pieces, as he fancied.

When morning came he was very stiff, but well pleased with his doings. "Now I have Nagaina to settle with, and she will be worse than five Nags, and there's no knowing when the eggs she spoke of will hatch. Goodness! I must go and see Darzee," he said.

Without waiting for breakfast, Rikki-tikki ran to the thorn-bush where Darzee was singing a song of triumph at the top of his voice. The news of Nag's death was all over the garden, for the sweeper had thrown the body on the rubbish heap.

"Oh, you stupid tuft of feathers!" said Rikki-tikki angrily. "Is this the time to sing?"

"Nag is dead – is dead – is dead!" sang Darzee. "The valiant Rikki-tikki caught him by the head and held fast. Then the big man brought the bang-stick, and Nag fell in two pieces! He will never eat my babies again."

"All that's true enough. But where's Nagaina?" said Rikki-tikki, looking carefully round him.

"Nagaina came to the bathroom and called for Nag," Darzee went on, "and the sweeper picked him up on the end of a stick and threw him upon the rubbish heap!" And Darzee filled his throat and sang.

"If I could get up to your nest, I'd roll your babies out!" said Rikki-tikki. "You're safe enough in your nest there, but it's war for me down here. Stop singing a minute, Darzee."

"For the great, the beautiful Rikki-tikki's sake I will

stop," said Darzee. "What is it that you want, oh killer of the terrible Nag?"

"Where is Nagaina, for the third time?"

"On the rubbish heap by the stables, mourning for Nag. Great is Rikki-tikki with the white teeth."

"Bother my white teeth! Have you ever heard where she keeps her eggs?"

"In the melon bed, on the end nearest the wall, where the sun strikes nearly all day. She hid them there weeks ago."

"And you never thought it worthwhile to tell me? The end nearest the wall, you said?"

"Rikki-tikki, you are not going to eat her eggs?"

"Not eat exactly, no. Darzee, if you have a grain of sense you will fly off to the stables and pretend that your wing is broken, and let Nagaina chase you away to this bush. I must get to the melon bed, and if I went there now she'd see me."

Darzee was a feather-brained little fellow who could never hold more than one idea at a time in his head. And just because he knew that Nagaina's children were born in eggs like his own, he didn't think at first that it was fair to kill them. But his wife was a sensible bird, and she knew that cobra's eggs meant young cobras later on. So she flew off from the nest, and left Darzee to keep the babies warm.

She fluttered in front of Nagaina by the rubbish heap and cried out, "Oh, my wing is broken! The boy in the house threw a stone at me and broke it."

Nagaina lifted up her head and hissed, "You warned Rikki-tikki when I would have killed him. Indeed and truly, you've chosen a bad place to be lame in." And she moved toward Darzee's wife, slipping along over the dust.

"The boy broke my poor wing with a stone!" shrieked Darzee's wife.

"Well! It may be some consolation to you when you're dead to know that I shall settle accounts with the boy. What is the use of running away? I am sure to catch you. Little fool, look at me!"

Darzee's wife knew better than to do that, for a bird who looks at a snake's eyes gets so frightened that she cannot move. Darzee's wife fluttered on, piping sorrowfully, and never leaving the ground, and Nagaina quickened her pace.

Rikki-tikki heard them going up the path, and he raced for the melon patch near the wall. There, in the warm litter above the melons, he found twenty-five

eggs, about the size of a bantam's eggs, but with whitish skin instead of shell.

"I was not a day too soon," he said, for he could see the baby cobras curled up inside the skin, and he knew that the minute they were hatched they could each kill a man or a mongoose. He bit off the tops of the eggs as fast as he could, taking care to crush the young cobras.

At last there were only three eggs left, and Rikki-tikki began to chuckle to himself, when he heard Darzee's wife screaming: "Rikki-tikki, I led Nagaina toward the house, and she has gone into the veranda, and – oh, come quickly – she means killing!"

Rikki-tikki smashed two eggs, and tumbled backward down the melon bed with the third egg in his mouth, and scuttled to the veranda as hard as he could put foot to the ground. Teddy and his mother and father were there at early breakfast, but they were not eating anything. They sat stone-still, and their faces were white. Nagaina was coiled up within easy striking distance of Teddy's bare leg, and she was swaying to and fro, singing a song of triumph.

"Son of the big man that killed Nag," she hissed, "stay still. I am not ready yet. Wait a little. Keep very still, all you three! If you move I strike, and if you do not move I strike!"

Teddy's eyes were fixed on his father. All his father could do was to whisper, "Sit very still, Teddy. You mustn't move."

Rikki-tikki came up and cried, "Turn round, Nagaina. Turn and fight!"

"All in good time," said she, without moving her eyes. "I will settle my account with you presently. Look at your friends, Rikki-tikki. They are still and white. They are afraid, and if you come a step nearer to me I will strike."

"Look at your eggs," said Rikki-tikki, "in the melon bed near the wall. Go and look, Nagaina!"

The big snake turned half around, and saw the egg on the veranda. "Ah-h! Give it to me," she said.

Rikki-tikki put his paws one on each side of the egg, and his eyes were blood-red. "What price for a snake's egg? For a young king cobra? For the last – the very last of the brood? The ants are eating all the others down by the melon bed."

Nagaina spun clear round, forgetting everything for the sake of the one egg. Rikki-tikki saw Teddy's father drag him across the little table, safe and out of reach of Nagaina.

"Tricked! Tricked! Tricked!" chuckled Rikki-tikki. "The boy is safe, and it was I—I—I that caught Nag by the hood last night in the bathroom." Then he began to jump up and down, all four feet together. "He threw me to and fro, but he could not shake me off. He was dead before the big man blew him in two. I did it! Rikki-tikki-tck-tck! Come then, Nagaina. Come and fight with me."

Nagaina saw that she had lost her chance of killing Teddy. "Give me the egg, Rikki-tikki, and I will go away from this house and never come back," she said, lowering her hood.

"Yes, you will go away, and you will never come back. For you will be thrown on the rubbish heap with Nag. Fight!"

Rikki-tikki was bounding all round Nagaina, keeping just out of reach of her stroke, his little eyes like hot coals. Nagaina gathered herself together and flung out at him. Rikki-tikki jumped up and backward. Again and again and again she struck, and each time her head came with a whack on the matting of the veranda and she gathered herself together like a watch spring. Then Rikki-tikki danced in a circle to get behind her, and Nagaina spun round to keep her head to his head.

He had forgotten the egg. It still lay on the veranda, and Nagaina came nearer and nearer to it, till at last, while Rikki-tikki was drawing breath, she caught it in her mouth, turned to the veranda steps, and flew like an arrow down the path, with Rikki-tikki behind her.

Rikki-tikki knew that he must catch her, or all the trouble would begin again. She headed straight for the long grass by the thorn-bush, and as he was running Rikki-tikki heard Darzee still singing his foolish little song of triumph. But Darzee's wife was wiser. She flew off her nest as Nagaina came along, and flapped her wings about Nagaina's head. But Nagaina only lowered her hood and went on. Still, the instant's delay brought Rikki-tikki up to her, and as she plunged into the rat-hole where she and Nag used to live, his little white teeth were clenched on her tail, and he went down with her – and very few mongooses, however wise and old they may be, care to follow a cobra into its hole.

It was dark in the hole, and Rikki-tikki never knew when it might open out and give Nagaina room to turn and strike at him. He held on savagely, and stuck out his feet to act as brakes on the dark slope.

Then the grass by the mouth of the hole stopped waving, and Darzee said, "It is all over with Rikki-tikki! We must sing his death song. The valiant Rikki-tikki is dead! For Nagaina will surely kill him underground."

So he sang a mournful song that he had just made up. Just as he got to the most touching part, Rikki-tikki, covered with dirt, dragged himself out of the hole. Darzee stopped with a little shout. Rikki-tikki shook some of the dust out of his fur and sneezed.

"It is all over," he said. "The widow will never come out again." And the red ants that live between the grass stems heard him, and began to troop down one after another to see if he had spoken the truth.

Rikki-tikki curled himself up in the grass and slept where he was – slept and slept till it was late in the afternoon, for he had done a hard day's work.

"Now," he said, when he awoke, "I will go back to the house. Tell the Coppersmith, Darzee, and he will tell the garden that Nagaina is dead."

The Coppersmith is a bird who makes a noise exactly like the beating of a little hammer on a copper

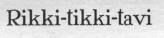

pot. He is the town crier to every Indian garden, and tells all the news to everybody who cares to listen.

When Rikki got to the house, Teddy and Teddy's mother and father came out and almost cried over him. That night he ate all that was given him till he could eat no more, and went to bed on Teddy's shoulder. Teddy's mother came to look in late at night and said to her husband, "Just think, he saved our lives."

Rikki-tikki woke up with a jump, for mongooses are light sleepers.

"What are you bothering for?" said he. "All the cobras are dead now. And if they weren't, I'm here."

Rikki-tikki had a right to be proud of himself. But he did not grow too proud, and he kept that garden as a mongoose should keep it, with tooth and jump and spring and bite, till never a cobra dared show its head inside the walls.

The Circus

From *The Wouldbegoods*
by E Nesbit

*The Bastables – Oswald, Dora, Dicky, Alice, Noel, and H.O.
(Horace Octavius) – are staying at the house of a writer they call
'Albert's uncle'. A brother and sister, Daisy and Denny, are also
staying. The children have formed a society to help them behave,
which they call 'The Wouldbegoods'.*

The ones of us who had started the Society of
the Wouldbegoods began, at about this time,
to bother. They said we had not done anything really
noble – not worth speaking of, that is – for over a
week, and that it was high time to begin again "with
earnest endeavour", Daisy said. So then Oswald said,
"All right, but there ought to be an end to everything.
Let's each of us think of one really noble and

unselfish act, and the others shall help to work it out.
Then when everybody's had their go we'll write every
single thing down in the Golden Deed book, and
we'll draw two lines in red ink at the bottom, like
Father does at the end of an account. And after that,
if anyone wants to be good they can jolly well be
good on their own, if at all."

Dora said, "It would be a noble action to have all
the school children from the village and give them tea
and games in the paddock. They would think it so
nice and good of us."

But Dicky showed her that this would not be our
good act, but Father's, because he would have to pay
for the tea, and it is in vain being noble and generous
when someone else is paying for it all the time, even if
it happens to be your own father. Then three others
had ideas at the same time and began to explain what
they were.

We were all in the dining-room, and perhaps we
were making a bit of a row. Anyhow, Oswald for one,
does not blame Albert's uncle for opening his door
and saying, "I suppose I must not ask for complete
silence. That would be too much. But if you could
whistle, or stamp your feet, or shriek or howl

instead – anything to vary the monotony of your well-sustained conversation."

Oswald said kindly, "We're awfully sorry. Are you very busy?"

"Busy?" said Albert's uncle. "My heroine is hesitating on the verge of an act which, for good or ill, must influence her whole subsequent career. You wouldn't like her to decide in the middle of such a row that she can't hear herself think?"

We said, "No, we wouldn't."

Then he said, "If any outdoor amusement should present itself to you this bright mid-summer day—" So we all went out.

Then Daisy whispered to Dora – they always hang together. Daisy is not nearly so white-micey as she was at first, but she still seems to fear public speaking.

Dora said, "Daisy's idea is a game that'll take us all day. She thinks keeping out of the way when he's making his heroine decide would be a noble act, and we might as well be playing at the same time."

We all said "Yes, but what?" There was a long interval of silence.

"Speak up please, Daisy, my child," Oswald said. "Fear not to lay bare the utmost thoughts of that

faithful heart."

Daisy giggled. (Our own girls never giggle – they laugh right out or hold their tongues. Their kind brothers have taught them this.)

Then Daisy said, "If we could have a sort of play to keep us out of the way. I once read a story about an animal race. Everybody had an animal, and the one that got in first got the prize. There was a tortoise in it, and a rabbit, and a peacock, and sheep, and dogs, and a kitten."

This proposal left us cold, as Albert's uncle says, as we knew there could not possibly be any prize worth bothering about.

Thus the idea was not followed up. Dicky yawned and said, "Let's go into the barn and make a fort."

So we did, with straw. It does not hurt straw to be messed about with like it does hay. This passed the time very agreeably till dinner, when there was roast mutton with onion sauce, and a roly-poly pudding.

Albert's uncle said we had effaced ourselves effectually, so we determined to do the same during the afternoon, for he told us his heroine was by no means out of the woods yet.

And at first it was easy. Jam roly gives you a

peaceful feeling and you do not at first care if you never play any runabout games ever any more. But after a while the torpor begins to pass. Oswald was the first to recover. He had been lying on his front in the orchard, but now he turned over on his back and said, "I say, look here, let's do something."

Daisy was looking thoughtful. I could see she was still thinking about that animal race. So I explained that it would be very poor fun without a tortoise and a peacock, and she saw this, though not willingly.

It was H.O. who said, "Doing anything with animals is prime, if they only will. Let's have a circus!"

At the word the last thought of the pudding faded from Oswald's memory, and he stretched himself, sat up, and said, "Bully for H.O. Let's!"

Never in all our lives had we had such a galaxy of animals at our command. Rabbits and guinea-pigs paled into insignificance before the number of live things on the farm.

"The worst of a circus is," Dora said, "that you've got to teach the animals things. A circus where the performing creatures hadn't learned performing would be a bit silly. Let's give up a week to teaching them and then have the circus."

The Circus

Some people have no idea of the value of time – and Dora is one of those who do not understand the fact that when you want to do something, you want to do it immediately, and not a week later.

Oswald said the first thing was to collect the performing animals. "We may find," he said, "that they have hidden talents hitherto unsuspected by their harsh masters."

So Denny took a pencil and wrote a list of the animals required. This is it:

List of animals requisite for the circus we are going to have:

1 bull — for bull-fight
1 horse — for ditto (if possible)
1 goat — to do Alpine feats of daring
1 donkey — to play see-saw
2 white pigs — one to be Learned, and the other to play with the clown
Turkeys — as many as possible, because they can make a noise that sounds like an audience applauding
The dogs — for any odd parts
1 large black pig — to be the Elephant in the procession
Calves (several) — to be camels, and to stand on tubs

TRICKS, TRAPS AND MISCHIEF

Oswald said, "The first thing is to get all the creatures together – the paddock at the side of the orchard is the place. Then we'll make a programme, and dress for our parts. It's a pity there won't be any audience but the turkeys."

We decided to collect the animals in the right order. The bull was first. Oswald and Alice went to fetch him. They took a halter to lead the bull by, and a whip, not to hurt the bull with, but just to make him mind. The others were to try to get one of the horses while we were gone.

The bull lives in a house made of wood and prickly furze bushes, and he has a yard to his house. When we got there he was half in his house and half out in his yard.

Oswald called to him. He said, "Bull! Bull! Bull! Bull!" because we did not know the animal's real name. The bull took no notice. Then Oswald picked up a stone and threw it at the bull, not angrily, but just to make it pay attention. But the bull did not pay a farthing's worth of it. So then Oswald leaned over the iron gate of the bull's yard and just flicked the bull with the whiplash.

And then the bull really did pay attention. He

started when the lash struck him, then suddenly he faced round. Uttering a roar and putting his head down close to his feet, he ran straight at the iron gate where we were standing.

Alice and Oswald turned away. They did not wish to annoy the bull any more, and they ran as fast as they could across the field (just so as not to keep the others waiting).

As they ran Oswald had a fancy that perhaps the bull had rooted up the gate with one paralyzing blow, and was now tearing across the field after him and Alice, with the broken gate balanced on its horns. We climbed the stile quickly and looked back – the bull was still on the right side of the gate.

Oswald said, "We'll do without the bull. He did not seem to want to come, and we must be kind to dumb animals."

We did not tell the others how we had hurried back. We just said, "The bull didn't seem to care about coming."

The others had not been idle. They had got old Clover, the cart-horse, but she would do nothing but graze, so we decided to let her be the Elephant. The Elephant's is a nice quiet part. Then the black pig could be Learned, and the other two could be something else.

They had also got the goat – he was tethered to a tree. The donkey was there. Denny was leading him in the halter. The dogs were there, of course – they always are. So now we only had to get the turkeys for the applause and the calves and pigs.

The calves were easy to get, because they were in their own house. There were five. And the pigs were in their houses too. We got them out after long and

198

patient toil, and persuaded them that they wanted to go into the paddock, where the circus was to be. This is done by pretending to drive them the other way. A pig only knows two ways – the way you want him to go, and the other.

But the turkeys knew thousands of different ways, and tried them all. They made such an awful row, we had to drop all ideas of ever hearing applause from their lips, so we came away and left them.

"Never mind," H.O. said, "they'll be sorry enough afterwards, because now they won't see the circus."

While the turkeys were baffling the rest of us, Dicky had found three sheep who seemed to wish to join the throng, so we let them. Then we shut the gate of the paddock, and left the circus performers to make friends while we dressed.

Oswald and H.O. were to be clowns, which is quite easy with Albert's uncle's pyjamas, and flour on your hair and face, and the red they do the brick-floors with.

Alice had pink and white skirts, and roses in her hair and round her dress. Her dress was the pink calico and white muslin stuff off the dressing-table in the girls' room fastened with pins and tied round the waist with a small bath towel. She was to be the Dauntless Equestrienne, and to give an enchanting act of barebacked daring, riding either a pig or a sheep. Dora was dressed for the Haute ecole, which means a riding-habit and a high hat. She took Dick's topper that he wears with his Etons, and a skirt of Mrs Pettigrew's. Daisy dressed the same as Alice, taking the muslin from Mrs Pettigrew's dressing-table without saying anything. We were thinking of trying to put it back, when Denny and Noel, who were highwaymen, with brown-paper top-boots and slouch hats and Turkish towel cloaks, suddenly stopped dressing and gazed out of the window.

"Crikey!" said Dick. "Come on, Oswald!" and he bounded like an antelope from the room.

Oswald and the rest followed, casting a hasty glance through the window. Noel had got brown-paper boots too, and a Turkish towel cloak. H.O. had been waiting for Dora to dress him up for the other clown. He had only his shirt and knickerbockers and his braces on. He came down as he was – as indeed we all did. And no wonder, for in the paddock, where the circus was to be, a blood-thrilling thing had transpired. The dogs were chasing the sheep.

The Circus

We all rushed into the paddock, calling to Pincher, and Martha and Lady. Pincher came back to us almost at once. He is a well-brought-up dog. Martha did not seem to hear – she is awfully deaf. But she did not matter so much, because the sheep could walk away from her easily. However, Lady is a deer-hound, and she was now far away in a distant region of the paddock, with a fat sheep just before her in full flight. I am sure if ever anybody's eyes did start out of their heads with horror (just like in narratives of adventure), ours did then.

There was a moment of panic. We expected to see Lady pull down her quarry, and we know what a lot of money a sheep costs, to say nothing of its own personal feelings.

Then we started to run for all we were worth. It is hard to run swiftly as the arrow from the bow when you happen to be wearing pyjamas belonging to a grown-up person – as I was – but even so I beat Dicky. Alice came in third. She held on the dressing-table muslin and ran jolly well. But ere we reached the fatal spot all was very nearly up with the sheep.

We heard a plop, Lady stopped and looked round. Then she came towards us, prancing with happiness and pride, but we said "Down!" and "Bad dog!" and ran sternly on.

When we came to the brook we saw the sheep struggling in the water. It is not very deep – I believe the sheep could have stood up if it had liked, but it absolutely would not try.

Alice and I got down and stuck our legs into the water, and then Dicky came down, and the three of us hauled that sheep up by its shoulders till it could rest on Alice and me as we sat on the bank. I tell you that sopping wet, heavy, panting, silly donkey of a sheep sat there on our laps like a pet dog. Dicky got his shoulder under it at the back and heaved to keep it from flumping off into the water again, while the others fetched the shepherd.

When the shepherd came he called us every name you can think of. He got the sheep up the bank, and took it and the others away. And the calves too. He did not seem to be interested in any of the other performing animals.

Alice, Oswald and Dick had had almost enough circus for just then, so we sat in the sun and dried ourselves and wrote the programme of the circus. This was it:

The Circus

PROGRAMME

1. Startling leap from the lofty precipice by the performing sheep. Real water, and real precipice. The gallant rescue. O., A. and D. Bastable. (We thought we might as well put that in, though it was over and had happened accidentally.)

2. Graceful barebacked equestrienne act on the trained pig, Eliza. A. Bastable.

3. Amusing clown interlude, introducing trained dog, Pincher, and the other white pig. H.O. and O. Bastable.

4. The See-Saw. Trained donkeys. (H.O. said we had only one donkey, so Dicky said H.O. could be the other. When peace was restored we went on to 5.)

5. Elegant equestrian act by D. Bastable. Haute ecole, on Clover, the incomparative trained elephant from the plains of Venezuela.

6. Alpine feat of daring. The climbing of the Andes, by Billy, the well known acrobatic goat. (We thought we could make the Andes out of hurdles and things, and so we could have but for what always happens. (This is the unexpected. (This is a saying Father told me, but I see I am three deep in brackets so I will close them before I get into any more).).).

7. The Black but Learned Pig. (I daresay he knows something, Alice said, if we can only find out what. We did find out all too soon.)

TRICKS, TRAPS AND MISCHIEF

After we finished the programme we went back to dress up the creatures. We had just tied the Union Jack we made out of Daisy's flannel petticoat round the waist of the Black and Learned Pig, when we heard screams from the back part of the house, and realized that Billy, the acrobatic goat, had got loose from the tree we had tied him to.

We hastily proceeded in the direction of the screams, and, guided by the sound, threaded our way into the kitchen. As we went, Noel, ever fertile in melancholy ideas, wondered aloud whether Mrs Pettigrew was being robbed, or only murdered.

In the kitchen we saw that Noel was wrong as usual. It was neither. Mrs Pettigrew, screaming like a steam-siren and waving a broom, occupied the foreground. In the distance the maid was shrieking and trying to shut herself up inside a clothes-horse on which washing was being aired.

On the dresser – which he had ascended by a chair – was Billy, the acrobatic goat, doing his Alpine daring act. He had found out his Andes for himself. The next moment he put one horn neatly behind the end plate of the next to the bottom row, and ran it along against the wall. The plates fell crashing on to

the soup tureen and vegetable dishes which adorned the lower range of the Andes.

Mrs Pettigrew's screams were almost drowned in the crash of the falling avalanche of crockery.

Oswald, though stricken with horror and polite regret, preserved dauntless cool. Disregarding the mop which Mrs Pettigrew kept on poking at the goat in a timid yet cross way, he sprang forward, crying out to his trusty followers, "Stand by to catch him!"

But Dick had thought of the same thing, and ere Oswald could carry out his design, Dicky had caught the goat's legs and tripped it up. The goat fell against another row of plates, righted itself hastily in the ruins of the soup tureen and the sauce-boats, and then fell again, this time towards Dicky. The two fell heavily on the ground together.

The goat was not hurt, but Dicky had a sprained thumb and a lump on his head like a black marble door-knob. He had to go to bed.

I will draw a veil over what Mrs Pettigrew said. Also Albert's uncle, who was brought to the scene of ruin by her screams. Few words escaped our lips. There are times when it is not wise to argue.

When they had said what they deemed enough

and we were let go, we all went out. Then Alice said, "Let's give up the circus. Let's put the creatures in their places – and drop the whole thing. I want to go and read to Dicky."

Oswald hates to be beaten, but he gave in to Alice. We all went out to collect the performing troop and sort it out into its proper places.

Alas! We came too late. In the interest we had felt about whether Mrs Pettigrew was the victim of burglars or not, we had left both gates open again. The old horse – I mean the trained elephant from Venezuela – was there. The dogs we had tied up after the first act, when the intrepid sheep bounded, as it says in the programme. The two white pigs were there, but the donkey was gone. We heard his hoofs down the road, growing fainter and fainter. And the pig was off in exactly the opposite direction. Why couldn't they have gone the same way? But no, one was a pig and the other was a donkey, as Denny said afterwards.

Daisy and H.O. started after the donkey. The rest of us pursued the pig. It trotted quietly down the road. We thought it would be easy to catch up to it. This was an error.

When we ran faster it ran faster, when we stopped it stopped and looked round at us. That pig led us on and on, o'er miles and miles of strange country. One thing, it did keep to the roads.

When we met people, which wasn't often, we called out to them to help us, but they roared with laughter. You remember Alice was still dressed up as the gay equestrienne in the dressing-table pink and white, with rosy garlands, now very droopy. Oswald was attired in red paint and flour, for a clown. It is really impossible to run speedfully in another man's pyjamas, so Oswald had taken these off, and wore his own brown knickerbockers. He had tied the pyjamas round his neck, to carry them easily.

Noel was a highwayman in brown-paper gaiters and bath towels and a cocked hat made of newspaper. I don't know how he kept it on.

The Circus

All the same, I think if I had seen a band of youthful travellers in bitter distress about a pig I should have tried to lend a hand, no matter how the travellers might have been dressed.

It was hotter than anyone would believe who has never had occasion to hunt the pig when dressed for quite another part. The flour got out of Oswald's hair into his eyes and his mouth. His brow was wet, and it ran down his face and washed the red off in streaks, and when he rubbed his eyes he only made it worse. Alice had to run holding the equestrienne skirts on with both hands, and I think the brown-paper boots bothered Noel from the first. Dora had her skirt over her arm and carried the topper in her hand.

At last we met a man who took pity on us. He stood in the middle of the road and waved his arms. The pig turned right, through a gate into a private garden. We followed. What else were we to do?

The Learned Black Pig turned first right and then left, and emerged on a lawn. "Now, all together!" cried Oswald, mustering his voice to give the word of command. "Surround him! Cut off his retreat!"

We almost surrounded him. The pig edged towards the house.

"Now we've got him!" cried Oswald, as the pig got on to a bed of yellow pansies close against the red house wall.

All would even then have been well, but Denny, at the last, shrank from meeting the pig face to face in a manly way, and the next moment the pig bolted into a French window. The pursuers halted not. This was no time for trivial ceremony. In another moment the pig was a captive. Alice and Oswald had their arms round him under the ruins of a table that had had teacups on it, and around the hunters and their prey stood the startled members of a parish society. You think they screamed when they saw the pig and us? You are right.

Oswald explained that it was the pig's doing, and asked pardon for any alarm the ladies had felt. Alice said how sorry we were but really it was not our fault this time.

When we had explained, we said, "Might we go?"

The Circus

But the Lady of the House asked for our names and addresses, and said she should write to our Father. (She did, and we heard of it too.)

They let us go. And we went, after we had asked for a piece of rope to lead the pig by. "In case it should come back into your nice room," Alice said. "And that would be such a pity, wouldn't it?" And as soon as the pig had agreed to let us tie it round his neck we came away. The scene in the drawing-room had not been long. The pig went slowly.

Dicky's act with the goat was the only thing out of that day that was put in the Golden Deed book, and he put that in himself while we were hunting the pig.

I will not seek to unfold to you how we got the pig home, or how the donkey was caught (that was poor sport compared to the pig). Nor will I tell you a word of all that was said and done to the intrepid hunters of the Black and Learned Pig. I have told you all the interesting part. Seek not to know the rest. It is better buried in obliquity.

THE HUNTERS

213

The Cow and the Python

By D G Mukerji

When I was about eight years old, I began to notice things as a whole. Until then the events of the day, such as morning prayers and evening silence, had seemed islands of peace in a chaos of meaningless unrelated events, and people went to work, came home from the fields, went to bed, and each one of these actions appeared an invention of the moment. It never occurred to my child's mind that they formed the parts of a whole and were not mere unrelated incidents.

But a little before my eighth birthday a change was wrought in my perceptions when one of our cows gave birth to a heifer. I was entrusted with the task of looking after the calf when she was weaned from her mother six weeks later. My first care was to go to the smith for a brass bell. After that I had to call on the weaver for a cotton string which would be thick but soft enough for the tender young neck of Goma, which was the name I gave my little charge. Whenever she mooed it sounded like 'Go-Ma', meaning 'O my mother, where are you?'

One more experience revealed to my poor little mind the unity of life. It occurred during the Dipavali festival – the feast of lanterns – which as you know, is held after the autumn rain is over, and is a kind of thanksgiving and harvest-home celebration. During that day in late October all the cows of our village were led in procession through its chief thoroughfare to the communal threshing floor, there to be let loose to wander home all by themselves.

My aunt owned the third largest flock of cattle in the village, consisting of twenty cows, so ours had the third place in the procession. I was charged with choosing our six finest beasts to walk in the procession. I took Goma, then her mother, three more cows and our bull Vrisa.

THE HUNTERS

The selection was made in the morning. The rest of the day I spent with one of our farm hands in washing and decorating the beasts. We took them to the river which ran at the south end of the village. The village ran from east to west and to our north bristled the Himalayas. After their bath the animals were brought home to be decorated. First of all we painted each adult animal's horns in yellow. Then we strung garlands of red oleanders around their necks, and over their backs we flung purple, blue, orange, green and silver shawls which were securely tied by strings round their glistening rumps. Next we painted their hoofs yellow. It took nearly the whole day before my flock was ready to march in the procession.

Goma, who had not yet grown horns, nor a back ample enough to be covered with a shawl, had to walk with nothing on but her brass bell.

My aunt ordered us to march along to the village temple whence the procession was to start. Our bull,

The Cow and the Python

Vrisa, garlanded in red oleander, his horns gleaming like spikes of gold, his back a shimmer of emerald, while his dewlap peeped out like shining steel in between clusters of flaming flowers, led our flock. Next to him marched our chief cowherd clad in spotless white and turbaned in tawny silk. He held a green bamboo stave in his left hand while his right rested on Vrisa's mountainous rump that swayed from side to side like the head of a sleepy child. I led the rear with Goma whose tinkling bell fretted the silence of the evening.

Our house was the last one at the northern end of the village, and we were obliged to go far to the west to reach the temple compound, for our village shrine lay at the western end so that at dawn the rising sun's light fell on it in its purest splendour. It was a miracle of yellow sandstone about three storeys high. In front of it spread a lawn large enough to accommodate more than five hundred people. Behind the shrine, out of sight, lay the low one-storeyed house of the priest. Soon from different directions came pouring flocks of cattle, their horns all yellow flame and their flanks dripping with stabbing colours. In no time the place was filled with the noise of men and beasts.

THE HUNTERS

Now the priest appeared on the temple steps to give his benediction. Slowly he lifted his hands and blessed us.

Just as the priest had finished, my little charge ran forward tinkling her bell. This was in good taste, I thought, for it marked the end of the ceremony at the temple. Now the procession formed itself, and we started for the communal threshing floor.

We passed between houses, some of clay with thatched roofs, some of brick and timber – but all filled with faces of men and women not only of our village but from the neighbouring city who had come to witness our festival. The usually dusty road that traversed our village had been swept and strewn with grains of rice and lotus leaves, and drawings and designs had been made by different families on their front walls and also in the dust of their thresholds. From every house rose a trumpeting sound of conch-shells blown by women, and over our heads were strewn flowers by young girls. One could hardly see the ruddy evening sky above our heads because of the cedar leaves and little flowers that swarmed in the air ere they fell upon us.

At last we reached the communal threshing floor

under the vast banyan tree where the village elders and my aunt Kuri received us and blessed us.

The oldest one said, "We are all brothers – man and beast. We share in toil and pain. We partake of one another's well-being – the life that is in the ox is the same life that beats in our blood, the milk that comes from the cow is the strength that is in our limbs. May you treat your animals well. May they in turn be moved by God to serve you abundantly."

With these words the gathering was dismissed. Just then Goma, that little mischief-maker, walked forward and began to devour the oleander garland from the neck of the bull at the head of the procession. This was both terrible and humiliating in spite of the fact that she was hungry and only two months old. Had the owner of the bull been a good man he would have understood and forgiven, but instead he rushed forward in a rage and began to beat her back. Instantly she switched her tail and frisked off in the direction of the jungle and I followed after! It did not take us long to be out of the reach of the men and women at the threshing floor. I saw nothing but Goma's vanishing white body before me. I stumbled, fell, rose and ran again after her. Before she had stopped running and before I knew where we were, it had grown quite dark.

Both of us suddenly realized that we had penetrated the outskirts of the jungle and were at the threshold of great danger. To ordinary observers the outer edges of a forest may seem safe, but to those who know, evening and early morning are the two occasions when animals are going out to hunt or returning from their night's outing. Any man who lingers on the outskirts of a dense jungle may be killed by a tiger or leopard. A boy and a calf are in greater danger, because wild dogs, wolves, hyenas, and black panthers all seek to devour them.

So there we stood wondering about our fate. In a moment there flashed through my mind the pictures of previous nights at Dipavali when the whole village was illuminated with lights, every house decorating its roof and walls with innumerable lamps. But now here I was lost in the jungle in the company of a cow hardly two months old!

Fortunately Goma had not yet learned to be afraid. Fear is taught by grown-up men and beasts to their young. Once we learn to be afraid, we rarely shake off the habit, and I believe our fear frightens other beasts, causing them to attack us. While Goma stood there looking at me between eating mouthfuls of leaves from the surrounding dense saplings, I thought how hard it would be to find a way out in the surrounding dark, eloquent with a thousand noises of insects and animals. These sounds, however, signalled comparative safety, for were a tiger moving in our direction, all voices would have been hushed.

I put my hand on Goma's shoulder and started to lead her back. We kept steadily to the windward of the noises, but we had to do a good deal of tacking to avoid the less noisy places. After we had gone about half an hour, we were able to discern through the

surrounding wall of foliage what I thought to be a
haze of light in the sky betokening our nearness to
the town of Mayavati. I felt happy, and Goma
switched her tail in pleasure. But danger swoops
down on you when you relax your vigilance.
Something fell at our feet crushing under it all the
insect and other noises that were running like water
in the undergrowth. Goma groaned, then leaped. In a
moment she was out of touch or hearing. I stood still,
wondering at the heavy thing lying on the floor of the
jungle. I kept on walking backwards and peering into
the midnight dark before me. Nothing could I see,
but I heard shush – sha – shush near me. It kept on
drawing nearer and nearer. I was convinced that it
must be a python. If there had been a strong tree
nearby I would have been lost, for the snake with its
tail around the trunk for a lever could have held me
so firmly in its coil that escape would have been
impossible. Luckily we were passing through grassy
fields interspersed with saplings hardly ten feet high,
too frail for the great snake to coil around. The
moment I realized the nature of my enemy, I turned
on my heels and ran, knowing that he could not catch
me if I ran zig-zagging away from him. I had not gone

very far when I met a search party from the village out with lanterns and spikes looking for me. I was indeed very glad to see them. They had been searching for Goma and myself for nearly an hour. On my arrival home we found the calf already there, for she had dashed from the jungle straight to the cowshed – how she found it I do not know.

When I told the men who found me and my aunt about my having encountered a python they would hardly believe me, saying: "This is the tale of a frightened child." Alas, they did not know that in another week's time they would pay for the folly of their scepticism.

I must give you some further description of our village before our story travels any further. As well as at the communal threshing floor and the temple grounds, people met and talked with one another by the river Avati, which was about a twentieth of a mile broad and too shallow for navigation, though during the spring when the snows melted in the Himalayas, or the rains swelled its waters in July, Avati attained the depth of nearly a dozen feet for a fortnight at a time. But the current was so swift at that season that swimming or floating on it meant utter disaster. The river ran between banks of ilex, deodar and pine trees, and here and there its northern shore was secured by stone walls and yellow sandstone stairways commonly known as Ghauts. During the rainy season Avati would turn as tawny as the steps themselves but at other times she was as clear and bright as the eyes of a bird.

There on the Ghauts people met when they came to fetch water, about nine in the morning, an hour before bathing began. Since it was a one-way current, without tides, whatever water was muddled after the drinking water was taken, became clear for the bathers downstream, and whatever they sullied, flowed out eastwards to the sea. The water was always clean. In the afternoon people bathed in it again before going to the temple, and about midday, the animals bathed in Avati, and drank from it. We always took our cattle there at half past eleven and gave them their bath.

One late November morning when women had come to fetch water from the river, they saw a python floating downstream. They came home and told their men-folk, but those of us in the fields did not hear of it, and at eleven thirty we brought our herds of cattle to give them their bath. With the help of one of our hired men, I was busy scrubbing my beasts with straw as they came out of the water, usually one by one, but when two came out together the hired man took one and I the other. After they had been rubbed, they were sent down for a final dip.

It was when Goma and her mother had come up from the stream and the hired man and I had begun to rub them – I of course taking Goma – that suddenly a black rope swung down from a tree above and gathered the cow, and then my poor man, in its swift circling coil. In a trice, where stood the two of them, groaned a dying man amid the bellows of a dying beast. Goma and the rest of the herd fled in panic. I will never forget how the few feet of that serpent's tail thinned itself almost to the size of a child's wrist as it hung from the tree, tightening as its body stretched and then letting go as the coils dropped upon its victims. Before he and the poor cow became crushed into pulp I fled from the spot.

It was not long before I met herds of cattle running through the village streets. Our stampeding

herd had run into other people's cattle coming down
to the river for their bath, and had communicated to
them their panic. I shouted to the herdsmen the news
of the calamity that I had witnessed on the riverbank.
Call after call was sounded by the priest at his temple
on his conch-shell.

Alas, by the time the village rallied to the river
they found neither python nor victims. None knew
where to search. But I told Kuri I was sure the
monster could be found very near the place of the
tragedy. So when in the evening we went to the
temple to hear the priest read the scriptures and the
epics, we drew him into a corner and I unburdened
my mind to him.

The grey-beard listened to me carefully, and said,
"Take me tomorrow morning. I must now take my
seat at the altar and read to you the story of Rama."

The following day, after I had brought flowers to
the temple and prayed there, the priest and I set out
to find the murderer. I took him first to the outer
jungle where I had encountered the enemy during the
Dipavali evening. It proved an easy task in daylight.
Lo, there lay long lines of grass and dry leaves crushed
in a certain pattern. We followed it wherever it led.

Those long sweeping lines thick as my waist could only have been made by a python.

It did not take us long to reach the riverbank. No doubt he had gone there to take a drink. And while he was at it something from behind had frightened him and he fell into the swift current. The latter had borne him down past the Ghaut where human beings bathed. At last he reached the place where the river takes a sharp turn and where we always bathed the cattle. There the current is retarded by a kind of dam made by fallen boulders. We traced him as far as the soft ground on which he had crawled and the tree around which he had coiled his muddy body. After that we faced a perfect blank.

Purohit, the priest, and I tried hard to locate his present whereabouts but in vain. Dejected in spirit and baffled in mind, we sat down on the shore about midday just to rest our tired limbs. Slowly herdsmen brought their herds and bathed them. One by one the cows and oxen went home. At last came our own herd led by a new hired man named Gokul. He plunged into the water ahead of his charge.

Then followed little Goma just to show that she too could share Gokul's fun. They played with each other in the water like children. It amused me so to see my little heifer so frisky and happy. I called her name. She obeyed instantly. She started toward the shore. Slowly, inch by inch, she struggled up. When she was ready to put her feet on dry ground, her eyes fell on something to her left. Then she stopped. As if she had seen death itself, her body quivered in terror.

That was enough for the keen eye of the priest. He dashed forward into the water and stood waist deep looking at the spot where the calf's eyes were riveted. He shouted, "Mila, Mila!" (Found! Found!) That noise dug into Goma's being like a goad. She was driven up the shore by that 'Mila, Mila,' and ran home. The other cattle followed her example. The drumming of their hoofs on the ground frightened the python apparently, for the priest called to me to look before he also ran away.

The python could not creep away nor fight. He had eaten too much. It would take him at least a month to digest a youth of twenty and a cow. I went into the water and stood near the priest. I looked and looked. At last under a tree from which the river, after eating half the ground, had receded, I saw something. Two eyes like dull crystals, and below them two

protruding brown things
like tusks. He looked like a most
sinister image of Satan lying under
the outer roots of a maple and the thick
shadows cast by its bough that overhung many
feet of water. A black mountain of half-coiled python
looking at us with glassy eyes and out of the corner of
its mouth protruding the two horns of our cow.

The uncanny sight filled me with loathing and
terror. It takes a serpent a long time to dissolve the
horns of its victim in its own saliva. As you know,
snakes, large or small, cannot chew – they partly
crush their food in their throats. The priest said, "Let
us catch him alive." We went to the village, which had
heard of the python's presence from our new
herdsman, Gokul. The able-bodied men asked advice
of the serpent charmers who said the snake was too

large to be caught by the flute, so the men set to work to erect a cage of bamboo and cowhide thongs which took a day to finish. When it was done it was lowered in front of the python. But now the problem was to get him to move into it. Noises, shouts, then men jumping over the roots of the tree, all failed to make him move an inch.

There he lay, gripped by the act of digesting his food, a process more powerful than himself. The open cage was pushed close enough to the cavern mouth under the tree to allow just room enough for the front door, which was held up by a rope to the overhanging branch, to fall guillotine fashion, once he was inside.

But he did not budge from his place. So all the people left in disgust, saying, "What a stupid snake."

It was about the fourth day after our finding his hiding place that I went alone to carry out a plan of my own. When I reached the spot there was no adult about. I fetched pick, shovel, straw and a lot of kindling wood. Next I dug a tunnel at the python's back, which was a slanting hole, descending deeper and deeper as it approached the beast. As I was halfway through Purohit appeared. When he saw me he approved of my plan, and threw aside his priest's beads and cudgel, and took the pick from my already tired hands. He kept on digging harder and harder, and after we had worked another two hours, at about four in the afternoon he said, "I can hear him breathe. Go and get a crowbar."

When I fetched it he took it and jammed it right through the thin partition of loose soil and struck the serpent. He moved. We heard the roots of the tree tremble as his heavy body fell against them. But he did not move enough to please the priest. He jabbed a few times more, without getting a satisfactory result from the sleepy monster.

Then we laid the straw thick in the tunnel, almost next to the python's skin, then covered it with dry autumn leaves. After placing the kindling wood on top, we set the tunnel on fire. I was ordered to go up the tree with a knife. I climbed away over and lay on the overhanging branch to which was tied the rope, that held up the door of the prison prepared for our enemy. My orders were to cut the rope as soon as the snake had entered the cage.

Slowly the smoke arose, and as luck would have it, lay in thick layers between me and everything below.

In time it rose higher and began to hurt my eyes. I shouted to the priest a warning, "Call to me as loud as you can when the python enters the cage and you want the door to snap down, for I can see nothing. When I hear you I shall cut the rope."

Purohit shouted, "If he gets into the cage I will shout so that it will make you deaf. As soon as you hear me, cut that rope."

Whirl upon whirl of smoke arose, choking my nostrils and blinding my eyes. There I sat with my face over that all-powerful incense fume. I shut my eyes and concentrated all attention to catching the priest's warning cry. Of course the more I listened the more I heard the hiss and crackle of the fire and the noise of human voices. Apparently the whole village had repaired there to witness the roasting of the python. They kept on talking to one another and sometimes shouting aloud. How on earth I could complete my task under those circumstances passed my comprehension.

It seemed as if hours passed. I was like one wrapped in midnight darkness of smoke and noise. Suddenly a dizzy spell seized me. I felt as if I should fall off the tree. I heard an awful uproar. In the midst of the thunderous racket I faintly heard someone say in a squeaking voice, "O thou grandsire of a monkey, cut the rope. Host thou not hear me, O half brother of a mule? Cut that rope."

But he who was abusing me did not know that I could see nothing in the smoke. All the same I blindly groped forward and slashed away under the bough with my knife, mostly cutting the air. But I persisted. Once I cut off a twig. Another time I thought I cut a branch. Then another branch – no, this was no branch! Ha, the rope! I went on sawing away at it. Harder and harder I worked. And by the increasing din and tumult I could make sure that I was cutting the rope. I redoubled my forces. Ultimately I put half my weight on the knife, then pulled. More noise from below. Then something snapped! That instant I lost my balance. But I had sense enough to throw away the knife as I fell from the tree. In a moment I was sinking in the river, down, down, down…

When I came to the surface of the water again, my face was almost against the thick and double bamboo bars of the cage in which writhed a huge grey-black mass of flesh. I looked more carefully. Yes, he had swallowed those two horns that had stuck out of his mouth when first we located him under the tree. That seemed to satisfy some strange curiosity in me. Another thing I noticed was the size of the brute. He must have been at least a foot in diameter. People around me said that they had never seen a python so large before. However, they were so glad that he was caged and ready to be sold to a museum that, except the priest and Kuri, no one interested himself in me, dripping, choking and bruised.

Tiger! Tiger!

From *The Jungle Book*
by Rudyard Kipling

*The boy Mowgli was found in the jungle, and raised by a family
of wolves. Shere Khan, the tiger, persuaded the rest of the pack to
reject their leader, Akela, who defends Mowgli. Mowgli used fire
('the red flower') to frighten Shere Khan away, saving Akela's life.
Then he decides to leave the jungle...*

Mowgli left the wolf's cave after the fight
with the Pack at the Council Rock, and
went down to the lands where the villagers lived. He
did not stop there because it was too near the jungle,
and he knew he had made at least one enemy at the
Council. So he hurried on, keeping to the rough road
that ran down the valley. The valley opened out into a
rocky plain. At one end stood a village, and at the

other the jungle came down in a sweep to the grazing grounds. All over the plain, cattle were grazing, and when the boys in charge of the herds saw Mowgli they shouted and ran away. Mowgli walked on, for he was hungry. When he came to the village gate he saw the big thorn bush that was drawn up before the gate at twilight, pushed to one side.

"Umph!" he said, for he had come across more than one such barricade in his nightly hunting rambles. "So men are afraid of the People of the Jungle here also." He sat down by the gate, and when a man came out he stood up, opened his mouth, and pointed down it to show that he wanted food. The man stared, and ran back into the village shouting for the priest, who was a big, fat man dressed in white, with a red and yellow mark on his forehead. The priest came to the gate, and with him many people, who stared and talked and pointed at Mowgli.

"They have no manners, these Men Folk," said Mowgli to himself. "Only the grey ape would behave as they do." So he threw back his long hair and frowned at the crowd.

"Look at the marks on his arms and legs," said the priest. "They are the bites of wolves. He is just a wolf-child who has run away from the jungle."

In playing, the cubs had often nipped Mowgli harder than they intended, and there were scars all over his arms and legs. But he would not have called these bites, for he knew what real biting meant.

"To be bitten by wolves, poor child!" said two or three women together. "He is a handsome boy. He has eyes like red fire. By my honour, Messua, he is not unlike thy boy that was taken by the tiger."

"Let me look," said a woman with copper rings on her wrists and ankles. She peered at Mowgli. "Indeed he is not. He has the very look of my boy."

The priest was a clever man, and he knew that Messua was wife to the richest villager in the place. He looked up at the sky and said solemnly, "What the jungle has taken the jungle has restored. Take the boy into thy house, my sister."

The woman beckoned Mowgli to her hut, where there was a red lacquered bedstead, a great earthen grain chest with funny raised patterns on it, half a dozen copper cooking pots, an image of a Hindu god in a little alcove, and on the wall a real looking glass.

She gave him a drink of milk and some bread, and then she laid her hand on his head and looked into his eyes. She said, "Dost thou not remember the day when I gave thee thy new shoes?" She touched his foot, and it was almost as hard as horn. "No," she said, "those feet have never worn shoes, but thou art very like my Nathoo, and thou shalt be my son."

Mowgli was uneasy, because he had never been under a roof before. But as he looked at the thatch, he saw that he could tear it out at any time if he wanted to get away, and that the window had no fastenings.

"What is the good of a man," he said to himself, "if he does not understand man's talk? I am as dumb as a man would be in the jungle. I must speak their talk."

He had learned while he was with the wolves to imitate the challenge of bucks in the jungle and the grunt of the wild pig. So, when Messua said a word, Mowgli would imitate it almost perfectly. Before dark he had learned the names of many things in the hut.

At bedtime Mowgli would not sleep under anything that looked so like a panther trap as the hut, and when they shut the door he went through the window.

"Give him his will," said Messua's husband. "He can never till now have slept on a bed. If he is indeed sent in the place of our son he will not run away."

So Mowgli stretched himself in some long, clean grass at the edge of the field, but before he had closed his eyes a soft grey nose poked him under the chin.

"Phew!" said Grey Brother (he was the eldest of Mother Wolf's cubs). "This is a poor reward for following thee twenty miles. Thou smellest of wood smoke and cattle – like a man already."

"Are all well in the jungle?" Mowgli asked, giving him a hug.

"All except the wolves that were burned with the Red Flower. Shere Khan has gone away till his coat grows again, for he is badly singed. When he returns he swears that he will lay thy bones in the river."

"I also have made a little promise. I am tired tonight, Grey Brother – but bring me the news always."

"Thou wilt not forget that thou art a wolf? Men will not make thee forget?" said Grey Brother anxiously.

"Never. I will always remember that I love thee and all in our cave. But also that I have been cast out of the Pack."

"And that thou mayest be cast out of another pack. Men are only men, Little Brother. When I come down here again, I will wait for thee in the bamboos at the edge of the grazing-ground."

For three months, Mowgli hardly left the village, he was so busy learning the ways of men. First he had to wear a cloth round him, which annoyed him horribly. Then he had to learn about money, which he did not understand, and about ploughing, of which he did not see the use. Luckily, the Law of the Jungle had taught him to keep his temper, but when the children made fun of him because he would not play games, or because he mispronounced some word, only the knowledge that it was unsportsmanlike to kill cubs kept him from picking them up and breaking them in two.

One day it was decided that Mowgli would go out with the buffaloes, and herd them while they grazed.

THE HUNTERS

No one was more pleased than Mowgli. The custom of most Indian villages is for a few boys to take the cattle and buffaloes out to graze in the early morning, and bring them back at night. So long as the boys keep with the herds they are safe, for not even a tiger will charge a mob of cattle. But if they straggle, they are sometimes carried off. Mowgli went through the village street in the dawn, sitting on the back of Rama, the great herd bull. The slaty-blue buffaloes, with their long, backward-sweeping horns and savage eyes, rose out of their byres, one by one, and followed him. Mowgli made it clear to the children with him that he was the master. He beat the buffaloes with a long bamboo, and told Kamya, one of the boys, to graze the cattle, while he went on with the buffaloes.

An Indian grazing ground is all rocks and scrub and tussocks and ravines, among which the herds scatter and disappear. The buffaloes generally keep to muddy places, where they lie wallowing or basking in the warm mud for hours. Mowgli drove them on to the edge of the plain where the river came out of the jungle. Then he dropped from Rama's neck, trotted off to a bamboo clump, and found Grey Brother.

"Ah," said Grey Brother, "I have waited here very

many days. What is the meaning of this cattle-herding work?"

"It is an order," said Mowgli. "I am a village herd for a while. What news of Shere Khan?"

"He has come back to this country, and has waited here a long time for thee. He has gone off again, for the game is scarce. But he means to kill thee."

"Good," said Mowgli. "So long as he is away do thou or one of the four brothers sit on that rock, so that I can see thee as I come out of the village. When he is back wait for me in the ravine by the dhak tree in the centre of the plain."

Then Mowgli picked out a shady place, and lay down and slept while the buffaloes grazed round him. Herding in India is one of the laziest things in the world. The cattle move and crunch, and lie down, and move on again, and they do not even low. They only grunt, and the buffaloes very seldom say anything, but get down into the muddy pools one after another, and work their way into the mud till only their noses and staring china-blue eyes show above the surface.

The sun makes the rocks dance in the heat, and the herd children sleep and wake and sleep again, and weave little baskets of dried grass and put grasshoppers in them, or catch two praying mantises and make them fight, or watch a lizard basking on a rock, or a snake hunting a frog near the wallows. The day seems longer than most people's whole lives. Then evening comes and the children call, and the buffaloes lumber up out of the sticky mud with noises like gunshots going off one after the other, and they all string across the grey plain back to the twinkling village lights.

Day after day Mowgli would lead the buffaloes out to their wallows, and day after day he would see Grey Brother across the plain (so he knew that Shere Khan had not come back), and day after day he would lie on the grass listening to the noises around him, and dreaming of old days in the jungle.

At last a day came when he did not see Grey

Brother, and he headed the buffaloes for the ravine by the dhak tree, which was all covered with golden-red flowers. There sat Grey Brother, every bristle on his back lifted.

"He has hidden for a month to throw thee off thy guard. He crossed the ranges last night with Tabaqui the jackal, hot-foot on thy trail," said the Wolf, panting.

Mowgli frowned. "I am not afraid of Shere Khan, but Tabaqui is very cunning."

"Have no fear," said Grey Brother, licking his lips a little. "I met Tabaqui in the dawn. Now he is telling all his wisdom to the kites, but he told me everything before I broke his back. Shere Khan's plan is to wait for thee at the village gate this evening. He is lying up now, in the big dry ravine."

"Has he eaten today, or does he hunt empty?" said Mowgli, for the answer meant life and death to him.

"He killed at dawn, and he has drunk too. Shere Khan could never fast, even for the sake of revenge."

"Oh, fool! Eaten and drunk, and he thinks I will wait till he has slept! These buffaloes will not charge unless they wind him. Can we get behind his track so that they may smell it?"

"He swam down the river to cut that off," said Grey Brother.

"Tabaqui told him that, I know. He would never have thought of it." Mowgli stood with his finger in his mouth, thinking. "The big ravine. That opens out on the plain not half a mile from here. I can take the herd round through the jungle to the head of the ravine and then sweep down – but he would slink out at the foot. We must block that end. Grey Brother, canst thou cut the herd in two for me?"

"Not I, perhaps – but I have brought a helper." Grey Brother trotted off. Then there lifted up a huge grey head that Mowgli knew well, and the hot air was filled with the hunting howl of a wolf at midday.

"Akela! Akela!" said Mowgli, clapping his hands. "I might have known that thou wouldst not forget me. Cut the herd in two, Akela. Keep the cows and calves together, and the bulls and the plough buffaloes by themselves."

The two wolves ran in and out of the herd, which snorted and threw up its head, and separated into two clumps. In one, the cow-buffaloes stood with their calves in the centre, and glared and pawed, ready, if a wolf would only stay still, to charge down and trample the life out of him. In the other, the bulls and the young bulls snorted – though they looked more imposing they were much less dangerous, for they had no calves to protect.

Mowgli slipped on to Rama's back. "Drive the bulls away to the left, Akela. Grey Brother, when we are gone, hold the cows together, and drive them into the foot of the ravine."

"How far?" said Grey Brother, panting.

"Till the sides are higher than Shere Khan can jump," shouted Mowgli. "Keep them there till we come down." The bulls swept off as Akela bayed, and Grey Brother stopped in front of the cows. They charged down on him, and he ran just before them to the foot of the ravine, as Akela drove the bulls far to the left.

"Well done! Another charge and they are fairly started. Careful, now – careful, Akela. A snap too much and the bulls will charge. Swiftly turn them! Rama is mad with rage. Oh, if I could only tell him what I need of him today."

Mowgli's plan was simple enough. He wanted to make a big circle uphill and get at the head of the ravine, and then take the bulls down it and catch

Shere Khan between the bulls and the cows, for he knew that after a meal and a full drink Shere Khan would not be in any condition to fight or to clamber up the sides of the ravine. He was soothing the buffaloes now by voice, and Akela had dropped far to the rear, only whimpering once or twice to hurry the rear-guard. It was a long circle, for they did not wish to get too near the ravine and give Shere Khan warning.

At last Mowgli rounded up the bewildered herd at the head of the ravine on a grassy patch that sloped steeply down to the ravine itself. From that height you could see across the tops of the trees down to the plain below, but what Mowgli looked at was the sides of the ravine, and he saw with satisfaction that they ran nearly straight up and down, while the vines and creepers that hung over them would give no foothold to a tiger who wanted to get out.

"Let them breathe, Akela," he said, holding up his hand. "They have not winded him yet. Let them breathe. I must tell Shere Khan who comes. We have him in the trap."

He put his hands to his mouth and shouted down the ravine, and the echoes jumped from rock to rock.

Tiger! Tiger!

After a long time there came back the drawling, sleepy snarl of a full-fed tiger just wakened.

"Who calls?" said Shere Khan, and a splendid peacock fluttered up out of the ravine screeching.

"Down – hurry them down, Akela! Down, Rama, down!"

The herd paused at the edge of the slope, but Akela gave tongue in the full hunting-yell, and they pitched over one after the other, sand and stones spurting up round them. Before they were fairly in the bed of the ravine Rama winded Shere Khan and bellowed.

"Ha! Ha!" said Mowgli, on his back. "Now thou knowest!" and the torrent of black horns, foaming muzzles, and staring eyes whirled down the ravine. They knew what the business was before them – the terrible charge of the buffalo herd against which no tiger can hope to stand. Shere Khan heard the thunder of their hoofs, picked himself up, and lumbered down the ravine, looking from side to side for some way of escape, but the walls of the ravine were straight. The herd splashed through the pool he had just left, bellowing till the narrow cut rang. Mowgli heard an answering bellow from the foot of the ravine, saw Shere Khan turn, and then Rama, with the bulls at his heels, crashed full into the other herd. That charge carried both herds out into the plain, goring and stamping and snorting. Mowgli watched his time, and slipped off Rama's neck, laying about him right and left with his stick.

"Quick, Akela! Break them up, or they will be fighting one another."

Akela and Grey Brother ran to and fro nipping the buffaloes' legs. Mowgli managed to turn Rama, and the others followed him to the wallows.

Shere Khan needed no more trampling. He was dead, and the kites were coming for him already.

"Brothers, that was a dog's death," said Mowgli, feeling for the knife he always carried in a sheath round his neck now that he lived with men. "But he would never have shown fight. His hide will look well on the Council Rock."

Tiger! Tiger!

A boy trained among men would never have dreamed of skinning a ten-foot tiger alone, but Mowgli knew better than anyone else how an animal's skin is fitted on, and how it can be taken off. But it was hard work, and Mowgli slashed and tore and grunted for an hour. Presently a hand fell on his shoulder, and looking up he saw the man Buldeo. The children had told the village about the buffalo stampede, and Buldeo went out angrily, only too anxious to correct Mowgli for not taking better care of the herd.

"What is this folly?" said Buldeo angrily. "To think that thou canst skin a tiger! Where did the buffaloes kill him? It is the Lame Tiger too, and there is a hundred rupees on his head. Well, we will overlook thy letting the herd run off, and perhaps I will give thee one of the rupees of the reward when I have taken the skin to Khanhiwara."

"Hum!" said Mowgli, half to himself. "So thou wilt take the hide to Khanhiwara for the reward, and perhaps give me one rupee? I need the skin."

"Thy luck and the stupidity of thy buffaloes have helped thee to this kill. The tiger has just fed, or he would have gone twenty miles by this time. Thou canst not even skin him properly. Mowgli, I will not give thee one anna of the reward, but only a very big beating. Leave the carcass!"

"By the Bull that bought me," said Mowgli, who was trying to get at the shoulder, "must I stay babbling to an old ape all noon? Here, Akela, this man plagues me."

Buldeo suddenly found himself sprawling on the grass, with a grey wolf standing over him, while Mowgli went on skinning.

"Ye-es," he said, between his teeth. "Thou art altogether right, Buldeo. Thou wilt never give me one anna of the reward. There is an old war between this tiger and myself – a very old war – and I have won."

To do Buldeo justice, if he had been ten years younger he would have taken his chance with Akela had he met the wolf in the woods, but a wolf who obeyed the orders of this boy who had private wars with man-eating tigers was not a common animal. He lay as still as still, expecting every minute to see Mowgli turn into a tiger too.

At last he said, in a husky whisper, "May I rise up and go away, or will thy servant tear me to pieces?"

"Go, and peace go with thee. Only, another time

do not meddle with my game. Let him go, Akela."

Buldeo hobbled away to the village as fast as he could. Mowgli went on with his work, but it was nearly twilight before he had drawn the great skin clear of the body.

"Now we must hide this and take the buffaloes home! Help me to herd them, Akela."

The herd rounded up in the misty twilight, and when they got near the village Mowgli saw lights, and heard the conches and bells in the temple blowing. Half the village seemed to be waiting for him by the gate. "That is because I have killed Shere Khan," he said to himself. But the villagers shouted: "Sorcerer! Wolf's brat! Jungle demon! Go away! Shoot, Buldeo, shoot!"

The old Tower musket went off with a bang, and a young buffalo bellowed in pain.

"Now, what is this?" said Mowgli, bewildered.

"They are not unlike the Pack, these brothers of thine," said Akela, sitting down composedly. "It is in my head that, if bullets mean anything, they would cast thee out."

"Wolf! Wolf's cub! Go away!" shouted the priest, waving a sprig of the sacred tulsi plant.

THE HUNTERS

"Again? Last time it was because I was a man. This time it is because I am a wolf. Let us go, Akela."

The buffaloes were anxious enough to get to the village. They hardly needed Akela's yell, but charged through the gate like a whirlwind, scattering the crowd right and left.

Mowgli turned on his heel and walked away with the Lone Wolf, and as he looked up at the stars he felt happy. "No more sleeping in traps for me, Akela. Let us get Shere Khan's skin and go away."

When the moon rose over the plain, the villagers saw Mowgli, with two wolves at his heels and a bundle on his head, trotting across at the steady wolf's trot that eats up the long miles like fire. Then they banged the temple bells and blew the conches louder than ever.

The moon was just going down when Mowgli and the two wolves came to the hill of the Council Rock, and they stopped at Mother Wolf's cave.

"They have cast me out from the Man-Pack, Mother," shouted Mowgli, "but I come with the hide of Shere Khan to keep my word."

Mother Wolf walked stiffly from the cave with the cubs behind her, and her eyes glowed in the dark as she saw the skin.

"I told him on that day, when he crammed his head into this cave, hunting for thy life, Little Frog – I told him that the hunter would be the hunted. It is well done."

"Little Brother, it is well done," said a deep voice in the thicket. "We were lonely here without thee," and Bagheera came running to Mowgli's bare feet.

They clambered up the Council Rock together, and Mowgli spread the skin out on the flat stone where Akela used to sit, and pegged it down with four slivers of bamboo, and Akela lay down upon it, and called the old call to the Council, "Look – look well, O Wolves," exactly as he had called when Mowgli was first brought there.

Ever since Akela had been deposed, the Pack had been without a leader, hunting and fighting at their own pleasure. But they answered the call from habit; and some of them were lame from the traps they had fallen into, and some limped from shot wounds, and some were mangy from eating bad food, and many were missing. But they came to the Council Rock, all that were left of them, and saw Shere Khan's striped hide on the rock, and the huge claws dangling at the end of the empty dangling feet. It was then that Mowgli made up a song that came up into his throat all by itself, and he shouted it aloud, leaping up and down on the rattling skin, and beating time with his heels till he had no more breath left, while Grey Brother and Akela howled between the verses.

"Look well, O Wolves. Have I kept my word?" asked Mowgli.

And the wolves bayed, "Yes".

One tattered wolf howled, "Lead us again,

O Akela. Lead us again, O Man-cub, for we be sick of this lawlessness, and we would be the Free People once more."

"Nay," purred Bagheera, "that may not be. When ye are full-fed, the madness may come upon you again. Not for nothing are ye called the Free People. Ye fought for freedom, and it is yours."

"Man-Pack and Wolf-Pack have cast me out," said Mowgli. "Now I will hunt alone in the jungle."

"And we will hunt with thee," said the four cubs.

So Mowgli went away and hunted with the four cubs in the jungle from that day on. But he was not always alone, because, years afterward, he became a man and married.

But that is a story for grown-ups.

The Calf's Childhood

From *The Story of a Red Deer*
by J W Fortescue

*The book this extract comes from is about the life of one of the
beautiful deer that roam Exmoor, in southwest England. These deer
used to be hunted, like foxes, by men riding horses with hounds.*

Once upon a time there was a little Red Deer
Calf. A very pretty little fellow he was, downy-
haired and white-spotted, though as yet his legs were
rather long and his ears were rather large, for he was
still only a very few weeks old.

The first thing that he remembered was that he
found himself lying very snug in a patch of fern, with
the most beautiful pair of brown eyes gazing straight
down upon him. And soon he was aware that they

The Calf's Childhood

were the eyes of the Hind his mother, that they followed him wherever he went, and watched over him whatever he did, and that, whatever he might want, she was there to provide it for him. She always had a cosy bed ready for him in grass or fern, she washed him clean with her tongue every morning, and she taught him two lessons – to lie as still as a mouse, and to do as he was bid. For every morning before dawn she had to go afield to feed herself – farther than the little Calf could travel with her. She just tucked him up as closely as she could, and told him to lie still till she came back. And like a good little fellow he obeyed her.

For some time they moved but little distance from the place where he was born, but as he grew stronger they wandered farther, till at last one day he found himself on high ground, and saw the world that he was to live in, his heritage of Exmoor. Fold upon fold of grass and heather, slashed by deep valleys and merry babbling streams, and bounded on the one hand by the blue sky and on the other by the blue sea. It was all his own, for he was a wild Red Deer.

Then they went down, leaving the song of the wind ever fainter behind them, and in its stead rose the song of the peat stream bidding them come down to it. They passed by a little shallow, and there the Calf saw dozens of little fry, scurrying about from stone to stone. Just below the shallow they came to a pool in a basin of rock. The Calf looked into it, and there he saw his own form, and behind it his mother's sweet eyes watching over him. For the first time he noticed that his own coat was spotted while his mother's was red. While he was staring at the water a fly suddenly came, and began to dance a reel over it, when all of a sudden a neat little body, all brown and gold and red spots, leaped up out of the water, seized the fly in his mouth and fell back with a splash which broke the pretty picture all to pieces.

He shrank back, for he was rather startled, but his

mother soon comforted him. "It was only a little Trout, my dear," she said, "only a greedy little Trout."

"But he was such a pretty little fellow," he said, for he had quite got over his fright. "I wish he would jump again."

But the Hind looked grave. "We are never unkind to the Trout," she said, "for they belong to the peat stream, but you must never become familiar with them. They are a lazy lot of fellows whose forefathers would not take the trouble to go down to the sea, whereby they might have grown into noble fish, with a coat as bright as the moon on the water. But they would not, and so they have remained small, and they never lose their spots. You must never be rude to them, but you must never make friends with them."

"But, mother," said the poor little Calf, "I've got a spotted coat."

"But you will lose it, my darling," she said tenderly.

So they left the water, and presently stopped while his mother plucked at a tuft of sweet grass, when to his astonishment a little ball of fur came bounding out of a hole in the ground, and another at his heels, and three more after them. And they ran round and round and played like mad things. And presently

another, far bigger than they, came up slowly out of another hole, sat up on her hind legs, pricked her ears, and began to look about her.

Then catching sight of the Calf she crouched down, and began in a very shrill voice, "Why, my dear tender heart, if it isn't my little maister, and her ladyship too, begging your pardon, my lady. And sweetly pretty he is, my lady, and butiful you'm looking too, in your summer coat, glossy as a chestnut, sure enough. And dear heart alive, how he groweth. Why, 'twas but a few days agone that my Bucky saith to me, 'Bunny,' saith he, 'you may depend that young maister will grow to be so fine a stag as ever was seen on Exmoor.'"

The Hind listened very graciously to this speech, for she loved to hear good words of her Calf, and she was just a little pleased to hear of her own good looks. But she could not help looking beautiful, and she looked all the more so because she very seldom thought about it. So she returned the compliment by asking after Bunny and her family.

"Oh! Thank you, my lady," answered Bunny, "I reckon we'm well. There han't been no man this way this long time, thanks be, and there's plenty of meat, and not too much rain. And the family's well, my lady, my third family this spring! But oh, my lady! They foxes, and they weasels! They do tell me that the old vixen from Cornham Brake hath five cubs, and I can't abide a vixen. And they weasels they'm small, but they'm worse than foxes. Now there's my Bucky. He can't bide home, he saith, these fine days, but must go and lie out. I says to mun, 'Bucky,' I says, 'tis very well for the likes of her ladyship to lie out every day, but you should bide home to bury'. But no, he would go. 'Well then, Bucky,' I says, 'I reckon that you'll grow a pair of horns like his lordship, brow, bay, and trey, Bucky,' I says, 'and turn to bay when the weasel's after 'ee'. And with that he layeth back his ears and away he goeth. Oh dear, dear, dear!" And she stopped for want of breath.

THE HUNTERS

"Well, good evening, Bunny," said the Hind very kindly, "I must take my little son home. I shall see you again soon."

"And good evening to your ladyship," answered Bunny, "and good evening to you, dear. Ah! You'm his lordship's son sure enough. I mind the time—"

But the Hind had moved out of hearing, for when once an old Doe Rabbit begins to talk she never stops. Then presently the Calf said, "Mother, who is his lordship?"

And she answered, "He is your father, my darling. For the Red Deer are lords of this forest, and he is the lord of them all. And brow, bay, trey is the coronet that every good Stag wears, and which you too shall wear in due time, when you grow up."

The next day the Hind led her Calf away from the valley, and after travelling some little way, they met a beautiful bird. His plumage was all of glossy black, which shone blue and green and purple in the sun, while to set it off he had a patch of pure white on each wing, and a spot of red above each eye. His tail was forked and bent outwards in two graceful curves, and his legs were feathered to the very heel.

"Well, good Master Blackcock," said the Hind,

264

"has my lord not moved?"

"Not a step, my lady," said the bird, "though the flies do worrit mun terrible."

"Then come along, son," she said. And she led him on and presently stopped and whispered, "Look." And there he saw a great Stag nearly twice the size of his mother, with horns half grown and velvet-black with flies, lying down motionless but for the constant twitching of his head.

The Calf could not see how big he was, till he rose on to his feet, and stretched himself. Then he stood for a minute or two blinking rather sleepily. His back was broad and his coat shone with good living, and the little Calf made up his mind then and there to stand just like that and to stretch himself just like that, when he had grown to be such a fine stag as that.

But presently the Hind led him away and asked the Blackcock, "And where is my sister?" And the Blackcock led them on, and after a time they came in sight of two more Hinds and another little Calf. One of the Hinds was very big and grey, and she had no Calf, but the other was smaller and bright red, and had at her foot as sweet a little Calf as ever you saw. Then both of the mothers laid their Calves down, and began to talk, but the old grey Hind broke in.

"So it's you, Tawny, is it?" she said, "You have brought a Calf with you, I see. Is it a stag or a hind?"

"A stag, Aunt Yeld," said the Lady Tawny (for that was the name of our Calf's mother).

"A stag, is it?" said Aunt Yeld with a little sniff. "Well, I suppose if people must have calves they had better have stags. Ruddy's here is a hind, but I never could see the attraction of any calf myself."

For Aunt Yeld, like some old maids (but by no means like all) that have no children of their own, thought it the right thing to look down on Calves.

Then Aunt Yeld turned round and said, "Now you two mustn't think of going. You are not fit to take care of yourselves, so you must stay with me. I'll take care of you." You see she had quite forgotten what she said at first, for she had really a kind heart, though nothing could keep her from patronising everyone.

So for many days they lived together, and Aunt Yeld always posted herself upwind of them to keep watch over them. Now and again, though very seldom, the Stag would join them and lie by them all day, chewing the cud and shaking his great head, which grew bigger every day. But he never uttered a

word, unless it was to say, "Very good that growing wheat was this morning, to be sure," to which the Hind would answer, "I am so glad, dearest," or it would be, "The turnips on Yarner farm are not coming on well in this dry weather. It's very annoying, for I was looking forward to my turnips," and then the Hind would say, "I am so sorry, dearest. How I hope it will rain soon!" For old stags are perhaps rather too fond of their dinners.

Once only he showed himself quite different, and that was when one day the Blackcock flew up to say that all the hills were coming down. He had been taking a bath in the dust at the foot of a great sheet of screes, and had enjoyed it greatly, fluffing out his feathers and flapping his great wings. While he was in the middle of it a Jackdaw came flying overhead, and seeing this great ball of feathers rolling about, pitched down upon the screes to see what strange thing it might be. As he came hopping down to look at it closer, he displaced one little stone, which displaced another stone, until quite a number of stones were moving, and came rushing down, close to the Blackcock's ear. Whereupon the Jackdaw flapped off, and the Blackcock flew away screaming to tell the deer that the hills were coming down.

The old Stag stood up at once and said, "Lady Yeld, take the lead, Ruddy and Tawny, follow her. Steadily now, no hurrying!" Then they moved on a little way and stopped, the Stag always remaining behind them – they could see that the hills were not coming down before them, and therefore they must have begun to fall behind them. That was why the Stag remained behind, to be nearest to danger, as a gentleman should be.

The Deer stopped for a time, and at last the Stag said, "I can see nothing, hear nothing, and wind nothing. Are you quite sure the hills are all coming down, Blackcock? I think that you must have made some mistake." For the old Stag was a gentleman, and always very civil and courteous.

Lady Tawny said kindly, "Thank you, Blackcock, for coming. You mustn't let us keep you from your dinner." And though it was not his dinner-time, he was so glad of the excuse that he flew off straight away.

But except on this one occasion the Stag never stirred, never opening his mouth except to munch his food or talk of it. He never spoke a word to the Calf, and you may be sure that the Calf never said a word to him, for he was terribly afraid of him – an old stag, while his head is growing, is very irritable indeed.

One day they were lying out in the grass as usual, and our little Calf was having a great game of romps with the little Hind. The Stag was not with them, but Aunt Yeld was standing sentry, when all of a sudden she came back in a great fluster.

"Quick!" she said. "I can wind them and see them. Call your Calves and go. Run as fast as you can!"

"But our Calves can't keep up if we go fast," pleaded the two mothers.

Then they looked down across the rolling waves of grass, and a mile and a half away they saw twenty-five couples of great hounds trotting over the heather with a horseman in a white coat at their heads and another at their sterns. A fresh puff of wind bore a wave of strange scent to the nostrils of the Deer, and our little Calf snuffed it and thought it the most unpleasant that he had ever tasted.

Aunt Yeld stood talking to herself. "I passed just in front of the place where they are now on my way back from breakfast this morning," she murmured. "I trust that scent has failed by this time. Ah!"

As she spoke some of the hounds swung suddenly with one impulse towards them, but the horseman behind them galloped forward and turned them back. Then the mass began to move faster, and the Deer watched it go further and further away from them till at last it vanished out of sight.

"Well, that is a mercy," said Aunt Yeld with a deep sigh. "I think that we are safe now, but I'll just make sure in case of accidents."

With that she began to trot about in a strange fashion. She made a great circle to the track by which she had come back from feeding in the morning, and ran back along it for some way. Then she turned off it, and made another circle which brought her to a stream. Then she ran up the water and made another circle which brought her back again.

"There," she said, "if they follow, at least that will puzzle them."

But the Lady Tawny spoke, "I am afraid to stay

here, Aunt Yeld. I will take my Calf far away to a quiet spot that I know of." So they parted, and very sad they were at parting.

Early one morning, it must have been almost the last week in September, the peace of the oak coppice was disturbed by a terrible clamour. The Hind started to her feet in alarm, and led the Calf out of the wooded valley to the moor above. The whole valley was filled with the tumult. It was hard to say exactly where the sound came from, but after a short time the clamour drew nearer to the Hind and Calf, and presently out came one of the Fox cubs, looking desperately weary. He went on for a little distance, as if to go away over the moor, but soon stopped and flung back with desperation into a thicket.

Then the noise drew closer and closer, and out bounded a pack of hounds, with bristles erect and gleaming eyes. They flashed over the scent for fifty yards, still yelling with all their might, and then they fell silent and spread out in all directions. Presently they found the line of the Cub, and turned, but two puppies had crossed the scent of the Hind and Calf and started after them as fast as they could run.

Then the Hind turned and fled and the Calf with

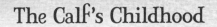

her, as he had never fled
before, but his poor
little legs began
speedily to
tire, and he could
not have held out for
much longer,
when suddenly
he found himself poked down quick as though by his
mother's nose into a tuft of fern.

"Lie still, my son, till I come back," she whispered,
and so she left him. He lay panting, while the voices
of the puppies came closer and closer to his hiding
place, but he never moved, for his mother had bid
him lie still. Then they rushed past him with a wild
cry, for his mother had waited to lead them after
herself; and their voices died away, and all was silent.

Presently he heard a dull sound, coming, drum,
drum, drum, louder and louder. The earth shook, and
a huge dark body seemed to be coming almost on to
the top of him, but suddenly swerved aside just in
time, and left him unharmed. Then the drumming
died away, and after a time he heard a dismal yelping
such as he had once heard before. He did not know

that it was a man and horse that had nearly galloped on to the top of him, and would have galloped quite on the top of him if the horse had not shied, nor that the man had given the puppies a thrashing for running a deer when they had been told to run a fox.

He was hoping that his mother would soon come back, when he heard two voices unlike any that he had ever heard before, and saw riding towards him two people. One was a man with fair hair and blue eyes, and the other a girl, a year or so younger than the man. She, too, had bright blue eyes, and fair hair, and a very pretty face, at least the man seemed to think so, for he was always looking at it. They came on till they were only at a little distance from him, and the man pulled up and, pointing to him, said very low, "Look."

And the girl whispered, "What a little duck! I wish I could take him home with me."

But the man said, "No, no. His mother will come and take him home, and the sooner we leave him the better she will be pleased." So they rode away, and he could hear them talking as they rode, for they seemed to have a great deal to say to each other.

Before very long his mother came back to him,

and you may guess how glad he was to see her, and how she rejoiced to see him. After looking round to see that all was quiet, she led him away over the heather, and then down a very steep hillside among stunted gorse.

"See, my son," she said, "this is the first time that you have been chased by hounds, and it may not be the last. Remember, no hound can run fast over this gorse, while we do not mind it. And these loose stones are almost better for us than the gorse, for our scent hardly lies on them and they hurt a hound's feet almost as much as the gorse."

So they went to the bottom of the hill, and there was a peat stream. The Hind led him up a shallow for a little way, and then she jumped out on to the opposite bank and followed it upwards for a little way, and then she jumped into the water again and went down for a full hundred yards till they came to a comfortable shady spot, where they both left the water and lay down together.

"Now, my son," said the Hind, "here is another lesson for you to learn. The water carries no scent. But a hound will try the bank to find out where we have left the water. If we enter it upstream he will try upward, and if we enter it downstream he will try downward. So always try to make them work upward when you mean to go down, and downward when you mean to go up, as I have shown you today."

They lay there together till the sun began to fall low, and then they rose and went down to the water to cross it. They made their way to the cliffs that overhang the sea, where they made their home in a great plantation of Scotch firs. Here they lay, and very much the Calf liked his new home.

They had not been there for three days when one morning they heard faint sounds of a great trampling of hoofs. They lay quite still, though the Hind was very uneasy. Then suddenly they heard the voice of hounds rise from the thickets on the cliff below them, and a man screaming at the top of his voice.

The sounds came nearer, and then there was a great clatter of branches, and the great Stag, whom they had known on the moor, came bounding leisurely through the thicket. His head was thrown back, and very proud and very terrible he looked as he cantered up to them. He jerked his head at them, and said sternly, "Off with you! Quick!"

The Hind jumped up in terror and the Calf with her. As they ran off they could see the old Stag lie down in their place with his horns laid back on his shoulders, and his chin pressed tight to the ground.

They had no time to lose, for the hounds were coming closer. The Hind led the Calf into a path, because his little legs could not keep pace with hers in the tangle of the plantation. Thus they ran on for a little way, till they heard the sound of a horse coming towards them, when they turned into the thicket again and lay down. A man in a red coat came trotting by, and meeting the hounds stopped them at once. Then he pulled out a horn, blew one single note, and trotted away with the hounds, just three couples of them, at his heels.

Presently they heard two more horses coming gently along the path, and two human voices chattering very fast. And who should ride by but the pretty girl whom he had seen a few days before! A man was riding with her, but he was dark, and rather older. As they passed they saw her smile at him, in a way that seemed to please him very well.

They rode on till their chattering could be heard no more, and then another man came riding by on a grey horse, whom the Calf recognized as the fair man that had been with the girl when first he saw her, and very miserable he seemed to be. For he stopped on the path opposite to them, looking down at the ground with a troubled face, and kept flicking savagely at the heather with his whip. All of a sudden the Hind and Calf heard a wild sound of men hallooing, and the horn sounding. Then the man's face brightened up, and he caught hold of the grey horse by the head and galloped off as fast as he could go.

Directly after this, the Deer heard a mighty rush of hoofs all hastening to the same spot, the sound growing gradually fainter until all was still. And then the Hind led the Calf cautiously out of the plantation to the open moor. As they went they saw a long string of horses, toiling one after the other, while far ahead the hounds kept creeping on and on, with a larger speck close to them which could be nothing else than a grey horse. So the Hind led the Calf on to a quiet valley. There they lay down in peace.

And when the sun began to sink they saw, far away, the hounds and a few horses with them, returning home. Presently they were startled by voices much closer to them, and they saw the fair man on the grey horse and the pretty girl, riding side by side. The pair were riding close together, and they seemed to be much occupied with each other. After they were gone there came a loose horse, saddled and bridled, but covered with mire, and with a stirrup missing.

Last of all came a man tramping wearily over the heather, with a stirrup in his hand – the Calf hardly recognized him as the dark man whom he had seen in the morning, for his hat was crushed in, and his clothes caked with mire from head to foot.

So he too passed out of sight, and the sun went down, and the mist stole over the face of the moor, and the Hind and Calf were left alone with the music of the flowing water to sing them to sleep. But they never saw that old Stag again.

The White Seal

From *The Jungle Book*
by Rudyard Kipling

All these things happened several years ago at a place called Novastoshnah, on the Island of St Paul, away and away in the Bering Sea.

Nobody comes to Novastoshnah except on business, and the only people who have regular business there are the seals. They come in the summer months by hundreds and hundreds of thousands out of the cold sea. For Novastoshnah Beach is the finest home for seals of any place in all the world.

Sea Catch knew that, and every spring would swim like a torpedo-boat straight for Novastoshnah and spend a month fighting with his companions for a good place on the rocks, as close to the sea as possible. Sea Catch was fifteen years old, a huge grey fur seal with almost a mane on his shoulders, and long, wicked teeth. When he heaved himself up on his front flippers he stood more than four feet clear of the ground, and his weight, if anyone had been bold enough to weigh him, was nearly seven hundred pounds. He was scarred all over with the marks of savage fights, but he was always ready for just one fight more. Yet Sea Catch never chased a beaten seal, for that was against the Rules of the Beach. He only wanted room by the sea for his nursery. But as there were forty or fifty thousand other seals hunting for the same thing each spring, the whistling, bellowing, and roaring on the beach was frightful.

From a little hill called Hutchinson's Hill, you could look over three-and-a-half miles of ground covered with fighting seals. Their wives never came to the island until late in May or early in June, for they did not care to be torn to pieces, and the young seals who had not begun housekeeping went inland about half a mile through the ranks of the fighters and played about on the sand dunes. They were called the holluschickie – the bachelors – and there were perhaps two or three hundred thousand of them at Novastoshnah alone.

Sea Catch had just finished his forty-fifth fight one spring when Matkah, his soft, gentle-eyed wife, came up out of the sea, and he caught her by the scruff of the neck and dumped her down on his reservation, saying gruffly, "Late as usual. Where have you been?"

It was not the fashion for Sea Catch to eat anything during the four months he stayed on the beaches, and so his temper was generally bad. Matkah knew better than to answer back. She looked round and cooed, "How thoughtful of you. You've taken the old place again."

"I should think I had," said Sea Catch. "Look at me!" He was scratched and bleeding in twenty places, one eye was almost out, and his sides were torn to ribbons.

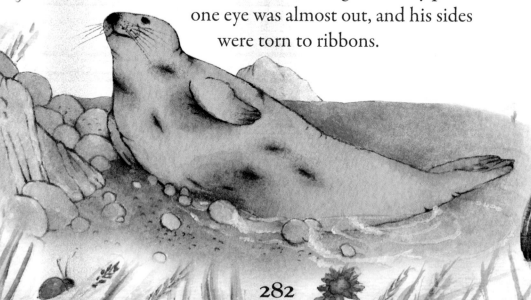

"Oh, you men, you men!" Matkah said, fanning herself with her hind flipper. "Why can't you be sensible and settle your places quietly? You look as though you had been fighting with the Killer Whale."

"I haven't been doing anything but fighting since the middle of May. The beach is disgracefully crowded this season. I've met at least a hundred seals from Lukannon Beach, house-hunting."

"I've often thought we should be much happier if we hauled out at Otter Island instead of this crowded place," said Matkah.

"Only the holluschickie go to Otter Island. If we went there they would say we were afraid." Sea Catch sunk his head proudly between his fat shoulders.

Now that all the seals were on the land, you could hear their clamour miles out to sea. At the lowest counting there were over a million seals on the beach – old seals, mother seals, tiny babies, and holluschickie, fighting, scuffling, bleating, crawling, and playing together – going down to the sea and coming up from it, lying over every foot of ground as far as the eye could reach, and skirmishing about in brigades through the fog. It is nearly always foggy at Novastoshnah, except when the sun comes out and makes everything look all rainbow-coloured for a little while.

Kotick, Matkah's baby, was born in the middle of that confusion, but there was something about his coat that made his mother look at him closely.

"Sea Catch," she said, at last, "our baby's going to be white!"

"Empty clam-shells!" snorted Sea Catch. "There never has been such a thing as a white seal."

"There will be now," said Matkah.

The little fellow paddled and scrambled about by his mother's side, and learned to scuffle out of the way when his father was fighting another seal, and the two rolled and roared up and down the slippery rocks.

The first thing he did was to crawl inland, and there he met tens of thousands of babies of his own age, and they played together like puppies, went to sleep on the clean sand, and played again. The old people in the nurseries took no notice of them, and the holluschickie kept to their own grounds, and the babies had a beautiful playtime.

When Matkah came back from her deep-sea fishing she would go straight to their playground and call as a sheep calls for a lamb, and wait until she heard Kotick bleat. Then she would take the straightest of straight lines in his direction, knocking the youngsters head over heels right and left.

Little seals can no more swim than little children, but they are unhappy till they learn. The first time that Kotick went down to the sea a wave carried him out beyond his depth, and his big head sank and his little hind flippers flew up, and if the next wave had not thrown him back again he would have drowned.

After that, he learned to lie in a beach pool and let the wash of the waves just cover him and lift him up while he paddled, but he always kept his eye open for big waves that might hurt. He was two weeks learning to use his flippers, and all that while he floundered in and out of the water, and coughed and grunted and crawled up the beach, and went back again, until at last he found that he truly belonged to the water.

Then you can imagine the times that he had with his companions, ducking under the rollers, or coming in on top of a comber and landing with a swash and a splutter as the big wave went whirling far up the beach, or standing up on his tail and scratching his head as the old people did, or playing 'I'm the King of the Castle' on slippery, weedy rocks that just stuck out of the wash. Now and then he would see a thin fin, like a big shark's fin, drifting along close to shore, and he knew that that was the Killer Whale, who eats young seals when he can get them, and Kotick would head for the beach like an arrow, and the fin would jig off slowly, as if it were looking for nothing at all.

Late in October the seals began to leave St Paul's for the deep sea, by families and tribes, and there was no more fighting over the nurseries, and the holluschickie played anywhere they liked. "Next year," said Matkah to Kotick, "you will be a holluschickie, but this year you must learn how to catch fish."

They set out together across the Pacific, and Matkah showed Kotick how to sleep on his back with his flippers tucked down by his side and his nose just out of the water. No cradle is so comfortable as the rocking swell of the Pacific. When Kotick felt his skin tingle all over, Matkah told him he was learning the 'feel of the water', and that tingly, prickly feelings meant bad weather coming, and he must swim hard and get away.

"In a little time," she said, "you'll know where to swim to, but just now we'll follow Sea Pig, the Porpoise, for he is very wise." A school of porpoises were tearing through the water, and little Kotick followed them as fast as he could.

"How do you know where to go to?" he panted. The leader of the school rolled his white eye and ducked under. "My tail tingles, youngster," he said. "That means there's a gale behind me. When you're south of the Sticky Water (he meant the Equator) and your tail tingles, that means there's a gale in front of you and you must head north."

This was one of very many things that Kotick learned. Matkah taught him to follow the cod and the halibut along the banks and wrench the rockling out of his hole among the weeds, how to skirt the wrecks lying a hundred fathoms below water and dart like a rifle bullet in at one porthole and out at another, how to dance on the top of the waves when the lightning was racing all over the sky, and wave his flipper politely to the stumpy-tailed Albatross and the Man-of-war Hawk as they went down the wind, how to jump three or four feet clear of the water like a dolphin, to leave flying fish alone because they are all bony, to take the shoulder-piece out of a cod at full speed ten fathoms deep, and never to stop and look at a boat or a ship, particularly a row-boat. At the end of six months what Kotick did not know about deep-sea fishing was not worth knowing. And all that time he never set flipper on dry ground.

One day, however, as he was lying in the warm water somewhere off the Island of Juan Fernandez, he remembered the good beaches of Novastoshnah seven thousand miles away, the games his friends played, the smell of the seaweed, and the fighting. That very minute he turned north, swimming steadily. As he went on he met scores of his mates, all bound for the same place, and they said, "Greeting, Kotick! This year we are all holluschickie. We can dance the Fire-dance in the breakers off Lukannon and play on the grass. Where did you get that coat?"

Kotick's fur was almost pure white now, and though he felt proud of it, he only said, "Swim quickly! My bones are aching for land." And so they all came to the beaches where they had been born.

That night Kotick danced the Fire-dance with the

yearling seals. The sea is full of fire on summer nights all the way down from Novastoshnah to Lukannon, and each seal leaves a wake like burning oil behind him and a flaming flash when he jumps. Then they went inland to the holluschickie grounds and told stories of what they had done while they had been at sea. The older holluschickie romped down from Hutchinson's Hill crying, "Out of the way, youngsters! The sea is deep and you don't know all that's in it yet. Wait till you've rounded the Horn. Hi, you yearling, where did you get that white coat?"

"I didn't get it," said Kotick. "It grew." And just as he was going to roll the speaker over, a couple of black-haired men with flat red faces came from behind a sand dune, and Kotick, who had never seen a man before, coughed and lowered his head. The holluschickie just bundled off a few yards and sat staring stupidly. The men were no less than Kerick Booterin, the chief of the seal-hunters on the island, and Patalamon, his son. They came from the village not half a mile from the sea nurseries, and they were deciding what seals they would drive up to the killing-pens to be turned into seal-skin jackets later.

"Look!" said Patalamon. "There's a white seal!"

THE HUNTERS

Kerick Booterin said, "Don't touch him, Patalamon. There has never been a white seal since I was born. Perhaps it is Zaharrof's ghost. He was lost last year in the big gale."

"I'm not going near him," said Patalamon. "He's unlucky. Do you really think he is old Zaharrof come back? I owe him for some gulls' eggs."

"Don't look at him," said Kerick. "Head off that drove of four-year-olds. The men ought to skin two hundred today, but they are new to the work. A hundred will do. Quick!"

Patalamon rattled a pair of seal's shoulder bones in front of a herd of holluschickie and they stopped dead, puffing and blowing. Then he stepped near and the seals began to move, and Kerick headed them inland, and they never tried to get back to their companions. Hundreds and hundreds of thousands of seals watched them being driven, but they went on playing just the same. Kotick was the only one who asked questions, and none of his friends could tell him anything, except that the men always drove seals in that way for six weeks or two months of every year.

"I am going to follow," he said, and he shuffled along in the wake of the herd.

"The white seal is coming after us," cried Patalamon.

"Hsh! Don't look," said Kerick. "It is Zaharrof's ghost! I must speak to the priest about this."

The distance to the killing-grounds was only half a mile, but it took an hour to cover, because if the seals went too fast Kerick knew that they would get heated and then their fur would come off in patches when they were skinned. So they went on very slowly, till they came to the Salt House just beyond the sight of the seals on the beach. Kotick followed, panting and wondering. Then Kerick sat down on the moss and pulled out a heavy pewter watch and let the drove cool off for thirty minutes. Then ten men, each with an iron-bound club three or four feet long, came up, and then Kerick said, "Let go!" and then the men clubbed the seals on the head as fast as they could.

Ten minutes later little Kotick did not recognize his friends any more, for their skins were ripped off from the nose to the hind flippers, whipped off and thrown down on the ground in a pile. That was enough for Kotick. He turned and galloped back to the sea. At Sea Lion's Neck, where the great sea lions sit on the edge of the surf, he flung himself into the cool water and rocked there, gasping miserably. "What's here?" said a sea lion gruffly, for as a rule the sea lions keep themselves to themselves.

"They're killing all the holluschickie!" said Kotick.

The Sea Lion turned his head inshore. "You must have seen old Kerick polishing off a drove. He's done that for thirty years."

"It's horrible," said Kotick, as a wave went over him, and he steadied himself with his flippers.

"Well done for a yearling!" said the Sea Lion, who could appreciate good swimming. "It is rather awful from your way of looking at it, but if you seals will come here year after year, the men get to know of it. Unless you find an island where no men come you will always be driven."

"Isn't there any such island?" began Kotick.

"I can't say I've found it yet. But go to Walrus Islet and talk to Sea Vitch. He may know something. Don't flounce off like that. It's a six-mile swim, and if I were you I should haul out and take a nap first."

Kotick thought that that was good advice, so he swam round to his own beach, and slept for half an hour. Then he headed for Walrus Islet, a little rocky island almost due northeast from Novastoshnah.

He landed close to old
Sea Vitch – the big, ugly,
bloated, long-tusked
walrus of the North
Pacific, who has no
manners except
when he is
asleep – as he
was then, with
his hind flippers half in and half out of the surf.

"Wake up!" barked Kotick, for the gulls were
making a great noise.

"Hah! Ho! Hmph! What's that?" said Sea Vitch,
and he struck the next walrus a blow with his tusks
and waked him up, and the next struck the next, and
so on till they were all awake and staring in every
direction but the right one.

"Hi! It's me," said Kotick, bobbing in the surf and
looking like a little white slug.

"Well! May I be – skinned!" said Sea Vitch, and
they all looked at Kotick as you can fancy a club full
of drowsy old gentlemen would look at a little boy.

Kotick called out, "Isn't there any place for seals to
go where men don't ever come?"

293

THE HUNTERS

"Go and find out," said Sea Vitch, shutting his eyes. "Run away. We're busy here."

Kotick made his dolphin-jump in the air and shouted as loud as he could: "Clam-eater! Clam-eater!" He knew that Sea Vitch never caught a fish in his life but always rooted for clams and seaweed; though he pretended to be a very terrible person. Naturally the Chickies and the Gooverooskies and the Epatkas – the Burgomaster Gulls and the Kittiwakes and the Puffins, who are always looking for a chance to be rude, took up the cry. All the population was yelling "Clam-eater! Stareek (old man)!" while Sea Vitch rolled from side to side grunting and coughing.

"Now will you tell?" said Kotick, all out of breath.

"Go and ask Sea Cow," said Sea Vitch. "If he is living still, he'll be able to tell you."

"How shall I know Sea Cow when I meet him?" said Kotick, sheering off.

"He's the only thing in the sea uglier than Sea Vitch!" screamed a gull.

Kotick swam back to Novastoshnah, but no one sympathized with him in his attempt to discover a quiet place for the seals. They said men had always driven the holluschickie and that he should not have gone to the killing-grounds. But none of the other seals had seen the killing, and that made the difference between him and his friends. Besides, Kotick was a white seal.

"What you must do," said old Sea Catch, after he had heard his son's adventures, "is to grow up and be a big seal like your father, and then they will leave you alone. In another five years you ought to be able to fight for yourself."

Even his mother said, "You will never be able to stop the killing. Go and play in the sea, Kotick." And Kotick went off and danced the Fire-dance with a very heavy little heart.

That autumn he left the beach as soon as he could, and set off alone. He was going to find Sea Cow, and he was going to find a quiet island with good beaches for seals to live on, where men could not get them. So he explored by himself from the North to the South Pacific. He met with more adventures than can be told, and narrowly escaped being caught by the Basking Shark, and the Spotted Shark, but he never met Sea Cow, and he never found an island that he could fancy.

THE HUNTERS

If the beach was good and hard, with a slope behind it for seals to play on, there was always the smoke of a whaler on the horizon. Or else he could see that seals had once visited the island and been killed off, and Kotick knew that where men had come once they would come again.

He picked up with an old albatross, who told him that Kerguelen Island was the very place for peace, and when Kotick went down there he was all but smashed to pieces against some wicked black cliffs in a heavy sleet-storm. Yet he could see that even there had once been a seal nursery. And it was so in all the other islands that he visited.

Kotick spent five seasons exploring, with a four months' rest each year at Novastoshnah, when the holluschickie used to make fun of him and his imaginary islands. He went to the Galapagos, where he was nearly baked to death, he went to the Georgia Islands, the Orkneys, Little Nightingale Island, Emerald Island, Gough's Island, Bouvet's Island, the Crossets, and even to a little speck of an island south of the Cape of Good Hope. But everywhere the People of the Sea told him that seals had come to those islands once, but men had killed them all off.

That nearly broke his heart, and he headed back to his own beaches. On his way he hauled out on an island full of green trees, where he found an old seal who was dying. Kotick caught fish for him and told him his sorrows. "Now," said Kotick, "I am going home, and if I am driven to the killing-pens with the holluschickie I shall not care."

The old seal said, "Try once more. I am the last of the Lost Rookery of Masafuera, and in the days when men killed us there was a story on the beaches that some day a white seal would come and lead the seal people to a quiet place. Try once more."

When he came back to Novastoshnah that summer his mother begged him to marry, for he was no longer a holluschick but a full-grown sea-catch, as big as his father. "Give me another season," he said.

There was another seal who thought that she would put off marrying till the next year, and Kotick danced the Fire-dance with her the night before he set off on his last exploration. This time he went westward, on the trail of a shoal of halibut. He chased them till he was tired, and then he curled up and went to sleep on the hollows of the ground swell that sets in to Copper Island. About midnight, he felt himself gently bumped on a weedbed, he turned over underwater, opened his eyes and stretched. Then he jumped like a cat, for he saw huge things nosing about in the water and browsing on the weeds.

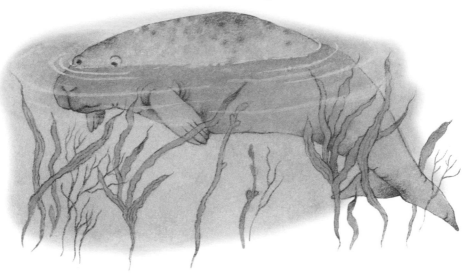

They were like no walrus, sea lion, seal, bear, whale, shark, fish, squid, or scallop that Kotick had ever seen. They were between twenty and thirty feet long, and they had no hind flippers, but a shovel-like tail. Their heads were the most foolish-looking things you ever saw, and they balanced on the ends of their tails in deep water when they weren't grazing, bowing solemnly to each other and waving their front flippers as a fat man waves his arm.

"Ahem!" said Kotick. "Good sport, gentlemen?" They answered by bowing and waving their flippers. When they began feeding again Kotick saw that their lip was split into two pieces that they could twitch apart and bring together again with a bushel of seaweed between the splits. They tucked the stuff into their mouths and chumped solemnly.

"Messy style of feeding, that," said Kotick, and he remembered what the gull had screamed to him at Walrus Islet, and he tumbled backward in the water, for he knew that he had found Sea Cow at last.

The sea cows went on schlooping and grazing and chumping in the weed, and Kotick asked them questions. But the sea cows did not answer because Sea Cow cannot talk. But, as you know, he has an extra joint in his foreflipper, and by waving it up and down and about he makes what answers to a sort of clumsy telegraphic code.

By daylight the Sea Cow began to travel slowly northward, stopping to hold absurd bowing councils from time to time. Kotick followed them, saying to himself, "Such idiots as these would have been killed long ago if they hadn't found a safe island."

As they went farther north they held a bowing

council every few hours, and Kotick was getting very impatient till he saw that they were following a warm current of water, and then he respected them more.

One night they sank through the shiny water like stones and for the first time began to swim quickly. They headed for a cliff by the shore, and plunged into a dark hole at the foot of it, twenty fathoms under the sea. It was a long swim, and Kotick badly wanted fresh air before he was out of the dark tunnel.

"My wig!" he said, when he rose into open water at the end. "It was a long dive, but it was worth it."

The sea cows had separated and were browsing along the edges of the finest beaches that Kotick had ever seen. There were long stretches of smooth rock, exactly fitted to make seal-nurseries, and playgrounds of hard sand sloping inland behind them, and sand dunes to climb up and down, and, best of all, Kotick knew by the feel of the water, which never deceives a true sea catch, that no men had ever come there.

First he assured himself that the fishing was good. Away to the north, out to sea, ran a line of bars and rocks that would never let a ship come within miles of the beach, and between the islands and the mainland was a stretch of deep water that ran up to the cliffs. Somewhere below the cliffs was the tunnel.

"It's like Novastoshnah, but ten times better," said Kotick. "If any place in the sea is safe, this is it."

He was six days going home, though he was not swimming slowly. The first person he met was the seal who had been waiting for him, and she saw by the look in his eyes that he had found his island at last.

But all the other seals laughed at him when he told them what he had discovered, and a young seal said, "Kotick, you can't come from no one knows where and order us off like this. We've been fighting for our nurseries. You preferred prowling about in the sea."

"I've no nursery to fight for," said Kotick. "I only want to show you all a place where you will be safe."

"Oh, if you're trying to back out, of course I've no more to say," said the young seal with an ugly chuckle.

"Will you come with me if I win?" said Kotick.

"Yes," said the young seal. "If you win, I'll come."

Kotick's teeth sunk into the blubber of the young seal's neck. Then he threw himself back on his haunches and hauled his enemy down the beach, shook him, and knocked him over. Then Kotick roared to the seals, "I've done my best for you for five seasons. I've found you the island where you'll be safe, but you won't believe. I'm going to teach you now!"

Kotick flung himself at the biggest sea catch he could find, choked him till he grunted for mercy, then attacked the next. He had never fasted for four months as the big seals did every year, and his swimming kept him in perfect condition. His white mane stood up with rage and his eyes flamed. His father saw him tearing past, and shouted, "He may be a fool, but he is the best fighter on the beaches! Don't tackle your father, my son! He's with you!"

Old Sea Catch waddled in, and the two fought as long as there was a seal that dared lift up his head. When there were none they grandly paraded up and down the beach side by side, bellowing.

At night, just as the Northern Lights were flashing, Kotick climbed a rock and looked down on the scattered nurseries and the torn and bleeding seals. "Now," he said, "I've taught you your lesson."

Sea Catch hauled himself up stiffly, for he was fearfully mauled, and said "Son, I'm proud of you, and I'll come with you to your island."

"Hear you, fat pigs of the sea. Who comes with me to the Sea Cow's tunnel?" roared Kotick.

There was a murmur up and down the beaches.

The White Seal

"We will follow Kotick, the White Seal," said thousands of tired voices.

A week later Kotick and nearly ten thousand seals went away north to the Sea Cow's tunnel. The seals that stayed at Novastoshnah called them idiots, but next spring, when they all met off the fishing banks of the Pacific, Kotick's seals told such tales of the new beaches beyond Sea Cow's tunnel that more and more seals left Novastoshnah.

Year after year more seals went away from Novastoshnah to the quiet, sheltered beaches where Kotick sits all the summer through, getting bigger and stronger each year, while the holluschickie play around him, in that sea where no man comes.

304

TALL TALES

The Giant Roc

From *The Second Voyage of Sinbad the Sailor*

The stories of Sinbad were based on the experiences of sailors from Iraq. Sinbad is a merchant who makes many voyages to trade his goods. In this extract he tells the story of one of his most amazing adventures.

We embarked on board a good ship, and, after recommending ourselves to God, set sail. We traded from island to island, and exchanged commodities with great profit. One day we landed on an island covered with several sorts of fruit trees, but we could see neither man nor animal. We walked in the meadows, along the streams that watered them. While some diverted themselves with gathering flowers, and others fruits, I took my wine and provisions, and sat down near a stream betwixt two high trees, which formed a thick shade. I made a good meal, and afterward fell asleep. I cannot tell how long I slept, but when I awoke the ship was gone.

I was ready to die with grief. I cried out in agony, beat my head and breast, and threw myself upon the ground. At last I resigned myself to the will of God. Not knowing what to do, I climbed to the top of a lofty tree, from whence I looked about on all sides, to see if I could discover anything that could give me hope. When I gazed towards the sea I could see nothing but sky and water, but looking over the land, I beheld something white, and coming down, I took what provision I had left and went toward it, the distance being so great that I could not distinguish what it was.

As I approached, I thought it to be a white dome, of a prodigious height and extent, and when I came up to it, I touched it, and found it to be very smooth. I went round to see if it was open on any side, but saw it was not, and that there was no climbing up to the top, as it was so smooth. It was at least fifty paces round.

By this time the sun was about to set, and all of a sudden the sky became as dark as if it had been covered with a thick cloud. I was much astonished at this sudden darkness, but much more when I found it was occasioned by a bird of a monstrous size that came flying toward me. I remembered that I had often heard mariners speak of a miraculous bird called the roc, and conceived that the great dome which I so much admired must be its egg.

The bird alighted, and sat over the egg. As I perceived her coming, I crept close to the egg, so that I had before me one of the legs of the bird, which was as big as the trunk of a tree. I tied myself strongly to it with my turban, in hopes that the roc next morning would carry me with her out of this desert island. After having passed the night in this condition, the bird flew away as soon as it was daylight, and carried me so high that I could not discern the earth. She afterward descended with so much rapidity that I lost my senses. But when I found myself on the ground, I speedily untied the knot, and had scarcely done so, when the roc, having taken up a serpent of a monstrous length in her bill, flew away.

The spot where it left me was surrounded on all sides by mountains that seemed to reach above the clouds, and so steep that there was no possibility of getting out of the valley. This was a new perplexity – when I compared this place with the island from which the roc

had brought me, I found that I had gained nothing by the change.

As I walked through this valley, I perceived it was strewn with diamonds, some of which were of surprising size. I took pleasure in looking upon them, but shortly I saw at a distance such objects as greatly diminished my satisfaction, and which I could not view without terror, namely, a great number of serpents, so monstrous that the least of them was capable of swallowing an elephant. They retired in the daytime to their dens, where they hid themselves from the roc, their enemy, and came out only in the night.

I spent the day in walking about in the valley, resting myself at times in such places as I thought most convenient. When night came on I went into a cave, where I thought I might repose in safety. I secured the entrance, which was low and narrow, with a great stone, to preserve me from the serpents, but not so far as to exclude the light. I supped on part of my provisions, but the serpents, which began hissing round me, put me into such extreme fear that I did not sleep. When day appeared the serpents retired, and I came out of the cave, trembling. I can justly say that I walked upon diamonds without feeling any inclination to touch them. At last I sat down and, after having eaten a little more of my provisions and not having closed my eyes during the night, I fell deeply asleep. But I had scarcely shut my eyes when something fell by me and awakened me. This was a large piece of raw meat, and at the same time I saw several others fall down from the rocks in different places.

I had always regarded as fabulous what I had heard sailors and others relate of the valley of diamonds, and of the stratagems employed by merchants to obtain jewels from thence, but now I found that they had stated nothing but the truth. For the fact is that the merchants come to the neighbourhood of this valley when the eagles have young ones, and throw great joints of meat into the valley. The diamonds, upon whose points the pieces of meat fall, stick to them. The eagles, which are stronger in this country than anywhere else, pounce with great force upon those pieces of meat, and carry them to their nests on the precipices of the rocks to feed their young. The merchants then run to the nests, drive off the eagles by their shouts, and take away the diamonds.

I perceived in this ingenious method the means of my deliverance.

TALL TALES

Having collected together the largest diamonds I could find, and put them into the leather bag in which I used to carry my provisions, I took the largest of the pieces of meat, tied it close round me with the cloth of my turban, and then laid myself upon the ground, with my face downward, the bag of diamonds being made fast to my girdle.

I had scarcely placed myself in this posture when one of the eagles, having taken me up with the piece of meat to which I was fastened, carried me to his nest on the top of the mountain. The merchants immediately began their shouting to frighten the eagles, and when they had obliged them to quit their prey, one of them came to the nest where I was. He was much alarmed when he saw me, but recovering himself, instead of inquiring how I came thither, began to quarrel with me, and asked why I stole his goods.

"You will treat me," replied I, "with more civility when you know me better. Do not be uneasy – I have diamonds enough for you and myself, more than all the other merchants together. Whatever they have they owe to chance, but I selected for myself, in the bottom of the valley, those which you see in this bag."

I had scarcely done speaking, when the other

merchants came crowding about us, much astonished to see me. But they were much more surprised when I told them my story.

They conducted me to their encampment, and there, having opened my bag, they were surprised at the largeness of my diamonds, and confessed that they had never seen any of such size and perfection. I prayed the merchant who owned the nest to which I had been carried (for every merchant had his own) to take as many for his share as he pleased. He contented himself with one, and that, too, the least of them, and when I pressed him to take more, without fear of doing me any injury, "No," said he, "I am very well satisfied with this, which is valuable enough to save me the trouble of making any more voyages, and will raise as great a fortune as I desire."

I spent the night with the merchants, to whom I related my story a second time, for the satisfaction of those who had not heard it. I could not moderate my joy when I found myself delivered from the danger I have mentioned. I thought myself in a dream, and could scarcely believe myself out of danger.

The merchants had thrown their pieces of meat into the valley for several days; and each of them being satisfied with the diamonds that had fallen to his lot, we left the place the next morning, and travelled near high mountains, where there were serpents of a prodigious length, which we had the good fortune to escape. We took shipping at the first port we reached, and touched at the isle of Roha, where the trees grow that yield camphor. This tree is so large, and its branches so thick, that one hundred men may easily sit under its shade. The juice, of which the camphor is made, exudes from a hole bored in the upper part of the tree, and is received in a vessel, where it thickens to a consistency, and becomes what we call camphor. After the juice is thus drawn out, the tree withers and dies.

In this island is also found the rhinoceros, an animal less than the elephant but larger than the buffalo. It has a horn upon its nose, about a cubit in length; this horn is solid, and cleft through the middle. The rhinoceros fights with the elephant, runs his horn into his belly, and carries him off upon his head, but the blood and the fat of the elephant running into his eyes and making him blind, he falls to the ground. Then, strange to relate, the roc comes and carries them both away in her claws, for food for her young ones.

I pass over many other things peculiar to this island,

The Giant Roc

lest I should weary you. Here I exchanged some of my diamonds for merchandise. From hence we went to other islands, and at last, having touched at several trading towns of the continent, we landed at Bussorah, from whence I proceeded to Bagdad. There I immediately gave large presents to the poor, and lived honourably upon the vast riches I had brought, and gained with so much fatigue.

The Mock Turtle's Story

From *Alice's Adventures in Wonderland*
by Lewis Carroll

Alice has fallen down a rabbit hole into a magical land where she encounters many strange creatures. In this extract, her companion is a gryphon, a creature with the body of a lion and the head and shoulders of an eagle.

They had not gone far before they saw the Mock Turtle in the distance, sitting sad and lonely on a little ledge of rock, and, as they came nearer, Alice could hear him sighing as if his heart would break. She pitied him deeply. "What is his sorrow?" she asked the Gryphon, and the Gryphon answered, very nearly in the same words as before, "It's all his fancy, that – he hasn't got no sorrow, you know. Come on!"

The Mock Turtle's Story

So they went up to the Mock Turtle, who looked at them with large eyes full of tears, but said nothing.

"This here young lady," said the Gryphon, "she wants for to know your history, she do."

"I'll tell it her," said the Mock Turtle in a deep, hollow tone. "Sit down, both of you, and don't speak a word until I've finished."

So they sat down, and nobody spoke for some minutes. Alice thought to herself, 'I don't see how he can even finish, if he doesn't begin.' But she waited patiently.

"Once," said the Mock Turtle at last, with a deep sigh, "I was a real Turtle."

These words were followed by a very long silence, broken only by an occasional exclamation of "Hjckrrh!" from the Gryphon, and the constant heavy sobbing of the Mock Turtle. Alice was very nearly getting up and saying, 'Thank you, sir, for your interesting story,' but she could not help thinking there must be more to come, so she sat still and said nothing.

"When we were little," the Mock Turtle went on at last, more calmly – though still sobbing a little now and then – "we went to school in the sea. The master was an old Turtle, and we used to call him Tortoise—"

"So why did you call him Tortoise, if he wasn't one?" Alice asked.

"We called him Tortoise because he taught us," said the Mock Turtle angrily. "Really you are very dull!"

"You ought to be ashamed of yourself for asking such a simple question," added the Gryphon, and then they both sat silent and looked at poor Alice, who felt ready to sink into the earth.

At last the Gryphon said to the Mock Turtle, "Drive on, old fellow! Don't be all day about it!" and he went on in these words, "Yes, we went to school in the sea, though you mayn't believe it—"

"I never said I didn't!" interrupted Alice.

"Oh yes, you did," said the Mock Turtle.

"Hold your tongue!" added the Gryphon, before Alice could say anything else. The Mock Turtle went on.

"We had the best of educations – in fact, we went to school every day—"

"*I've* been to a day-school, too," said Alice, "you needn't be so proud as all that."

"With extras?" asked the Mock Turtle a little anxiously.

"Yes," said Alice, "we learned French and music."

"And washing?" said the Mock Turtle.

"Certainly not!" said Alice indignantly.

"Ah! Then yours wasn't a really good school," said the Mock Turtle in a tone of great relief. "Now at ours they had at the end of the bill, 'French, music, *and washing* – extra.'"

"You couldn't have wanted it much," said Alice, "living at the bottom of the sea."

"I couldn't afford to learn it," said the Mock Turtle with a sigh. "I only took the regular course."

"What was that?" inquired Alice.

"Reeling and Writhing, of course, to begin with," the Mock Turtle replied; "and then the different branches of Arithmetic – Ambition, Distraction, Uglification, and Derision."

"I never heard of 'Uglification,'" Alice ventured to say. "What is it?"

The Gryphon lifted up both its paws in surprise. "What! Never heard of uglifying!" it exclaimed. "You know what to beautify is, I suppose?"

"Yes," said Alice doubtfully, "it means... to... make... anything... prettier."

"Well, then," the Gryphon went on, "if you don't know what to uglify is, you *are* a simpleton."

Alice did not feel encouraged to ask any more questions about uglification, so she turned instead to the Mock Turtle, and said, "What else had you to learn?"

"Well, there was Mystery," the Mock Turtle replied, counting off the subjects on his flappers, "Mystery, ancient and modern, with Seaography. Then Drawling – the Drawling-master was an old conger-eel, that used to come once a week. *He* taught us Drawling, Stretching, and Fainting in Coils."

"What was *that* like?" said Alice.

"Well, I can't show it you myself," the Mock Turtle said. "I'm too stiff. And the Gryphon never learnt it."

"Hadn't time," said the Gryphon, "I went to the

Classics master, though. He was an old crab, he was."

"I never went to him," the Mock Turtle said with a sigh. "He taught Laughing and Grief, they used to say."

"So he did, so he did," said the Gryphon, sighing in his turn, and both creatures hid their faces in their paws.

"And how many hours a day did you do lessons?" said Alice, in a hurry to change the subject.

"Ten hours the first day," said the Mock Turtle, "nine the next, and so on."

"What a curious plan!" exclaimed Alice.

"That's the reason they're called lessons," the Gryphon remarked, "because they lessen from day to day."

This was quite a new idea to Alice, and she thought it over a little before she made her next remark. "Then the eleventh day must have been a holiday?"

"Of course it was," said the Mock Turtle.

"And how did you manage on the twelfth?" Alice went on eagerly.

"That's enough about lessons," the Gryphon interrupted in a very decided tone. "Tell her something about the games now."

The Mock Turtle sighed deeply, and drew the back of one flapper across his eyes. He looked at Alice, and tried to speak, but for a minute or two sobs choked his voice. "As if he had a bone in his throat," said the Gryphon, and it set to work shaking him and punching him in the back.

At last the Mock Turtle recovered his voice, and, with tears running down his cheeks, he went on again, "You may not have lived much under the sea," ("I haven't," said Alice) "and perhaps you were never even introduced to a lobster," (Alice began to say "I once tasted—" but checked herself hastily, and said "No, never") "—so you can have no idea what a delightful thing a Lobster Quadrille is!"

"No, indeed," said Alice. "What sort of a dance is it?"

"Why," said the Gryphon, "you first form into a line along the sea-shore—"

"Two lines!" cried the Mock Turtle. "Seals, turtles, salmon, and so on. Then, when you've cleared all the jellyfish out of the way—"

"*That* takes some time," interrupted the Gryphon.

"—you advance twice—"

The Mock Turtle's Story

"Each with a lobster as a partner!" cried the Gryphon.
"Of course," the Mock Turtle said, "advance twice,
set to partners—"

"—change lobsters, and
retire in the same order,"
continued the Gryphon.
"Then, you know," the
Mock Turtle went on,
"you throw the—"
"The lobsters!" shouted the
Gryphon, with a bound into the air.
"—as far out to sea as you can—"
"Swim after them!" screamed
the Gryphon.
"Turn a somersault in the sea!" cried
the Mock Turtle, capering wildly about.
"Back to land again, and that's all the first
figure," said the Mock Turtle, suddenly dropping
his voice, and the two creatures, who had been jumping
about like mad things all this time, sat down again very
sadly and quietly, and looked at Alice.

"It must be a very pretty dance," said Alice timidly.

"Would you like to see a little of it?" said the
Mock Turtle.

"Very much indeed," said Alice.

"Come, let's try the first figure!" said the Mock Turtle to the Gryphon. "We can do without lobsters, you know. Which shall sing?"

"Oh, *you* sing," said the Gryphon. "I've forgotten the words."

So they began solemnly dancing round and round Alice, every now and then treading on her toes when they passed a little too close, and waving their forepaws to mark the time, while the Mock Turtle took a deep breath and sang this, very slowly and sadly:

> "'Will you walk a little faster?'
>   said a whiting to a snail.
> 'There's a porpoise close behind us,
>   and he's treading on my tail.'
> See how eagerly the lobsters and
>   the turtles all advance!
> They are waiting on the shingle
>   – will you come and join the dance?
> Will you, won't you, will you,
>   won't you, will you join the dance?
> Will you, won't you, will you,
>   won't you, won't you join the dance?

The Mock Turtle's Story

'You can really have no notion
   how delightful it will be
When they take us up and throw us,
   with the lobsters, out to sea!'
But the snail replied 'Too far, too far!'
   and gave a look askance
Said he thanked the whiting kindly,
   but he would not join the dance.
Would not, could not, would not,
   could not, would not join the dance.
Would not, could not, would not,
   could not, could not join the dance.

'What matters it how far we go?'
   his scaly friend replied.
'There is another shore, you know,
   upon the other side.
The further off from England
   the nearer is to France
Then turn not pale, beloved snail,
   but come and join the dance.
Will you, won't you, will you,
   won't you, will you join the dance?
Will you, won't you, will you,
   won't you, won't you join the dance?'"

"Thank you, it's a very interesting dance to watch," said Alice, feeling very glad that it was over at last. "And I do so like that curious song about the whiting!"

"Oh, as to the whiting," said the Mock Turtle, "they – you've seen them, of course?"

"Yes," said Alice, "I've often seen them at dinn—" she checked herself hastily.

"I don't know where Dinn may be," said the Mock Turtle, "but if you've seen them so often, of course you know what they're like."

"I believe so," Alice replied thoughtfully. "They have their tails in their mouths – and they're all over crumbs."

"You're wrong about the crumbs," said the Mock Turtle. "Crumbs would all wash off in the sea. But they *have* their tails in their mouths, and the reason is—" here the Mock Turtle yawned and shut his eyes. "Tell her about the reason and all that," he said to the Gryphon.

"The reason is," said the Gryphon, "that they *would* go with the lobsters to the dance. So they got thrown out to sea. They had to fall a long way. So they got their tails fast in their mouths. And they couldn't get them out again. That's all."

"Thank you," said Alice, "it's very interesting. I never knew so much about a whiting before."

The Mock Turtle's Story

"I can tell you more than that, if you like," said the Gryphon. "Do you know why it's called a whiting?"

"I never thought about it," said Alice. "Why?"

"*It does the boots and shoes*," the Gryphon replied very solemnly.

Alice was thoroughly puzzled. "Does the boots and shoes!" she repeated in a wondering tone.

"Why, what are *your* shoes done with?" said the Gryphon. "I mean, what makes them so shiny?"

Alice looked down at her shoes, and considered a little before she gave the Gryphon her answer. "They're done with blacking, I believe."

"Boots and shoes under the sea," the Gryphon went on in a deep, serious voice, "are all done with a whiting. So now you know."

"And what are they made of?" Alice asked in a tone of great curiosity.

"Soles and eels, of course," the Gryphon replied rather impatiently, "any shrimp could have told you that."

"If I'd been the whiting," said Alice, whose thoughts were still running on the song, "I'd have said to the porpoise, 'Keep back, please, we don't want *you* with us!'"

"They were obliged to have him with them," the Mock Turtle said, "for no wise fish would think of

going anywhere without a porpoise."

"Wouldn't it really?" said Alice in great surprise.

"Of course not," said the Mock Turtle. "Why, if a fish came to *me*, and told me he was going on a journey, I should say 'With what porpoise?'"

"Don't you mean 'purpose'?" said Alice.

"I mean what I say," the Mock Turtle replied in an offended tone.

Then the Gryphon said to Alice, "Come, let's hear some of *your* adventures."

"I could tell you my adventures – beginning from this morning," said Alice a little timidly, "but it's no use going back to yesterday, because I was a different person then."

"Explain all that," said the Mock Turtle.

"No, no! The

adventures first," said the Gryphon in an impatient tone, "explanations take such a dreadful time."

So Alice began telling them her adventures from the time when she first saw the White Rabbit. She was a little nervous about it just at first, the two creatures got so close to her, one on each side, and opened their eyes and mouths so very wide, but she gained courage as she went on. Her listeners were very quiet till she got to the part about her repeating *You are old, Father William*, to the Caterpillar, and the words all coming different, and then the Mock Turtle drew a long breath, and said "That's very curious."

"It's all about as curious as it can be," said the Gryphon.

"It all came different!" the Mock Turtle repeated thoughtfully. "I should like to hear her try and repeat something now, and we'll all see what happens. Tell her to begin." He looked haughtily at the Gryphon as if he thought it had some

329

kind of authority over Alice.

"Stand up and repeat *Tis the Voice of the Sluggard,*" said the Gryphon.

'How the creatures order one about, and make one repeat lessons!' thought Alice, 'I might as well be at school at once.' However, she got up, and began to repeat it, but her head was so full of the Lobster Quadrille, that she hardly knew what she was saying, and the words came very queer indeed:

> *"Tis the voice of the Lobster;*
> *I heard him declare,*
> *'You have baked me too brown,*
> *I must sugar my hair.'*
> *As a duck with its eyelids,*
> *so he with his nose*
> *Trims his belt and his buttons,*
> *and turns out his toes."*

"That's different from what I used to say when I was a child," said the Gryphon.

"Well, I never heard it before," said the Mock Turtle, "but it sounds uncommon nonsense."

Alice said nothing. She had sat down with her face in

her hands, wondering if anything would ever happen in a natural way again.

"I should like to have it explained," said the Mock Turtle.

"She can't explain it," said the Gryphon hastily. "Go on with the next verse."

"But about his toes?" the Mock Turtle persisted. "How *could* he turn them out with his nose, you know?"

"It's the first position in dancing." Alice said, but was dreadfully puzzled by the whole thing, and longed to change the subject.

"Go on with the next verse," the Gryphon repeated impatiently, "it begins 'I passed by his garden.'"

Alice did not dare to disobey the Gryphon, though she felt sure it would all come wrong, and she went on in a trembling voice:

"I passed by his garden, and marked, with one eye,
How the Owl and the Panther were sharing a pie—"

"What is the use of repeating all that stuff," the Mock Turtle interrupted, "if you don't explain it as you go on? It's by far the most confusing thing I ever heard!"

"Yes, I think you'd better leave off," said the Gryphon, and Alice was only too glad to do so.

"Shall we try another figure of the Lobster Quadrille?" the Gryphon went on. "Or would you like the Mock Turtle to sing you a song?"

"Oh, a song, please, if the Mock Turtle would be so kind," Alice replied, so eagerly that the Gryphon said, in a rather offended tone, "Hm! No accounting for tastes! Sing her 'Turtle Soup', will you, old fellow?"

The Mock Turtle sighed deeply, and began, in a voice sometimes choked with sobs, to sing this:

The Mock Turtle's Story

"Beautiful Soup, so rich and green,
Waiting in a hot tureen!
Who for such dainties would not stoop?
Soup of the evening, beautiful Soup!
Soup of the evening, beautiful Soup!
Beau-ootiful Soo-oop! Beau-ootiful Soo-oop!
Soo-oop of the e-e-evening,
    Beautiful, beautiful Soup!

"Beautiful Soup! Who cares for fish,
Game, or any other dish?
Who would not give all else for two
Pennyworth only of beautiful Soup?
Pennyworth only of beautiful Soup?
Beau-ootiful Soo-oop! Beau-ootiful Soo-oop!
Soo-oop of the e-e-evening,
    Beautiful, beautiful Soup!"

"Chorus again!" cried the Gryphon, and the Mock Turtle had just begun to repeat it, when a cry of "The trial's beginning!" was heard in the distance.

"Come on!" cried the Gryphon, and, taking Alice by the hand, it hurried off, without waiting for the end of the song.

333

"What trial is it?" Alice panted as she ran; but the Gryphon only answered "Come on!" and ran the faster, while more and more faintly came, carried on the breeze that followed them, the melancholy words:

"Soo-oop of the e-e-evening, Beautiful, beautiful Soup!"

The Curly-haired Hen

By Auguste Vimar

"Oh Grandfather, tell us a story, do. You know, the one you began the other evening about Mother Etienne's big farm. You remember. The weather is so horrible and we aren't allowed to go outside. Go on, Grandfather, please."

Coaxingly the three children clung round their grandfather, looking at him beseechingly. At last he began, "Since you have been very good, and you want it so much, I will tell you the wonderful story of Mother Etienne's farm and the still more wonderful story of what happened to one of its occupants.

"Love animals, my children, be kind to them, care

for them, and you will surely have your reward.

"Mother Etienne was a good stout woman with a very kind heart. While still young she was so unfortunate as to lose her husband and her son of whom she was very fond. This made her, as you can imagine, very, very sad. She wouldn't listen to any new offers of marriage, though she had plenty of them. Instead, she devoted her life, her whole existence, to the attentive, nay I ought to say, the maternal care, of the animals on her farm, making them as comfortable as could be.

"She had, as I said before, a most excellent heart, the good Mother Etienne. You shall see that presently.

"This good woman lived on her big farm very spacious and admirably situated. A slate roof covered the large house, and the granaries, stables and outhouses were sheltered by old thatching upon which grew moss and lichen.

"Let me tell you now, dear children, who were the chief occupants of the farm. First there was big Coco – a fine Normandy horse – bay-coloured and very fat, whose silky coat had a purple sheen; he had a star on his forehead and a pink mark between his eyes. He was very gentle and answered to the voice of his mistress. If

Mother Etienne passed by his stable he never failed to scent her and whinnied at once. That was his way of showing his friendliness and saying, 'Good morning'.

"His good mistress spoiled him with all sorts of dainties. Sometimes a crust of bread, sometimes a handful of carrots, but what he loved best of all was sugar. If you had given him a whole loaf he would soon have eaten it up.

"Coco had for stable companions three fine Swiss cows. Their names were La Blonde, Blanchotte and Nera. You know what the colours were for the names, don't you?

"Petit-Jacques, the stable boy, took care of them. On fine days he led them to pasture into a bog paddock near the farm up against a pretty wood of silver beeches. A large pond of clear water covered one corner of the meadow and lost itself in the reeds and iris. There the fine big cows went to quench their thirst. Quantities of frogs went there, too, to play leap-frog. It was a veritable earthly Paradise.

"From the farm Mother Etienne caught the sound of the bronze bells, each with its different low note, which hung round the necks of the cows. Thus she knew their comings and goings without interrupting her various occupations. For the farm was very big, with many animals on it.

"After the stables and coachhouses came the piggery, the rabbit hutches, and finally an immense poultry-yard divided into a thousand compartments, and sheltering a whole horde of poultry of all sorts – fowls of all kinds and of all breeds, geese, guinea fowl, pigeons, ducks, and what all besides. What wasn't there in that prodigious poultry-yard?

"Mother Etienne spent most of her time there, for the smaller and more delicate the creatures the more interest and care she gave them. 'The weak need protection,' this excellent woman would say, and she was right.

"So for the baby ducks her tenderness was limitless. What dangers had to be avoided to raise successfully all these tiny folks! Did a pig escape? Immediately danger threatened the poultry-yard. For a pig has terrible teeth and he doesn't care what he eats – he would as soon crunch a little duckling as a carrot. So she had to watch every minute, every second even. For besides, in spite of the vigilance of Labrie, the faithful watchdog, sometimes rats would suck the blood of the young pigeons. Once even a whole litter of rabbits was destroyed that way.

The Curly-haired Hen

"To dispose of the products of her farm, Mother Etienne drove twice a week to market in her market-cart drawn by Coco. She was famed for the best vegetables, the purest and creamiest milk – in short, the eggs she sold were the freshest, the poultry and rabbits the tenderest and most juicy to be had. As soon as she and Coco came trotting into the market there was a rush to get to her first. There, as everywhere, everyone loved Mother Etienne.

"Thus time passed peacefully at the big farm.

"One day, however, the quiet was disturbed by a little drama which convulsed the calm but busy spot.

"Mother Etienne had given to a Cochin-China hen, which she had christened Yollande, some white duck's eggs to sit on. The batch of fifteen eggs had all come out.

It was really wonderful to see these fifteen baby ducks, yellow as canaries, beaks and webbed feet pink, swarming around the big

patient sitting mother, ducking under her wings, to come out presently and clamber helter-skelter onto her broad back. As often happens with nurses, Yollande loved the ducklings as her own children, and without worrying about their shape or plumage, so different from her own, she showered upon them proofs of the tenderest affection. Did a fly pass within their reach, all these little ones jumped at it, tumbling in their efforts to catch it. The little yellow balls with their wide-awake air never took a second's rest.

"Well cared for and well fed, they grew so rapidly that soon they needed to have more space. Mother Etienne housed them then on the edge of the pond in a latticed coop opening onto a sloping board which led down to the water. It was, as it were, a big swimming bath, which grew gradually deeper and deeper. The ducks and geese loved to plunge in. In fact, they hardly left the water except to take their meals.

"Yollande felt very out of place in this new dwelling. The ducklings on the contrary, urged on by their instinct, madly enjoyed it and rushed pell-mell into the water. This inexplicable impulse terrified their mama. She was, in fact, 'as mad as a wet hen'.

"She ran up and down, her feathers on end, her face

swollen, her crest red, clucking away, trying to persuade her babies not to venture into the water. For hens, like cats, hate the water. It was unspeakable torture to her. The children would not listen; deaf to her prayers, her cries, these rascally babies ventured farther and farther out. They were at last and for the first time in their favourite element, lighter than little corks, they floated, dived, plunged, raced, fought, playing all sorts of tricks.

"Meanwhile, Yollande was eating her heart out. She rushed to and fro, keeping her eyes glued on the disobedient ones. Suddenly she saw a mother-duck chasing her darlings. This was more than she could bear – driven by her maternal instinct she leapt like a fury to the aid of her family.

"A flap or two of her wings and she was above the water into which she fell at the deepest part.

"Splashing, struggling madly in the midst of her frightened brood, she quickly became exhausted and sank to the bottom.

"The surface of the water closed above her. The little ones did not realize what had happened – very quickly they recovered from their momentary fright, and then went on with their games – splashing the water with their beaks and amusing themselves once again as though nothing were the matter.

"Mother Etienne, busy giving green apples to the pigs, bran to the rabbits, and corn to the pigeons, came back presently, and could not see the big Yollande beside the pond, only her children floating far, far away on the water. Surprised she drew nearer, called, but in vain. The mother-hen had disappeared. Then only did she understand the tragedy that had occurred. She called for help. Petit-Jacques immediately opened the big sluice and the water ran out, but much too slowly for their impatience. At last they began to see the bottom, and soon the body of poor Yollande was discovered stiff and motionless.

"There was general consternation at the farm. Petit-Jacques, by means of a long pole, seized her and drew her to land at Mother Etienne's feet. Labrie came up and sniffed sadly at the body of the unhappy hen. In vain they dried her and rubbed her – nothing did any good. 'She's quite dead, alas,' said Mother Etienne with tears in her eyes, 'but it was my own fault. I ought to have closed down the lattice and this misfortune would not have happened. It really is a great pity – such a fine hen. She weighs at least eight pounds. There, Germaine, take her and weigh her.'

The Curly-haired Hen

"Germaine was the maid and also the cousin of Petit-Jacques, of whom she was very fond. She was a fine buxom girl of eighteen, strong and well-grown. She loved animals, too, but her feeling for them could not be compared to Mother Etienne's.

"'Germaine, take away poor Yollande, I am quite upset by this trouble. You will bury her this evening, in a corner of the kitchen-garden – deep enough to prevent any animal digging her up. I leave it to you – do it carefully.'

"The girl bore away the fine hen in her apron. 'How heavy she is – it is a shame,' and blowing apart the feathers, she saw the skin underneath as yellow and plump as you could wish. Mechanically she plucked a few feathers. 'After all,' she said, 'it isn't as though she had died – she was drowned, quite a clean death; she's firm and healthy, only an hour ago she was as strong and well as could be. Why shouldn't we eat her? We'll stew her because, though she is not old, she is not exactly in her first youth, but there's a lot on her – with a dressing of carrots and nutmeg, a bunch of herbs and a tomato, with a calf's foot to make a good jelly, I believe she'd make a lovely dinner.'

"Saying this she went on plucking Yollande. All the

feathers, large and small, gone, a little down was left, so to get rid of this she lit an old newspaper and held her over it. 'Madame won't know anything and will enjoy her as much as we shall. There's enough on her for two good meals.'

"Quite decided, instead of burying her, she wrapped the future stew carefully in a perfectly clean cloth and put it on a shelf in the kitchen out of the way of flies or accident.

"During this time Mother Etienne was busy making as warm a home as she could for the fifteen little orphans. Poor darlings. In a wicker-basket she covered a layer of straw with another of wadding and fine down. Upon this she put the ducklings one by one, and covered the whole with feathers. Then closing the lid, she carried the basket to the stable where the air was always nice and warm. All this took time – it was about six o'clock in the evening, the sun was going down, throwing a last oblique smile into the kitchen, gleaming here and there on the shining copper which hung on the walls.

"As for Germaine, she, with Petit-Jacques to help her, had gone to milk the cows. Mother Etienne soon joined them, and the two women came back to the house together.

344

"Horror of horrors! What a terrible sight. Pale with fear they stood on the threshold of the kitchen not daring to move – to enter. Their hearts were in their mouths. A ghost stood there in front of them – Yollande – and Germaine fell at Mother Etienne's feet in utter consternation. Yollande? Yes, Yollande, but what a Yollande! Heavens! Yollande plucked, literally plucked! Yollande emerging from her shroud like Lazarus from his tomb! Yollande risen from the dead! A cry of anguish burst from the heart of kind Mother Etienne. 'Yollande, oh, Yollande!' The Cochin-China replied by a long shudder.

"This is what had happened. On falling into the water, Yollande after struggling fiercely, lost consciousness, and her lungs ceasing to act she had ceased to breathe, so the water had not entered her lungs. That is why she was not drowned. Life was, so to speak, suspended. This lasted some time.

345

The considerable heat to which she was subjected when Germaine held her above the flaming newspaper had brought about a healthy reaction and in the solitude of the kitchen she had recovered consciousness.

"After the first moment of terror was over, Germaine confessed her plan to Mother Etienne, who, glad to find Yollande still alive, forgave Germaine the disobedience which had saved her.

"But the hen was still shivering, shaking in every limb, her skin all goose-flesh. Dragging after her travesty of a tail, she jumped onto the kitchen table which she shook with her shivering.

"'We can't leave her like that any longer,' said Mother Etienne, 'we must cover her up somehow,' and straight away she wrapped her up in all the cloths she could lay her hands on. Germaine prepared some hot wine with sugar in it, and the two women fed her with it in spoonfuls – then they took a good drink of it themselves. All three at once felt the better for it. Yollande spent the night in these hastily-made swaddling clothes between two foot-warmers which threw out a gentle and continuous heat and kept away the catarrh with which the poor Cochin-China was threatened. The great question which arose now was how they were to protect her from the cold in future. Both of them cogitated over it.

"Several times during the night, Mother Etienne and the maid came to look at the hen, who, worn out by such a long day of fatigue and suffering, at last closed her eyes, relaxed, and slept till morning.

"Nevertheless she was the first in the house to wake up, and at dawn began to cackle vigorously. Germaine hastened to her, bringing a quantity of corn which the hen, doubtless owing to her fast of the day before, ate greedily.

"Now the important thing was to find her a practical costume. The weather was mild but there was great danger in allowing her to wander about in a garb as light as it was primitive. The mornings and evenings were cool and might bring on a cold, inflammation or congestion of the lungs, rheumatism, or what not.

"At all costs a new misfortune must be avoided. At last they dressed her in silk cunningly fashioned and lined with wadding. Thus garbed her entry into the poultry-yard was a subject of astonishment to some, fear to others, and excitement to most of the birds she met on her way.

"In vain Mother Etienne strove to tone down the

347

colours of the stuffs, to modify the cut of the garments, but Yollande long remained an object of surprise and antipathy to the majority of the poultry.

"The scandal soon reached its climax. 'That hen must be mad,' said an old duck to his wife.

"'Just imagine dressing up like that – she'll come along one of these days in a bathing suit,' cried a young rooster who prided himself on his wit.

"A young turkey tugged at her clothes, trying to pull them off, and all the others looked on laughing and hurling insults. They vied with one another in sarcastic speeches. At last, after a time, as the saying goes, familiarity bred contempt. The fear which her companions had felt at first soon changed into a familiarity often too great for the unhappy Cochin-China. They tried to see who could play her the shabbiest trick. Hens are often as cruel as men, which is saying a great deal.

"Poor Yollande, in spite of her size, her solidity, and strength, nearly always emerged half-dressed. Her companions could not stand her dressed like that, the sight of her irritated them. Not content with tearing her clothes they often pecked at the poor creature as well.

"Mother Etienne did her best to improve these

costumes in every way, but it was as impossible to find perfection as the philosopher's stone.

"They hoped at the farm that in time the feathers would grow again. Meanwhile it was hard on the hen.

"Nothing of the sort happened – one, two, three months passed and not the slighest vestige of down appeared on the hen, with the result that she had to be protected like a human being from the changes of climate and so forth. Like a well-to-do farmer's wife Yollande had her linen-chest and a complete outfit.

"It was, I assure you, my dear children, kept up most carefully. There was always a button to sew on, a buttonhole to remake, or a tear to be mended. Thus constantly in touch with the household Madame Hen soon thought she belonged to it. Indeed, worn out by the teasing of her companions, by the constant arguments she had with them, and touched on the other hand by the affectionate care of her mistresses, Yollande stayed more and more in the house. Coddled and swathed in her fantastic costumes, she sat in the chimney corner like a little Cinderella changed into a hen. From this corner she quietly watched – nothing escaped her notice.

"Meanwhile her reputation had grown, not only

amongst her comrades, but amongst all the animals of the neighbourhood, who, hearing her discussed, were anxious to see her.

"Woe to the cat or dog who dared venture too far into the room! Very annoyed at this impertinent curiosity, Yollande would leap upon the importunate stranger and punish him terribly with her sharp beak. Of course he would run off howling and frightened to death. It was very funny to watch.

"Mother Etienne and Germaine were much amused at these little comedies, and whenever visitors came to the farm they would try to provoke one. Everyone enjoyed them hugely.

"Germaine treated Yollande like a doll. She made her all sorts of fashionable clothes. The Cochin-China would be dressed sometimes like a man, sometimes like a woman. She had made her quite a collection of little trousers and vests, which had style, I can tell you. She had copied, too, from a circus she had seen, an English clown's costume which was most becoming. Nothing could be funnier than to watch this tiny dwarf, to see her strut, jump, dance, coming and going, skipping around suddenly – one moment skittish, the next very important.

The Curly-haired Hen

"Petit-Jacques loved to tease her, but he was never rough with her. He would push her gently with his foot, which would make her jump at him impatiently, looking perfectly ridiculous in her quaint little outfits. You could have sworn she was a miniature clown. Add to all this, the queer inarticulate sounds she made when she was angry, and even then you can have no idea how very amusing these pantomimes were.

"Soon the fame of Yollande spread far and wide. She became celebrated throughout the district. Instead of asking Mother Etienne how she was, people asked, 'How's your hen today, Mother Etienne?'

"One day a pedlar, such as often come round to visit the villages, laden like a mule, and leading slowly by the bridle an ass still more laden, appeared at the farm. Both the pedlar and his beast of burden looked well but tired and dusty – they seemed to have had a long journey.

"Father Gusson, for such was the good man's name, sold all sorts of different things, from toothbrushes to shoes, including hardware, glassware, notions, drugs, and even patent medicines.

"Mother Etienne received him kindly and after letting him show her the things in which she was interested, she offered him refreshment and suggested that he should take a little rest at the farm. This he accepted without needing any pressing.

"The donkey, relieved straightaway from his load, was led into the paddock, where he wallowed in the tall grass, rolling on his back, his feet in the air. He enjoyed cleaning himself up like this after his long and dusty journey, then, rested, he took his luncheon, choosing here and there the daintiest morsels, after which he lay down and philosophized at length.

"All this time, Mother Etienne and Germaine were buying, tempted by one thing after another, silks, laces, stuffs for dresses, and a number of toilet articles, for both were, though you would not have suspected it, rather coquettish. Father Gusson – delighted with his visit to the farm and the business he had done there – was anxious to leave Mother Etienne a little remembrance.

"'Madame,' he said, holding out a small china jar carefully sealed with parchment, 'assuredly you do not need this just now, but if I should never come back, and if it should happen that one day your beautiful hair should grow thin, turn grey, or fall out, you have only to rub your head with this sweet-scented ointment and at once your hair will grow again thick and of its original

The Curly-haired Hen

colour. I cannot – alas! – give you the recipe, it is a family secret left to me by my parents.'

"Then Father Gusson bade a fond farewell to the two women and went on his way with Neddy the donkey, both of them much refreshed by their pleasant rest.

"Mother Etienne handed Germaine the precious pot of ointment to put away with their other purchases into the big cupboard. Germaine stowed it safely, and they didn't give it another thought.

"One day as she sat by the fire with Yollande, watching the dinner, a bright and whimsical idea occurred to the maid. 'Supposing I were to try the ointment on the hen? It might be good for feathers too. Anyhow, it could not do any harm.'

"Saying this she went, found the ointment, and delicately rubbed a little onto Yollande's head. Yollande did not appear to mind at all, so Germaine repeated the treatment three days running.

"Two weeks later Mother Etienne, while dressing her hen as she did each day, found a thick reddish down sprouting round her head like a little flat wig. She showed it to Germaine, who paid no attention, having quite forgotten her childish trick.

"But during the next few days the wig prospered. The hair was two finger-breadths long, very thick and curly. Mother Etienne could not understand it at all. Germaine could not, at first, make up her mind to confess to her mistress what she had done.

"At last one evening, Mother Etienne being in a particularly good humour, the young girl took courage and told her all about it. Far from scolding her, her mistress was delighted, and so pleased at the news that she there and then undressed Yollande and rubbed her from head to foot with Father Gusson's marvellous ointment. She did the thing thoroughly, rubbing it into every pore. Then they made a good fire so that the poor little model, thus exposed, should not take cold.

"After that they watched her every instant. They were forever undressing her to see if the cure was working – they could hardly bear to wait. Just think, if it were to succeed, it would be the end and aim of all their care, and Yollande would once again be able to take her proper place in the outside world.

"At last what had happened to the head, happened to the body too. Before a week had gone by a thick down completely covered the big hen. The good women, much wondering, imagined that as it grew stronger the hair would change into feathers. Anxiously they awaited the change. Nothing of the sort happened. The hair remained hair, red – Titian red – fine and soft, curling round your fingers, admirable in quality and colour.

"The hair on the head, older than that on the rest of the body, was much longer, which suggested to the mischievous Germaine the idea of making her an elaborate headdress. Nothing like it had ever been seen before.

"Soon Yollande was able to discard some of her clothes. Her breast and back required for a time yet a little covering, but this grew gradually less and less.

"Naturally the phenomenon was much discussed in the neighbourhood, and it attracted many and delightful visitors to the farm, all of whom Mother Etienne welcomed cordially. Yollande was less pleased with this desire to inspect her. Generally some

unbeliever would tug at her hair, a painful experience
for her. So, except towards her mistress and Germaine,
she had become exceedingly vindictive and watchful.
Every time she had the chance she pecked with her
short, stout beak at the person indiscreet enough to
take such liberties. One little visitor, more daring than
the rest, nearly lost his finger over it.

The Curly-haired Hen

"The fame of the curly-haired hen was tremendous, it spread even beyond the limits of the district. It was really worth a journey to see her. They wrote of it in the newspapers. The Daily Mirror, I think it was, had a fine long article about her.

"But in certain quarters, the whole thing was looked upon as a 'fish story.'"

The Cat-hood of Maurice

By E Nesbit

To have your hair cut is not painful, nor does it hurt to have your whiskers trimmed. But round wooden shoes are not comfortable wear, however much it may amuse the onlooker to see you try to walk in them. If you have a nice fur coat, it is most annoying to be made to swim in it. And if you had a tail, surely it would be solely your own affair – that anyone should tie a tin can to it would strike you as an impertinence, to say the least.

Yet it is difficult for an outsider to see these things from the point of view of both the persons concerned. To Maurice, scissors in hand, it seemed the most natural

358

thing in the world to shorten the stiff whiskers of Lord Hugh Cecil by a generous inch. He did not understand how useful those whiskers were to Lord Hugh, both in sport and in the more serious business of getting a living.

Also it amused Maurice to throw Lord Hugh into ponds, and to put walnuts on Lord Hugh's feet and then to watch him walk on ice was, in Maurice's opinion, as good as a play. Lord Hugh was a very favourite cat, but Maurice was discreet, and Lord Hugh, except under violent suffering, was at that time anyhow, dumb.

But the empty sardine-tin attached to Lord Hugh's tail – this had a voice, and, rattling against stairs and the legs of furniture, it cried aloud for vengeance. Lord Hugh added his voice, and this time the family heard. There was a chase, a chorus of "Poor pussy!" and the tail and the tin and Lord Hugh were caught under Jane's bed. The tail and the tin acquiesced in their rescue. Lord Hugh did not. He fought, and Jane carried the scars of that rescue for many a week.

When all was calm Maurice was sought and, after some little natural delay, found – in the boot-cupboard.

"Oh, Maurice!" his mother almost sobbed, "how can

you? What will your father say?"

Maurice thought he knew what his father would do.

"Don't you know," the mother went on, "how wrong it is to be cruel?"

"I didn't mean to be cruel," Maurice said. And, what is more, he spoke the truth. The unwelcome attentions he had showered on Lord Hugh had not been intended to hurt – it was interesting to see what a cat would do if you threw it in the water, or cut its whiskers, or tied things to its tail.

"Oh, but you must have meant to be cruel," said his mother, "and you will have to be punished."

"I wish I hadn't," said Maurice, from the heart.

"So do I," said his mother, with a sigh. "You'd better go to your room and think it over. I shall have to tell your father directly he comes home."

Maurice went to his room and thought it over. And the more he thought the more he hated Lord Hugh. Why couldn't the beastly cat have held his tongue and sat still? He sat on the edge of his bed and savagely kicked the edge of the green Kidderminster carpet, and hated the cat.

He hadn't meant to be cruel. He wouldn't have pinched the cat's feet or squeezed its tail in the door, or poured hot water on it. He felt himself ill-used, and knew that he would feel still more so after the interview with his father.

But that interview did not take the immediately painful form expected by Maurice. No, his father was calm and reasonable – with a dreadful calm, a terrifying reason.

"Look here, my boy," he said. "This cruelty to dumb animals must be checked – severely checked."

"I didn't mean to be cruel," said Maurice.

"Evil," said Mr Basingstoke, for such was Maurice's surname, "is wrought by want of thought as well as want of heart. What about your putting the hen in the oven?"

"You know," said Maurice, pale but determined, "I only wanted to help her to get her eggs hatched quickly. It says in 'Fowls for Food and Fancy' that heat hatches eggs."

"But she hadn't any eggs," said Mr Basingstoke.

"But she soon would have," urged Maurice. "I thought a stitch in time—"

"That," said his father, "is the sort of thing that you must learn not to think."

"I'll try," said Maurice, miserably hoping for the best.

"I intend that you shall," said Mr Basingstoke. "This

afternoon you go to Dr Strongitharm's for the remaining week of term. If any more cruelty takes place during the holidays you will go there permanently. Go and get ready."

"Oh, father, please not," was all Maurice found to say.

"I'm sorry, my boy," said his father, much more kindly. "It's all for your own good, and it's as painful to me as it is to you – remember that. The cab will be here at four. Go and put your things together, and Jane shall pack for you."

So the box was packed, and Mabel, Maurice's kiddy sister, cried over everything as it was put in. It was a very wet day.

"If it had been any school but old Strong's," she sobbed.

She and her brother knew that school well: its windows, dulled with wire blinds, its big alarm bell, the high walls of its grounds, the iron gates through which gloomy boys scowled on a free world. Dr Strongitharm's was a school 'for backward and difficult boys'. Need I say more?

Well, there was no help for it. The box was packed, the cab was at the door. The farewells had been said. Maurice determined that he wouldn't cry and he didn't,

which gave him the one touch of pride and joy that such a scene could yield. Mother and Mabel had retired in tears. Maurice hurried to pack his postage-stamp album. Already he was planning how to impress the other boys at old Strong's, and his was a very fair collection. He ran up into the schoolroom, expecting to find it empty. But someone was there: Lord Hugh, in the very middle of the ink-stained table-cloth.

"You brute," said Maurice. "You know I'm going away, or you wouldn't be here."

"Meaow," said Lord Hugh.

"Mew!" said Maurice, with scorn. "That's what you always say. All that fuss about a sardine-tin. I wonder how you'd like being a boy? Lickings, and lessons, and sent back from breakfast to wash your ears – I wonder what they'd say to me if I washed my ears on the drawing-room hearthrug?"

"Meaow," said Lord Hugh, and washed an ear.

"Mew," said Maurice again. "That's all you can say."

"Oh, no, it isn't," said Lord Hugh, and stopped his ear-washing.

"I say!" said Maurice in awestruck tones.

"If you think cats have such a jolly time," said Lord Hugh, "why not be a cat?"

"I would if I could," said Maurice, "and fight you—"

"Thank you," said Lord Hugh.

"But I can't," said Maurice.

"Oh, yes, you can," said Lord Hugh. "You've only got to say the word."

"What word?"

Lord Hugh told him the word, but I will not tell you, for fear you should say it by accident and then be sorry.

"And if I say that, I shall turn into a cat?"

"Of course," said the cat.

"Oh, yes, I see," said Maurice. "But I'm not taking any, thanks. I don't want to be a cat for always."

"You needn't," said Lord Hugh. "You've only got to get someone to say to you, 'Please leave off being a cat and be Maurice again', and there you are."

Maurice thought of Dr Strongitharm's. He also thought of the horror of his father when he should find Maurice gone. 'He'll be sorry, then,' Maurice told

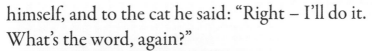

himself, and to the cat he said: "Right – I'll do it. What's the word, again?"

"—," said the cat.

"—," said Maurice. Suddenly the table shot up to the height of a house, the pattern on the carpet became enormous, and Maurice found himself on all fours. He tried to stand up on his feet, but he could only rear himself upright for a moment, and then fell heavily on his hands. He looked down at them – they had grown shorter and fatter, and were encased in black fur gloves. He felt a desire to walk on all fours – tried it – did it. It was very odd.

"I am asleep," said Maurice. "I am dreaming this. I am dreaming I am a cat. I hope I dreamed that about the sardine-tin and Lord Hugh's tail, and Dr Strong's."

"You didn't," said a voice he knew and yet didn't know, "and you aren't dreaming this."

"Yes, I am," said Maurice. "And now I'm going to dream that I fight that beastly black cat, and give him the best licking he ever had in his life. Come on, Lord Hugh."

A loud laugh answered him.

"Excuse my smiling," said the voice he knew and didn't know, "but don't you see – you are Lord Hugh!"

A great hand picked Maurice up from the floor and held him in the air. He felt the position to be undignified and unsafe, and gave himself a shake of relief and resentment when the hand set him down on the table-cloth.

"You are Lord Hugh now, my dear Maurice," said the voice, and a huge face came quite close to his. It was his own face, as it would have seemed through a magnifying glass. And the voice – oh, horror! – the voice was his own voice – Maurice Basingstoke's voice. Maurice shrank from the voice, and he would have liked to claw at the face, but he had had no practice.

"You are Lord Hugh," the voice repeated, "and I am Maurice. I like being Maurice. I am so large and strong. I could drown you

in the water-butt – oh, ever so easily. No, don't spit and swear. It's bad manners – even in a cat."

"Maurice!" shouted Mr Basingstoke from between the door and the cab.

Maurice, from habit, leaped towards the door.

"It's no use your going," said the thing that looked like a giant reflection of Maurice. "It's me he wants."

"But I didn't agree to your being me."

"That's poetry, even if it isn't grammar," said the thing that looked like Maurice. "Why, my good cat, don't you see that if you are I, I must be you? Otherwise we should interfere with time and space and as likely as not destroy the solar system. Oh, yes – I'm you, right enough, and shall be, till someone tells you to change from Lord Hugh into Maurice. And now you've got to find someone to do it."

("Maurice!" thundered the voice of Mr Basingstoke.)

"That'll be easy enough," said Maurice.

"Think so?" said the other.

"But I shan't try yet. I want to have some fun first. I shall catch heaps of mice!"

"Think so? You forget that your whiskers are cut off – Maurice cut them. Without whiskers, how can you judge of the width of the places you go through?

367

Take care you don't get stuck in a hole, my good cat."

"Don't call me a cat," said Maurice, and felt that his tail was growing thick and angry.

"You are a cat, you know – and that little bit of temper that I see in your tail reminds me—"

Maurice felt himself gripped round the middle, abruptly lifted, and carried swiftly through the air. The quickness of the movement made him giddy. He saw nothing, felt nothing, except a sort of long sea-sickness, and then suddenly he was not being moved. He was being held tight in a sort of vice – a vice covered with chequered cloth. It looked like the pattern, very much exaggerated, of his school knickerbockers. He was being held between the hard, relentless knees of that creature that had once been Lord Hugh, and to whose tail he had tied a sardine-tin. Now he was Lord Hugh, and something was being tied to his tail. Something mysterious, terrible. Very well, he would show he was not afraid of things that could be attached to tails. The string rubbed his fur the wrong way – it was that that annoyed him. And as for what was at the end of the string, what could that matter to any sensible cat?

The string, however, and the uncomfortable, tight position between those chequered knees – something

368

or other was getting on his nerves.

"Maurice!" shouted his father below, and the be-catted Maurice bounded between the knees of the creature that wore his clothes and his looks.

"Coming, father," this thing called, and sped away, leaving Maurice on the servant's bed. The stairs re-echoed to the loud boots which Maurice had never before thought loud – he had often, indeed, wondered that anyone could object to them. He wondered now no longer.

He heard the front door slam. That thing had gone to Dr Strongitharm's. That was one comfort. Lord Hugh was a boy now – he would know what it was to be a boy. He, Maurice, was a cat, and he meant to taste fully all catty pleasures, from milk to mice. Meanwhile he was without mice or milk, and, unaccustomed as he was to a tail, he could not but feel that all was not right with his own. There was a feeling of weight, a feeling of discomfort, of positive terror. If he should move, what would that thing that was tied to his tail do? Rattle, of course. Oh, but he could not bear it if that thing rattled. Nonsense – it was only a sardine-tin. But if it did rattle! He moved his tail the least little soft inch. No sound. Perhaps really there wasn't anything tied to his tail. But he couldn't be sure unless he moved. But if he moved the thing would rattle, and if it rattled Maurice felt sure that he would expire or go mad. A mad cat. What a dreadful thing to be! Yet he couldn't sit on that bed for ever, waiting for the dreadful thing to happen.

"Oh, dear," sighed Maurice the cat. "I never knew what people meant by 'afraid' before."

His cat-heart was beating heavily against his furry side. His limbs were getting cramped – he must move. He did. And instantly the awful thing happened. The sardine-tin touched the iron of the bed-foot. It rattled.

"Oh, I can't bear it, I can't," cried poor Maurice, in a heartrending meaow that echoed through the house. He leaped from the bed and tore through the door and down the stairs, and behind him came the most terrible thing in the world. People might call it a sardine-tin, but it was the soul of all the fear that ever had been.

Maurice who was a cat flew down the stairs, and down the rattling horror followed. At the foot of the stairs the horror, caught by something – a banister – stopped. The string on Maurice's tail tightened, his tail was jerked, he was stopped. But the noise had stopped too. Maurice lay only just alive at the foot of the stairs.

It was Mabel who untied the string and soothed his

terrors with kind strokings and tender words. Maurice was surprised to find what a nice little girl his sister really was.

"I'll never tease you again," he tried to say, softly – but that was not what he said to her. What he actually said to her was "Purrrr."

"Nice poor pussy, then," said Mabel, and she hid away the sardine-tin and did not tell anyone. This seemed unjust to Maurice until he remembered that Mabel thought that he was really Lord Hugh, and that the person who had tied the tin to his tail was her brother Maurice. Then he was half-grateful. She carried him down, in soft, safe arms, to the kitchen, and asked cook to give him some milk.

"Tell me to change back into Maurice," said Maurice who was quite worn out by his cattish experiences. But no one heard him. They heard, "Meaow-Meaow-Meeeaow!"

Then Maurice saw how he had been tricked. He could be changed back into a boy as soon as anyone said to him, 'Leave off being a cat and be Maurice again,' but his tongue had no longer the power to ask anyone to say it.

He did not sleep well at all that night. For one thing

he was not accustomed to sleeping on the kitchen hearthrug, and the kitchen floor was very hard. He was glad when cook came down and turned him out into the garden, where frost still lay white on the yellowed stalks of sunflowers and nasturtiums. He took a walk, climbed a tree, failed to catch a bird, and felt better. He began to feel hungry. A delicious scent came stealing out of the kitchen door. Oh, joy, there were to be herrings for breakfast! Maurice hastened in to the dining room and took his place on his usual chair at the table.

His mother immediately said, "Down, puss," and tilted the chair back so that Maurice fell off it onto the floor. Then the family had herrings. Maurice said loudly, "You might give me some," and he carried on saying it so that his father, who, of course, could hear only mewings, said, "For goodness' sake put that cat out of the room."

Maurice breakfasted later, in the dustbin, on herring heads. But he kept himself up with a splendid idea. They would give him milk presently, and then they should see.

He spent the afternoon sitting on the sofa in the dining-room, listening to the conversation of his father and mother. It is said that listeners never hear any good of themselves. Maurice heard so much that he was surprised and humbled. He heard his father say that he was a fine, plucky little chap, but he needed a severe lesson, and Dr Strongitharm was the man to give it to him. He heard his mother say things that made his heart throb and the tears prick behind those cat-eyes of his. He had always thought his parents a bit unjust. Now they did him so much justice that he felt quite small inside his cat-skin.

"He's a dear, good, affectionate boy," said his mother. "It's only his high spirits. Don't you think, darling, perhaps you were a little hard on him?"

"It was for his own good," said his father.

"Of course," said his mother, "but I can't bear to think of him at that dreadful school."

"Well—" his father said, but Jane came in with the tea on a clattering tray, whose sound made Maurice tremble in every leg. Father and mother began to talk about the weather.

Maurice felt very affectionately to both his parents. He showed it by jumping on to the sideboard and thence on to his father's shoulders. He landed there on his four padded feet, light as a feather, but father was not pleased.

"Bother the cat!" he cried. "Jane, put it out of the room."

Maurice was put out. He sought the kitchen, and, seeing a milk-can on the window-ledge, jumped up beside the can and patted it as he had seen Lord Hugh do.

"My!" said a friend of Jane's who happened to be there, "Ain't that cat clever."

"He's nothing to boast of this time," said cook. "I will say for Lord Hugh he's not often taken in with an empty can."

This was naturally mortifying for Maurice, but he pretended not to hear, and jumped from the window to the tea-table and patted the milk jug.

"Come," said the cook, "that's more like it," and she poured him out a full saucer and set it on the floor.

Now was the chance Maurice had longed for. Now he could carry out his idea. He carefully dipped his right paw in it, for his idea was to make letters with it on the kitchen oil-cloth. He meant to write 'Please tell me to leave off being a cat and be Maurice again,' but he found his paw a very clumsy pen, and he had to rub out the first 'P' because it only looked like an accident. Then he tried again and actually did make a 'P' that any fair-minded person could have read quite easily.

'I wish they'd notice,' he said, and before he got the 'l' written they did notice.

"Drat the cat," said cook. "Look how he's messing the floor up." And she took away the milk.

Very weary, very thirsty, and very tired of being Lord Hugh, he found his way to the schoolroom, where Mabel was doing her lessons. She took him on her lap and stroked him while she learned her French verb. He felt that he was growing very fond of her. People were right to be kind to dumb animals. Presently she had to stop stroking him and do a map. After that she kissed him and put him down and went away. All the time she had been doing the map, Maurice had had but one thought: Ink.

The moment the door had closed behind her – how sensible people were who closed doors gently – he stood up in her chair with one paw on the map and the other on the ink. Unfortunately, the inkstand top was made to dip pens in, and not to dip paws. But Maurice was desperate. He deliberately upset the ink. Most of it fell on the carpet, but with what was left he wrote quite plainly, across the map:

PLEASE TELL LORD HUGH
TO STOP BEING A CAT
AND BE MAURICE AGAIN

"There!" he said. "They can't make any mistake about that." They didn't. But they made a mistake about who had done it, and Mabel was deprived of jam with her supper.

Her assurance that some naughty boy must have come through the window and done it while she was not there convinced nobody, and with good reason, for the window was shut and bolted.

Maurice, wild with indignation, did not mend matters by then seizing the opportunity of a few minutes' solitude to write:

IT WAS NOT MABEL
IT WAS MAURICE,
I MEAN LORD HUGH

When that was seen Mabel was instantly sent to bed. "It's not fair!" cried Maurice.

"My dear," said Maurice's father, "if that cat goes on mewing to this extent you'll have to get rid of it."

Maurice said not another word. It was bad enough to be a cat, but to be a cat that was 'got rid off'! He knew how people got rid of cats. In a stricken silence he left the room and slunk up the stairs – he dared not mew again, even at the door of Mabel's room. But when Jane went in to put Mabel's light out Maurice crept in too, and in the dark tried with stifled mews and purrs to explain to Mabel how sorry he was. Mabel stroked him and he went to sleep, his last waking thought amazement at the blindness that had once made him call her a silly little kid.

The Cat-hood of Maurice

If you have ever been a cat you will understand some of what Maurice endured during the days that followed. If you have not, I can never make you understand fully. There was the affair of the fishmonger's tray balanced on the wall by the back door. Maurice knew as well as you do that one mustn't steal fish out of other people's trays, but the cat that he was didn't know – and Maurice was beaten by the cat-nature. Later he was beaten by the cook.

Then there was that very painful incident with the butcher's dog, the flight across gardens, the safety of the plum tree gained only just in time.

Worst of all, despair took hold of him, for he saw that nothing he could do would make anyone say those simple words that would release him. He had hoped that Mabel might be made to understand, but the ink had failed him, she did not understand his mewings, and when he got the cardboard letters and made the same sentence with them Mabel only thought it was that naughty boy who came through locked windows. Somehow he could not spell before anyone – his nerves were not what they had been. He felt that he was really growing like a cat in his mind. He hunted mice with enthusiasm, though the loss of his whiskers made hunting difficult.

He grew expert in bird-stalking, and often got quite near to a bird before it flew away. But all the time, in his heart, he was very, very miserable. And so the week went by.

Maurice in his cat shape dreaded more and more the time when Lord Hugh in the boy shape should come back from Dr Strongitharm's. He knew – who better? – exactly the kind of things boys do to cats, and he trembled to the end of his handsome half-Persian tail.

And then the boy came home from Dr Strongitharm's. At the sound of his boots in the hall Maurice in the cat's body fled with silent haste to hide in the boot-cupboard.

Here, ten minutes later, the boy that had come back from Dr Strongitharm's found him.

Maurice fluffed up his tail and unsheathed his claws. Whatever this boy was going to do to him Maurice meant to resist.

"Come out, you old duffer," said Lord Hugh in the boy shape of Maurice. "I'm not going to hurt you. Oh, I've had such a time!" said Lord Hugh. "I've been caned and shut up in a dark room and given thousands of lines to write out."

"I've been beaten, too, if you come to that," mewed Maurice. "Besides the butcher's dog."

It was an intense relief to speak to someone who could understand his mews.

"Well, I suppose it's Pax for the future," said Lord Hugh. "Please leave off being a cat and be Maurice again."

And instantly Maurice felt with a swelling heart that he was no longer a cat. No more of those undignified four legs, those tiresome pointed ears (so difficult to wash), that furry coat, that contemptible tail, and that terrible inability to express all one's feelings in two words: 'mew' and 'purr'.

He scrambled out of the cupboard, and the boots and galoshes fell off him like spray off a bather.

He stood upright, and found himself face to face with another boy, exactly like himself.

"You haven't changed, then – but there can't be two Maurices."

"There shan't be," said the other boy. "A boy's life is a dog's life. Quick, before anyone comes."

"Quick what?" asked Maurice.

"Why tell me to leave off being a boy, and to be Lord Hugh Cecil again."

Maurice told him at once. And at once the boy was gone, and there was Lord Hugh in his own shape, purring politely, yet with a watchful eye on Maurice's movements.

"Oh, you needn't be afraid, old chap. It's Pax right enough," Maurice murmured in the ear of Lord Hugh. And Lord Hugh, arching his back under Maurice's stroking hand, replied with a *purrrr-meaow* that spoke volumes.

"Oh, Maurice, here you are. It is nice of you to be nice to Lord Hugh, when it was because of him you—"

"He's a good old chap," said Maurice, carelessly. "And you're not half a bad old girl. See?"

Mabel almost wept for joy at this most magnificent compliment, and Lord Hugh himself took on a more happy and confident air.